'The undisputed queen of the comedy beat . . . A hilarious rollercoaster ride with a heroine who would have Bridget Jones for breakfast'   *Guardian*

'Janet Evanovich's characters are eccentric and exaggerated, the violence often surreal and the plot dizzily speedy; but she produces as many laughs as anyone writing crime today'   Marcel Berlins, *The Times*

'One of the rising stars of American crime fiction'
Daily Telegraph

'Pithy, witty and fast-paced'   *Sunday Times*

'Stephanie Plum in ass-kicking form . . . utterly delightful'   *Cosmopolitan*

'Janet Evanovich's name raises expectations of a laugh-aloud story . . . An entertaining frolic'
Sunday Telegraph

FOUR TO SCORE

Janet Evanovich now lives in New Hampshire but, like Stephanie Plum, grew up in New Jersey. She has won major crime fiction awards for her Stephanie Plum novels, including the CWA John Creasey Memorial, the Dilys on two occasions, the CWA Last Laugh and the CWA Silver Dagger for *Three to Get Deadly*.

JANET EVANOVICH

A STEPHANIE PLUM NOVEL

FOUR TO SCORE

PAN BOOKS

First published in Great Britain 1998 by Macmillan

This edition published 2013 by Pan Books
an imprint of Pan Macmillan, a division of Macmillan Publishers Limited
Pan Macmillan, 20 New Wharf Road, London N1 9RR
Basingstoke and Oxford
Associated companies throughout the world
www.panmacmillan.com

ISBN 978-1-4472-4058-7

1 3 5 7 9 8 6 4 2

A CIP catalogue record for this book is available from
the British Library.

Typeset by Intype Libra Ltd
Printed and bound by CPI Group (UK) Ltd, Croydon, CR0 4YY

Visit www.panmacmillan.com to read more about all our books
and to buy them. You will also find features, author interviews and
news of any author events, and you can sign up for e-newsletters
so that you're always first to hear about our new releases.

Thanks to Shannon Hendrix for suggesting the title for this book.

CHAPTER ONE

LIVING IN TRENTON in July is like living inside a big pizza oven. Hot, airless, aromatic.

Because I didn't want to miss any of the summer experience I had the sunroof open on my Honda CRX. My brown hair was pulled up into a wind-snarled, curls-gone-to-frizz ponytail. The sun baked the top of my head, and sweat trickled under my black spandex sports bra. I was wearing matching spandex shorts and a sleeveless over-sized Trenton Thunders baseball jersey. It was an excellent outfit except it gave me no place to stick my .38. Which meant I was going to have to borrow a gun to shoot my cousin Vinnie.

I parked the CRX in front of Vinnie's storefront bail bonds office, lunged out of the car, stalked across the sidewalk, and yanked the office door open. 'Where is he? Where is that miserable little excuse for a human being?'

'Uh oh,' Lula said from behind the file cabinet. 'Rhino alert.'

Lula is a retired hooker who helps clean up the filing and sometimes rides shotgun for me when I do my fugitive apprehension thing. If people were cars, Lula would be a big, black '53 Packard with a high-gloss chrome grill, oversized headlights, and a growl like a junkyard dog. Lots of muscle. Never fit in a compact space.

Connie Rosolli, the office manager, pushed back at her desk when I entered. Connie's domain was this one front room where friends and relatives of miscreants came to beg money. And to the rear, in an inner office, my cousin Vinnie slapped Mr. Johnson around and conversed with his bookie.

'Hey,' Connie said, 'I know what you're bummed about, and this wasn't my decision. Personally, if I were you, I'd kick your cousin's pervert ass around the block.'

I pushed a clump of hair that had strayed from the ponytail back from my face. 'Kicking isn't good enough. I think I'll shoot him.'

'Go for it!' Lula said.

'Yeah,' Connie agreed. 'Shoot him.'

Lula checked out my clothes. 'You need a gun? I don't see no gun bulges in that spandex.' She hiked up her T-shirt and pulled a Chief's Special out of her cut-off denim shorts. 'You could use mine. Just be careful; it sights high.'

'You don't want a little peashooter like that,' Connie said, opening her desk drawer. 'I've got a forty-five. You can make a nice big hole with a forty-five.'

Lula went for her purse. 'Hold on here. If that's what you want, let me give you the big stud. I've got a forty-four magnum loaded up with hydroshocks. This baby'll do *real* damage, you see what I'm saying? You could drive a Volkswagen through the hole this sweetheart makes.'

'I was sort of kidding about shooting him,' I told them.

'Too bad,' Connie said.

Lula shoved her gun back in her shorts. 'Yeah, that's damn disappointing.'

'So where is he? Is he in?'

'Hey, Vinnie!' Connie yelled. 'Stephanie's here to see you!'

The door to the inner office opened and Vinnie poked his head out. 'What?'

Vinnie was 5'7", looked like a weasel, thought like a weasel, smelled like a French whore and was once in love with a duck.

'You know what!' I said, hands fisted on hips. 'Joyce Barnhardt, that's what. My grandma was at the beauty parlor and heard you hired Joyce to do skip tracing.'

'So what's the big deal? I hired Joyce Barnhardt.'

'Joyce Barnhardt does makeovers at Macy's.'

'And you used to sell ladies' panties.'

'That was entirely different. I blackmailed you into giving me this job.'

'Exactly,' Vinnie said. 'So what's your point?'

'Fine!' I shouted. 'Just keep her out of my way! I *hate* Joyce Barnhardt!'

And everybody knew why. At the tender age of twenty-four, after less than a year of marriage, I'd caught Joyce bare-assed on my dining room table, playing hide-the-salami with my husband. It was the only time she'd ever done me a favor. We'd gone through school together, where she'd spread rumors, told fibs, ruined friendships and peeked under the stall doors in the girls' bathroom to see people's underpants.

She'd been a fat kid with a terrible overbite. The overbite had been minimalized by braces, and by the time Joyce was fifteen she'd trimmed down to look like Barbie on steroids. She had chemically enhanced red hair done up in big teased curls. Her nails were long and painted, her lips were high gloss, her eyes were rimmed in navy liquid liner, her lashes gunked up with blue-black mascara. She was an inch shorter than me, five pounds heavier and had me beat by two cup sizes. She had three ex-husbands and no children. It was rumored she had sex with large dogs.

Joyce and Vinnie were a match made in heaven. Too bad Vinnie was already married to a perfectly nice woman whose father happened to be Harry the Hammer. Harry's job description read 'expediter,' and Harry spent a lot of his time in the presence of men who wore fedoras and long black overcoats.

'Just do your job,' Vinnie said. 'Be a professional.' He waved his hand at Connie. 'Give her something. Give her that new skip we just got in.'

Connie took a manila folder from her desktop. 'Maxine Nowicki. Charged with stealing her former boyfriend's car. Posted bond with us and failed to show for her court appearance.'

By securing a cash bond Nowicki had been free to leave the lockup behind and return to society at large while awaiting trial. Now she'd failed to appear. Or in bounty-hunter speak, she was FTA. This lapse of judicial etiquette changed Nowicki's status to felon and had my cousin Vinnie worrying that the court might see fit to keep his bond money.

As a bond enforcement officer I was expected to find Nowicki and bring her back into the system. For performing this service in a timely manner I'd get ten percent of her bond amount. Pretty good money since this sounded like a domestic dispute, and I didn't think Maxine Nowicki would be interested in blowing the back of my head off with a .45 hollow tip.

I riffled through the paperwork, which consisted of Nowicki's bond agreement, a photo, and a copy of the police report.

'Know what I'd do?' Lula said. 'I'd talk to the boy-friend. Anybody pissed off enough to get his girlfriend arrested for stealing his car is pissed off enough to snitch on her. Probably he's just waiting to tell someone where to go find her.'

It was my thought too. I read aloud from Nowicki's charge sheet. 'Edward Kuntz. Single white male. Age Twenty-seven. Residing at Seventeen Muffet Street. Says here he's a cook.'

I PARKED IN front of Kuntz's house and wondered about the man inside. The house was white clapboard with aqua trim around the windows and tangerine paint on the door. It was half of a well-cared-for duplex with a minuscule front yard. A three-foot-tall statue of the Virgin Mary dressed in pale blue and white had been planted on the perfectly clipped patch of lawn. A carved wood heart with red lettering and little white daisies had been hung on the neighboring door, proclaiming that the Glicks lived there. The Kuntz side was free of ornamentation.

I followed the sidewalk to the porch, which had been carpeted in green indoor-outdoor carpet, and rang the Kuntz doorbell. The door opened and a sweaty, muscle-bulging, half-naked man looked out at me. 'What?'

'Eddie Kuntz?'

'Yeah?'

I passed him my business card. 'Stephanie Plum. I'm a bond enforcement officer, and I'm looking for Maxine Nowicki. I was hoping you could help me.'

'You bet I can help you. She took my car. Can you believe it?' He jerked his stubbled chin toward the curb. 'That's it right there. Lucky for her she didn't scratch it up. The cops picked her up driving through town in it, and they brought the car back to me.'

I glanced back at the car. A white Chevy Blazer. Freshly washed. I almost was tempted to steal it myself.

'You were living together?'

'Well, yeah, for a while. About four months. And then we had this disagreement, and next thing I know, she's gone with my car. It wasn't that I wanted her arrested . . . it was just that I wanted my car back. That was why I called the police. I wanted my car.'

'Do you have any idea where she might be now?'

'No. I tried to get in touch with her to sort of patch things up, but I couldn't find her. She quit her job at the diner and nobody's seen her. I stopped around her apartment a couple times, and there was never anybody home. I tried calling her mother. I called a couple of her girlfriends. No one seems to know anything. I guess they could have been lying to me, but I don't think so.' He winked at me. 'Women don't lie to me, you know what I mean?'

'No,' I said. 'I don't know what you mean.'

'Well, I don't like to brag, but I have a way with women.'

'Uh huh.' It must have been the pungent aroma they found so attractive. Or maybe the overdeveloped, steroid-pumped muscles that made him look like he needed a bra. Or maybe it was the way he couldn't conduct a conversation without scratching his balls.

'So what can I do for you?' Kuntz asked.

Half an hour later I left with a list of Maxine's friends and relatives. I knew where Maxine banked, bought her booze, shopped for groceries, dry-cleaned her clothes and had her hair done. Kuntz promised to call me if he heard from Maxine, and I'd promised to reciprocate in kind if I turned up anything interesting. Of course, I'd had my fingers crossed when I'd made the promise. I suspected Eddie Kuntz's way with women was to make them run screaming in the opposite direction.

He stood on the porch and watched me angle into my car.

'Cute,' he called. 'I like when a chick drives a sporty little car.'

I sent him a smile that felt a lot like a grimace and peeled away from the curb. I'd gotten the CRX in February, sucked in by a shiny new paint job and an odometer that read 12,000 miles. Cherry condition, the owner had said. Hardly ever driven. And that was partly true. It was hardly ever driven with the odometer cable connected. Not that it mattered. The price had been right, and I looked good in the driver's seat. I'd recently developed a dime-sized lesion on my exhaust pipe, but if I played Metallica loud enough I could hardly hear the muffler noise. I might have thought twice about buying the car if I'd known Eddie Kuntz thought it was cute.

My first stop was the Silver Dollar Diner. Maxine had worked there for seven years and had listed no other source of income. The Silver Dollar was open twenty-four hours. It served good food in generous portions and was always packed with overweight people and penny-pinching seniors. The families of fatties cleaned their plates, and the seniors took leftovers home in doggy bags . . . butter pats, baskets of rolls, packets of sugar, half-eaten pieces of deep-fried haddock, coleslaw, fruit cup, grease-logged french fries. A senior could eat for three days off one meal at the Silver Dollar.

The Silver Dollar was in Hamilton Township on a

stretch of road that was clogged with discount stores and small strip malls. It was almost noon, and diner patrons were scarfing down burgers and BLTs. I introduced myself to the woman behind the register and asked about Maxine.

'I can't believe she's in all this trouble,' the woman said. 'Maxine was responsible. Real dependable.' She straightened a stack of menus. 'And that business about the car!' She did some eye rolling. 'Maxine drove it to work lots of times. He gave her the keys. And then all of a sudden she's arrested for stealing.' She gave a grunt of disgust. 'Men!'

I stepped back to allow a couple to pay their bill. When they'd pocketed their complimentary mints, matchbooks and toothpicks and exited the diner I turned back to the cashier. 'Maxine failed to show for her court appearance. Did she give any indication that she might be leaving town?'

'She said she was going on vacation, and we all thought she was due. Been working here for seven years and never once took a vacation.'

'Has anyone heard from her since she's left?'

'Not that I know of. Maybe Margie. Maxine and Margie always worked the same shift. Four to ten. If you want to talk to Margie you should come back around eight. We get real busy with the early bird specials at four, but then around eight it starts to slack off.'

I thanked the woman and went back to my CRX. My next stop would be Nowicki's apartment. According to Kuntz, Nowicki had lived with him for four months but had never gotten around to moving out of her place. The apartment was a quarter mile from the diner, and Nowicki had stated on her bond agreement that she'd resided there for six years. All previous addresses were local. Maxine Nowicki was Trenton clear to the roots of her bleached blond hair.

The apartment was in a complex of two-story, blocky, red-brick buildings anchored in islands of parched grass, arranged around macadam parking lots. Nowicki was on the second floor with a first-floor entrance. Inside private stairwell. Not good for window snooping. All second-floor apartments had small balconies on the back side, but I'd need a ladder to get to the balcony. Probably a woman climbing up a ladder would look suspicious.

I decided to go with the obvious and knock on the door. If no one answered I'd ask the super to let me in. Many times the super was cooperative in this way, especially if he was confused as to the authenticity of my fake badge.

There were two front doors side by side. One was for upstairs and one was for downstairs. The name under the upstairs doorbell read Nowicki. The name under the downstairs doorbell read Pease.

I rang the upstairs doorbell and the downstairs door opened and an elderly woman looked out at me.

'She isn't home.'

'Are you Mrs. Pease?' I asked.

'Yes.'

'Are you sure Maxine isn't home?'

'Well, I guess I'd know. You can hear everything in this cheapskate apartment. If she was home I'd hear her TV. I'd hear her walking around. And besides, she'd stop in to tell me she was home and collect her mail.'

Ah hah! The woman was collecting Maxine's mail. Maybe she also had Maxine's key.

'Yes, but suppose she came home late one night and

didn't want to wake you?' I said. 'And then suppose she had a stroke?'

'I never thought of that.'

'She could be upstairs right now, gasping her last breath of air.'

The woman rolled her eyes upward, as if she could see through walls. 'Hmmm.'

'Do you have a key?'

'Well, yes . . .'

'And what about her plants? Have you been watering her plants?'

'She didn't ask me to water her plants.'

'Maybe we should go take a look. Make sure everything is okay.'

'Are you a friend of Maxine's?'

I held up two fingers side by side. 'Like this.'

'I suppose it wouldn't hurt to check. I'll be right back with the key. I've got it in the kitchen.'

Okay, so I fibbed a little. But it wasn't such a bad fib because it was for a good cause. And besides, she *could* be dead in her bed. And her plants *could* be dying of thirst.

'Here it is,' Mrs. Pease said, brandishing the key.

She turned the key in the lock and pushed the door open.

'Hell-*oo*-o,' she called in her warbling old lady's voice. 'Anybody home?'

No one answered, so we crept up the stairs. We stood in the little entrance area and looked into the living room–dining room.

'Not much of a housekeeper,' Mrs. Pease said.

Housekeeping had nothing to do with it. The apartment had been trashed. It wasn't a fight because nothing was smashed. And it wasn't clutter from a last-minute scurry to leave. Cushions were pulled off the couch and flung onto the floor. Cupboard doors were open. Drawers were pulled from the hutch and turned upside down, contents spilled out. I did a quick walk-through and saw more of the same in the bedroom and bath. Someone had been looking for something. Money? Drugs? If it was robbery it had been very specific, because the TV and VCR were untouched.

'Someone has ransacked this apartment,' I said to Mrs. Pease. 'I'm surprised you didn't hear the drawers being flung around.'

'If I was home I would have heard it. It must have been when I was out to bingo. I go to bingo every Wednesday and Friday. I don't get home until eleven. Do you think we should report this to the police?'

'It wouldn't serve much purpose right now.' Except to notify the police that I'd been in Maxine's apartment sort of illegally. 'We don't know if anything's been taken. Probably we should wait for Maxine to come home and let her call the police.'

We didn't see any plants to water, so we tippytoed back down the stairs and locked the door.

I gave Mrs. Pease my card and asked her to call me if she should see or hear anything suspicious.

She studied the card. 'A bounty hunter,' she said, her voice showing surprise.

'A woman's got to do what a woman's got to do,' I said.

She looked up and nodded in agreement. 'I suppose that's true.'

I squinted into the lot. 'According to my information Maxine owns an '84 Fairlane. I don't see it here.'

'She took off in it,' Mrs. Pease said. 'Wasn't much of a

car. Always something or other broken on it, but she loaded it up with her suitcase and took off.'

'Did she say where she was going?'

'On vacation.'

'That was it?'

'Yep,' Mrs. Pease said, 'that was it. Usually Maxine's real talkative, but she wasn't saying anything this time. She was in a hurry, and she wasn't saying anything.'

NOWICKI'S MOTHER LIVED on Howser Street. She'd posted the bond and had put up her house as collateral. At first glance this seemed like a safe investment for my cousin Vinnie. Truth was, getting a person kicked out of his or her house was a chore and did nothing to endear a bail bondsman to the community.

I got out my street map and found Howser. It was in north Trenton, so I retraced my route and discovered that Mrs. Nowicki lived two blocks from Eddie Kuntz. Same neighborhood of well-kept houses. Except for the Nowicki house. The Nowicki house was single-family, and it was a wreck. Peeling paint, crumbling roof shingles, saggy front porch, front yard more dirt than grass.

I picked my way over rotting porch steps and knocked on the door. The woman who answered was faded glory in a bathrobe. It was getting to be mid-afternoon, but Mrs. Nowicki looked like she'd just rolled out of bed. She was a sixty-year-old woman wearing the ravages of booze and disenchantment with life. Her doughy face showed traces of makeup not removed before calling it a night. Her voice had the rasp of two packs a day, and her breath was hundred proof.

'Mrs. Nowicki?'

'Yeah,' she said.

'I'm looking for Maxine.'

'You a friend of Maxy's?'

I gave her my card. 'I'm with the Plum Agency. Maxine missed her court date. I'm trying to find her so we can get her rescheduled.'

Mrs. Nowicki raised a crayoned brown eyebrow. 'I wasn't born yesterday, honey. You're a bounty hunter, and you're out to get my little girl.'

'Do you know where she is?'

'Wouldn't tell you if I did. She'll get found when she wants to.'

'You put your house up as security against the bond. If Maxine doesn't come forward you could lose your house.'

'Oh yeah, that'd be a tragedy,' she said, rummaging in the pocket of her chenille robe, coming up with a pack of Kools. '*Architectural Digest* keeps wanting to do a spread, but I can't find the time.' She stuck a cigarette in her mouth and lit up. She sucked hard and squinted at me through the smoke haze. 'I owe five years' back taxes. You want this house you're gonna hafta take a number and get in line.'

Sometimes bail jumpers are simply at home, trying to pretend their life isn't in the toilet, hoping the whole mess will go away if they ignore the order to appear in court. I'd originally thought Maxine would be one of these people. She wasn't a career criminal, and the charges weren't serious. She really had no reason to skip out.

Now I wasn't so sure. I was getting an uncomfortable feeling about Maxine. Her apartment had been trashed, and her mother had me thinking maybe Maxine didn't want to be found right now. I slunk back to my car and decided my deductive reasoning would be vastly improved if I ate a doughnut. So I cut across town to Hamilton and parked in front of Tasty Pastry Bakery.

I'd worked part-time at Tasty Pastry when I was in high school. It hadn't changed much since then. Same green-and-white linoleum floor. Same sparkling clean display cases filled with Italian cookies, chocolate chip cannoli, biscotti, napoleons, fresh bread and coffee cakes. Same happy smell of fried sweet dough and cinnamon.

Lennie Smulenski and Anthony Zuck bake the goodies in the back room in big steel ovens and troughs of hot oil. Clouds of flour and sugar sift onto table surfaces and slip under foot. And lard is transferred daily from commercial-sized vats directly to local butts.

I chose two Boston cremes and pocketed some napkins. When I came out I found Joe Morelli lounging against my car. I'd known Morelli all of my life. First when he was a lecherous little kid, then as a dangerous teen. And finally as the guy who at age eighteen, sweet-talked me out of my underwear, laid me down on the floor behind the eclair case one day after work and relieved me of my virginity. Morelli was a cop now, and the only way he'd get back into my pants would be at gunpoint. He worked Vice, and he looked like he knew a lot about it firsthand. He was wearing washed-out Levi's and a navy T-shirt. His hair needed cutting, and his body was perfect. Lean and hard-muscled with the best ass in Trenton . . . maybe the world. Buns you wanted to sink your teeth into.

Not that I intended to nibble on Morelli. He had an annoying habit of periodically popping up in my life, frustrating the hell out of me and then walking off into the sunset. I couldn't do much about the popping up or the walking off. I *could* do something about the frustrating. From here on out, Morelli was erotica non grata. Look but Don't Touch, that was my motto. And he could keep his tongue to himself, thank you.

Morelli grinned by way of hello. 'You're not going to eat both those doughnuts all by yourself, are you?'

'That was the plan. What are you doing here?'

'Drove by. Saw your car. Thought you'd need some help with those Boston cremes.'

'How do you know they're Boston cremes?'

'You always get Boston cremes.'

Last time I saw Morelli was back in February. One minute we were in a clinch on my couch with his hand halfway up my thigh, and the next thing I knew, his pager went off and he was gone. Not to be seen for five months. And now here he was . . . sniffing at my doughnuts.

'Long time, no see,' I said.

'I've been undercover.'

Yeah, right.

'Okay,' he said. 'I could have called.'

'I thought maybe you were dead.'

The smile tightened. 'Wishful thinking?'

'You're scum, Morelli.'

He blew out a sigh. 'You're not going to share those doughnuts, are you?'

I got into my car, slammed the door, squealed out of the lot and headed for home. By the time I got to my apartment I'd eaten both the doughnuts, and I was feeling much better. And I was thinking about Nowicki. She was five years older than Kuntz. High school graduate. Twice married. No children. Her file photo showed me a blowzy blonde with big Jersey hair, lots of makeup and a slim frame. She was squinting into the sun and smiling, wearing four-inch heels, tight black stretch pants and a loose flowing sweater with sleeves pushed up to her elbows and a V neck deep enough to show cleavage. I half expected to find writing on the back of the picture . . . 'If you want a good time, call Maxine Nowicki.'

Probably she'd done exactly what she'd said. Probably she'd stressed out and gone on vacation. Probably I shouldn't exert myself because she'd come home any day now.

And what about her apartment? The apartment was bothersome. The apartment told me Maxine had bigger problems than a simple auto theft charge. Best not to think about the apartment. The apartment only muddied the waters and had nothing to do with my job. My job was simple. Find Maxine. Bring her in.

I locked the CRX and crossed the lot. Mr. Landowsky stepped out the building's back door as I approached. Mr. Landowsky was eighty-two and somehow his chest had shrunk over the years, and now he was forced to hike his pants up under his armpits.

'Oi,' he said. 'This heat! I can't breathe. Somebody should do something.'

I assumed he was talking about God.

'That weatherman on the morning news. He should be shot. How can I go out in weather like this? And then when it gets so hot they keep the supermarkets too cold. Hot, cold. Hot, cold. It gives me the runs.'

I was glad I owned a gun, because when I got as old as Mr. Landowsky I was going to eat a bullet. The first time I got the runs in the supermarket, that was it. BANG! It would all be over.

I took the elevator to the second floor and let myself into my apartment. One bedroom, one bath, living room—dining room, uninspired but adequate kitchen, small foyer with a strip of pegs for hanging coats and hats and gun belts.

My hamster, Rex, was running on his wheel when I came in. I told him about my day and apologized for not saving him some doughnut. He looked disappointed at the doughnut part so I rooted around in my refrigerator and came up with a few grapes. Rex took the grapes and disappeared into his soup can. Life is pretty simple when you're a hamster.

I moseyed back into the kitchen and checked my phone messages.

'Stephanie, this is your mother. Don't forget about dinner. I have a nice roast chicken.'

Saturday night and I was having chicken dinner with my parents. And it wasn't the first time. It was a weekly occurrence. I had no life.

I dragged myself into the bedroom, flopped onto the bed and watched the minute hand creep around the dial on my wristwatch until it was time to go to my parents'. My parents eat dinner at six o'clock. Not a minute sooner or later. That's the way it is. Dinner at six or your life is ruined.

MY PARENTS LIVE in a narrow duplex on a narrow lot on a narrow street in a residential part of Trenton called the burg. When I arrived my mother was waiting at the door.

'What is this outfit you're wearing?' she asked. 'You have no clothes on. How is this to dress?'

'This is a Thunders baseball jersey,' I told her. 'I'm supporting local sports.'

My Grandma Mazur peeked from behind my mother. Grandma Mazur moved in with my parents shortly after my grandfather went heavenward to dine with Elvis. Grandma figures she's of an age to be beyond convention. My father thinks she's of an age to be beyond life.

'I need one of those jerseys,' Grandma said. 'Bet I'd have men following me down the block if I was dressed up like that.'

'Stiva, the undertaker,' my father murmured from the living room, head buried in the paper. 'With his tape measure.'

Grandma linked her arm in mine. 'I've got a treat for you today. Just wait till you see what I've cooked up.'

In the living room the paper was lowered, and my father's eyebrows raised.

My mother made the sign of the cross.

'Maybe you should tell me,' I said to Grandma.

'I was gonna keep it as a surprise, but I suppose I could let you in on it. Being that he'll be here any minute now.'

There was dead silence in the house.

'I invited your boyfriend over for dinner,' Grandma said.

'I don't have a boyfriend!'

'Well, you do now. I arranged everything.'

I spun on my heel and headed for the door. 'I'm leaving.'

'You can't do that!' Grandma yelled. 'He'll be real disappointed. We had a nice long talk. And he said he didn't mind that you shoot people for a living.'

'I don't shoot people for a living. I *almost never* shoot people.' I thunked my head against the wall. 'I hate fix-ups. Fix-ups are always awful.'

'Can't be any more awful than that bozo you married,' Grandma said. 'Only one way to go after that fiasco.'

She was right. My short-lived marriage had been a fiasco.

There was a knock on the door, and we swiveled our heads to look down the hall.

'Eddie Kuntz!' I gasped.

'Yep,' Grandma said. 'That's his name. He called up here looking for you, and so I invited him to dinner.'

'Hey,' Eddie said through the screen.

He was wearing a gray short-sleeved shirt open half-way down his chest, pleated slacks and Gucci loafers, no socks. He had a bottle of red wine in his hand.

'Hello,' we said in unison.

'Can I come in?'

'Sure you can come in,' Grandma said. 'I guess we don't leave handsome men standing at the door.'

He handed the wine to Grandma and winked. 'Here you go, cutie.'

Grandma giggled. 'Aren't you the one.'

'I almost never shoot people,' I said. '*Almost* never.'

'Me too,' he said. 'I hate unnecessary violence.'

I took a step backward. 'Excuse me. I need to help in the kitchen.'

My mother hurried after me. 'Don't even think about it!'

'What?'

'You know what. You were going to sneak out the back door.'

'He's not my type.'

My mother started filling serving dishes with food from the stove. Mashed potatoes, green beans, red cabbage. 'What's wrong with him?'

'He's got too many buttons open on his shirt.'

'He could turn out to be a nice person,' my mother

said. 'You should give him a chance. What would it take? And what about supper? I have this nice chicken that will go to waste. What will you eat for supper if you don't eat here?'

'He called Grandma *cutie*!'

My mother had been slicing up the chicken. She took a drumstick and dropped it on the floor. She kicked it around a little, picked it up and put it on the edge of the plate. 'There,' she said, 'we'll give him this drumstick.'

'Deal.'

'And I have banana cream pie for desert,' she added to seal the bargain. 'So you want to make sure you stay to the end.'

Be still my heart.

CHAPTER TWO

I TOOK MY place at the table, next to Eddie Kuntz. 'You were trying to get in touch with me?'

'Yeah. I lost your card. I put it down somewhere and couldn't find it. So I looked you up in the phone book . . . only I got your parents. Good thing, too. Granny told me you're hard up for a man, and it turns out I'm between women right now, and I don't mind older chicks. So I guess this is your lucky day.'

The chick made a valiant effort not to stab her fork into Eddie Kuntz's eyeball. 'What did you want to talk to me about?'

'I got a call from Maxine. She said she had a message for me and it was coming by airmail tomorrow. I said tomorrow was Sunday, and there was no airmail on Sunday, so why doesn't she just tell me the message. Then she called me some names.' He gave me a face like Maxine had hurt his feelings for no good reason. 'Real abusive,' he said.

'Was that it?'

'That was it. Except she said she was going to make me squirm. And then she hung up.'

*

BY THE TIME we got to the banana cream pie I was feeling antsy. Nowicki had called Kuntz, so Nowicki was alive, and that was good. Unfortunately, she was sending him airmail. Airmail meant distance. And distance was bad. Even more bothersome was the fact that Eddie Kuntz's napkin was moving on his lap without benefit of hands. My first inclination was to shout 'Snake!' and shoot, but probably that wouldn't hold up in court. Besides, as much as I disliked Eddie Kuntz, I could sort of identify with a man who got a stiffie over banana cream pie.

I scarfed down a piece of pie and cracked my knuckles. I glanced at my watch. 'Gee, look at the time!'

My mother gave me her resigned mother look. The one that said, So go . . . at least I got you to stay through dessert and now I know you had one good meal this week. And why can't you be more like your sister Valerie, who's married and has two kids and knows how to cook a chicken.

'Sorry, I have to run,' I said, pushing back from the table.

Kuntz paused with his fork midway to his mouth. 'What? We leaving?'

I retrieved my shoulder bag from the kitchen. '*I'm* leaving.'

'He's leaving too,' my father said, head bent over his pie.

'Well, this was nice,' Grandma said. 'This didn't go so bad.'

KUNTZ DANCED BEHIND me when I opened my car door. Up on the balls of his feet. Lots of energy. Tony Testosterone. 'How about we go somewhere for a drink?'

'Can't. I've got work to do. I need to finish up a lead.'

'Is this about Maxine? I could go with you.'

I slid behind the wheel and cranked the engine over. 'Not a good idea. But I'll give you a call if anything turns up.'

Look out world. Bounty hunter in action.

The diner was less than half filled when I arrived. Most of the people were lingering over coffee. In another hour a younger crowd would straggle in for dessert or fries after the movies let out.

The shift had changed, and I didn't recognize the woman working the register. I introduced myself and asked for Margie.

'Sorry,' the woman said. 'Margie didn't come in today. Called in sick. Said she might not be here tomorrow, either.'

I retreated to my car and rummaged through my bag, searching for the list of family and friends I'd gotten from Kuntz. I ran down the list in the fading light. There was one Margie. No last name, no phone, and for address Kuntz had written 'yellow house on Barnet Street.' He'd also added that Margie drove a red Isuzu.

The sun was a thin scarlet smudge on the horizon when I got to Barnet, but I was able to spot the yellow bungalow and red car. A woman with a heavily bandaged hand stepped out of the yellow house to fetch her cat just as I crept to a stop at the curb. She grabbed the gray cat when she saw me and disappeared behind her door. Even from the curb I could hear the bolt being thrown.

At least she was home. My secret fear had been that she'd disappeared and was sharing rent with Maxine in Cancún.

I hitched my bag onto my shoulder, plastered a

friendly smile on my face, marched up the short cement walk and knocked on her door.

The door opened with the security chain in place. 'Yes?'

I passed my card through to her. 'Stephanie Plum. I'd like to talk to you about Maxine Nowicki.'

'Sorry,' she said. 'I have nothing to say about Maxine. And I'm not feeling good.'

I peeked through the crack in the door and saw she held her bandaged hand to her chest. 'What happened?'

She looked at me slack faced and dead eyed, obviously medicated. 'It was an accident. A kitchen accident.'

'It looks pretty bad.'

She blinked. 'I lost a finger. Well, I didn't actually lose it. It was on the kitchen counter. I took it to the hospital and got it sewed back on.'

I had an instant vision of her finger lying on the kitchen counter. Little black dots danced in front of my eyes, and I felt sweat pop out on my upper lip. 'I'm sorry!'

'It was an accident,' she said. 'An accident.'

'Which finger was it?'

'The middle finger.'

'Oh man, that's my favorite finger.'

'Listen,' she said. 'I gotta go.'

'Wait! Just one minute more. I really need to know about Maxine.'

'There's nothing to know. She's gone. There's nothing more I can tell you.'

I SAT IN my car and took a deep breath. From now on, I was going to be more careful in the kitchen. No more fishing around the garbage disposal looking for bottle caps. No more flamboyant whacking away at salad greens.

It was too late to hit any more people on the list, so I headed home. The temperature had dropped a few degrees, and the air getting sucked through the sunroof was pleasant. I cruised across town, parked behind my apartment building and swung through the rear entrance.

Rex stopped running on his wheel when I walked into the living room. He looked at me, whiskers twitching.

'Don't ask,' I said. 'You don't want to know.' Rex was squeamish about things like chopped-off fingers.

My mother had given me some chicken and some pie to take home. I broke off a chunk of the pie and gave it to Rex. He shoved the crust into his cheek pouch, and his shiny black eyes almost popped out of his head.

Probably I'd looked like that earlier today when Morelli had asked for a doughnut.

I ALWAYS KNOW it's Sunday because I wake up feeling apologetic. That's one of the cool things about being a Catholic . . . it's a multifaceted experience. If you lose the faith, chances are you'll keep the guilt, so it isn't as if you've been skunked altogether. I rolled my head and looked at the digital readout on my clock. Eight. Still time to make late mass. I really should go. My eyes grew heavy at the thought.

Next time I opened my eyes it was eleven. Gosh. Too late to go to church. I heaved myself out of bed and padded to the bathroom, telling myself it was okay because God was willing to forgive little things like skimpy church attendance. Over the years I'd evolved my religion and constructed the Benevolent God. The

Benevolent God also didn't care about such trifles as cussing and fibbing. The Benevolent God looked into a person's heart and knew if she'd been naughty or nice in the grand scheme of things. In my world, God and Santa Claus did not micromanage lives. Of course, that meant you couldn't count on them to help you lose weight, either.

I stepped out of the shower and shook my head by way of styling my hair. I dressed in my usual uniform of spandex shorts and halter-style sports bra and topped it off with a Rangers hockey jersey. I took another look at my hair and decided it needed some help, so I did the gel, blow-dry, hair spray routine. When I was done I was several inches taller. I stood in front of the mirror and did the Wonder Woman thing, feet spread, fists on hips. 'Eat dirt, scumbag,' I said to the mirror. Then I did the Scarlett thing, hand to my heart, coy smile. 'Rhett, you handsome devil, how you do go on.'

Neither of those felt exactly right for the day, so I took myself into the kitchen to see if I could find my identity in the refrigerator. I was plowing through a Sara Lee frozen cheese-cake when the phone rang.

'Hey,' Eddie Kuntz said.

'Hey,' I answered.

'I got the letter from Maxine. I thought you might want to take a look.'

I CRUISED OVER to Muffet Street and found Eddie Kuntz standing on his minuscule front lawn, hands dangling loose at his sides, staring at his front window. The window was smash city. Big hole square in the middle. Lots of fracture lines.

I slammed the door when I got out of the car, but Kuntz didn't turn at the sound, nor at my approach. We stood there for a moment, side by side, studying the window disaster.

'Nice job,' I said.

He nodded. 'Square in the middle. Maxine was on the softball team in high school.'

'She do this last night?'

Another nod. 'I was going to bed. I turned the light off and CRASH . . . a brick came sailing through my front window.'

'Air mail,' I said.

'Yeah, goddamn airmail. My aunt is apeshit. She's my landlady. Her and Uncle Leo live in the other half of this piece of crap. The only reason she isn't out here wringing her hands is on account of she's at church.'

'I didn't realize you were renting.'

'What, you think I'd pick out these paint colors? Do I look like one of those poofie guys?'

Hell no. Poofie guys don't think a rip in an undershirt represents a fashion statement.

He handed me a piece of white paper. 'This was tied around the brick.'

The letter was handwritten and addressed to Kuntz. The message was simple. It told him he'd been a jerk, and if he wanted his property back, he was going to have to go on a treasure hunt. It said his first clue was 'in the big one.' And then a bunch of mixed-up letters followed.

'What does this mean?' I asked him.

'If I knew I wouldn't be calling you, would I? I'd be out on a goddamn treasure hunt.' He threw his hands into the air. 'She's wacko. I should have known she was wacko from the beginning. She had a thing about spies. Was always watching those stupid Bond movies. I'd be banging her from behind, and she'd be watching James Bond on the television. Can you believe it?'

Oh yeah.

'You snoop around, right?' he said. 'You know all about being a spy? You know about cracking codes?'

'I don't know anything about being a spy,' I told him. 'And I don't know what this says.'

In fact, not only didn't I know anything about being a spy, I didn't even know much about being a bounty hunter. I was just bumbling along, trying to pay my rent, praying I'd win the lottery.

'So now what?' Kuntz asked.

I reread the note. 'What is this property she's talking about?'

He gave me a minute-long, blank look. 'Love letters,' he finally said. 'I wrote her some love letters, and I want them back. I don't want them floating around now that we're broken up. There's some embarrassing things in them.'

Eddie Kuntz didn't seem like the type to write love letters, but what do I know? He *did* seem like the type to trash an apartment. 'Did you go to her apartment looking for the letters?'

'Yeah, but the apartment was all locked up.'

'You didn't break in? You didn't have a key?'

'Break in? You mean like bash down the door?'

'I walked through Maxine's apartment yesterday. Someone has torn it apart.'

Again, the blank look. 'I don't know anything about it.'

'I think someone was looking for something. Could Maxine have been keeping drugs?'

He shrugged. 'Who knows with Maxine. Like I said, she's screwy.'

It was nice to know Maxine was in the area, but aside from that I couldn't get too excited about a note I couldn't read. And I definitely didn't want to hear more about Kuntz's sex life.

He draped an arm around my shoulders and leaned close. 'I'm gonna level with you, sweetie-pie. I want to get those letters back. It might even be worth something to me. You know what I mean? Just because you're working for this bail bonds guy doesn't mean you can't work for me, too, right? I'd pay good money. All you have to do is let me talk to Maxie before you turn her over to the cops.'

'Some people might consider that to be double-dipping.'

'A thousand dollars,' Kuntz said. 'That's my final offer. Take it or leave it.'

I stuck out my hand. 'Deal.'

Okay, so I can be bought. At least I don't come cheap. And besides, it was for a good cause. I didn't especially like Eddie Kuntz, but I could understand about embarrassing love letters since I'd written a few myself. They'd gone to my slimy ex-husband, and I'd consider a thousand dollars well spent if I could get them back.

'I'll need the letter,' I said to him.

He handed it over and gave me a punch in the shoulder. 'Go for it.'

THE NOTE SAID the first clue was 'in the big one.' I looked at the jumble of letters that followed, and I saw no pattern. Not such a surprise, since I was missing the puzzle chromosome and couldn't do puzzles designed for nine-year-olds. Fortunately, I lived in a building filled with seniors who sat around all day doing crosswords. And this was sort of like a crossword, right?

My first choice was Mr. Kleinschmidt in 315.

'Ho,' Mr. Kleinschmidt said when he answered the door. 'It's the fearless bounty hunter. Catch any criminals today?'

'Not yet, but I'm working on it.' I handed him the airmail message. 'Can you unscramble this?'

Mr. Kleinschmidt shook his head. 'I do crosswords. This is a jumble. You have to go ask Lorraine Klausner on the first floor. Lorraine does jumbles.'

'Everyone's a specialist today.'

'If Mickey Mouse could fly he'd be Donald Duck.'

I wasn't sure what that meant, but I thanked Mr. Kleinschmidt and I tramped two flights down and had my finger poised to ring Lorraine's bell when her door opened.

'Sol Kleinschmidt just called and told me all about the jumbled-up message,' Lorraine said. 'Come in. I have cookies set out.'

I took a chair across from Lorraine at her kitchen table and watched her work her way through the puzzle.

'This isn't exactly a jumble,' she said, concentrating on the note. 'I don't know how to do this. I only do jumbles.' She tapped her finger on the table. 'I do know someone who might be able to help you, but . . .'

'But?'

'My nephew, Salvatore, has a knack for this sort of thing. Ever since he was little he's been able to solve all kinds of puzzles. One of those freak gifts.'

I looked at her expectantly.

'It's just that he can be a little odd sometimes. I think he's going through one of those conformity things.'

I hoped he didn't have a tongue stud. I had to struggle not to make guttural animal sounds when I talked to people wearing tongue studs. 'Where does he live?'

She wrote an address on the back of the note. 'He's a musician, and he mostly works nights, so he should be home now, but maybe it would be best if I call first.'

SALVATORE SWEET LIVED in a high-rise condo overlooking the river. The building was sandblasted cement and black glass. The landscaping was minimal but well maintained. The lobby was newly painted and carpeted in tones of mauve and gray. Hardly a nonconformist's paradise. And not low-rent, either.

I took the elevator to the ninth floor and rang Sweet's doorbell. A moment later the door opened and I found myself face-to-face with either a very ugly woman or a very gay guy.

'You must be Stephanie.'

I nodded my head.

'I'm Sally Sweet. Aunt Lorraine called and said you had a problem.'

He was dressed in tight black leather pants held together at the sides with leather lacing that left a strip of pale white flesh from ankle to waist, and a black leather vest that molded around cone-shaped, eat-your-heart-out-Madonna breasts. He was close to seven feet tall in his black platform pumps. He had a large hook nose, red roses tattooed on his biceps and—thank you, Lord—he didn't have a tongue stud. He was wearing a blond Farrah Fawcett wig, fake eyelashes and glossy maroon lipstick. His nails had been painted to match his lips.

'Maybe this isn't a good time . . .' I said.

'As good as any.'

I had no idea what to say or where to look. The truth is, he was fascinating. Sort of like staring at a car crash.

He looked down at himself. 'You're probably wondering about the outfit.'

'It's very nice.'

'Yeah, I had the vest made special. I'm lead guitar for the Lovelies. And let me tell you, it's fucking impossible to keep a good manicure through the weekend as a lead guitarist. If I'd known how things would turn out for me, I'd have taken up the fucking drums.'

'Looks like you're doing okay.'

'Success is my middle name. Two years ago I was straight as an arrow, playing for Howling Dogs. You ever hear of Howling Dogs?'

I shook my head. 'No.'

'Nobody fucking heard of Howling Dogs. I was fucking living in a fucking packing crate in the alley behind Romanos Pizza. I've been punk, funk, grunge and R&B. I've been with the Funky Butts, the Pitts, Beggar Boys, and Howling Dogs. I was with Howling Dogs the longest. It was a fucking depressing experience. I couldn't stand fucking singing all those fucking songs about fucking hearts fucking breaking and fucking goldfish fucking going to heaven. And then I had to fucking look like some western dude. I mean, how can you have any self-respect when you have to go on stage in a cowboy hat?'

I was pretty good at cussing, but I didn't think I could keep up with Sally. On my best day, I couldn't squeeze all those 'f' words into a sentence. 'Boy, you can really curse,' I said.

'You can't be a fucking musician without fucking cursing.'

I knew that was true, because sometimes I watched rock-umentaries on MTV. My eyes strayed to his hair. 'But now you're wearing a Farrah Fawcett wig. Isn't that kind of like a cowboy hat?'

'Yeah, only this is a fucking statement. This is fucking politically correct. See, this is the ultimate sensitive man. This is taking my female shit out of the closet. And like I'm saying, here it is, you know?'

'Un huh.'

'And besides, I'm making a shitload of money. I caught the wave on this one. This is the year of the drag queen. We're like a freaking fucking invasion.' He took the note from my hand and studied it. 'Not only am I booked solid for every weekend for two years . . . I get money stuffed in my goddamn pants. I got money I don't know what to do with.'

'So I guess you feel lucky to be gay.'

'Well, just between you and me, I'm not actually gay.'

'You're a cross-dresser.'

'Yeah. Something like that. I mean, I wouldn't mind being sort of gay. Like, I guess I could dance with a guy, but I'm not doing any of that butt stuff.'

I nodded. I felt like that about men, too.

He got a pen from a hall table and made some marks on the note. 'Lorraine said you're a bounty hunter.'

'I almost never shoot anybody,' I said.

'If I was a bounty hunter I'd fucking shoot *lots* of people.' He finished scribbling on the paper and gave it back to me.

'You're probably gonna find this hard to believe, but I was sort of weird when I was a kid.'

'No!'

'Yeah. I was like . . . out there. So I used to spend a lot of time talking to Spock. And Spock and me, we'd send messages to each other in code.'

'You mean Spock from *Star Trek*?'

'Yeah, that's the dude. Boy, Spock and I were tight. We did this code thing every day for years. Only our codes were hard. This code is too easy. This code is just a bunch of run-together letters with some extra shit thrown in. "Red and green and blue. At Cluck in a Bucket the clue waits for you." '

'I know Cluck in a Bucket,' I said. 'It's just down from the bonds office.'

The trash containers in the Cluck in a Bucket parking lot are colored red, green and blue. The green and the blue are for recycling paper and aluminum. The big red one is for garbage. I'd bet my apprehension fee the next clue was in the garbage.

A second man came to the door. He was neatly dressed in Dockers and a perfectly pressed button-down shirt. He was shorter than Sweet. Maybe 5'9". He was slender and totally hairless, like a bald Chihuahua, with soft brown eyes hidden behind thick glasses, and a mouth that seemed too wide, too sensuous for his small pinched face and little button nose.

'What's going on?' he asked.

'This is Stephanie Plum,' Sally said. 'The one Lorraine called about.'

The man extended his hand. 'Gregory Stern. Everyone calls me Sugar.'

'Sugar and I are roommates,' Sally said. 'We're in the band together.'

'I'm the band tart,' Sugar said. 'And sometimes I sing.'

'I always wanted to sing with a band,' I said. 'Only, I can't sing.'

'I bet you could,' Sugar said. 'I bet you'd be wonderful.'

'You'd better go get dressed,' Sally said to Sugar. 'You're going to be late again.'

'We have a gig this afternoon,' Sugar explained. 'Wedding reception.'

Yeeesh.

CLUCK IN A BUCKET is on Hamilton. It's housed in a cement cube with windows on three sides. And it's best known not for its outstanding food but for the giant rotating chicken impaled on a thirty-foot flagpole anchored in the parking lot.

I cruised into the lot and stopped short of the red Dumpster. The temperature had to be a hundred in the shade with a hundred percent humidity. My sunroof was open, and when I parked the car I felt the weight of the heat settling around me. Maybe when I found Nowicki I'd have my air-conditioning fixed, or maybe I'd spend a few days at the beach . . . or maybe I'd pay my rent and avoid eviction.

I walked to the Dumpster, thinking about ordering lunch. Two pieces of chicken plus a biscuit and slaw and an extra large soda sounded about right.

I peeked over the edge of the Dumpster, gave an involuntary gasp and staggered back a few feet. Most of the garbage was in bags, but some of the bags had split and had spewed out guts like bloated roadkill. The stench of vegetable rot and gangrenous chicken boiled over the Dumpster and had me reassessing my lunch plans. It also had me reassessing my job. There was no way I was scrounging in this mess for the stupid clue.

I returned to my car and called Eddie Kuntz on my cell phone. 'I've deciphered the note,' I told him. 'I'm at Cluck in a Bucket, and there's another clue here. I think you'd better come see for yourself.'

Half an hour later, Kuntz pulled into the lot. I was sitting in my car, slurping down my third giant-sized Diet Coke, and I was sweating like a pig. Kuntz looked nice and cool in his new sport utility vehicle and factory-installed air. He'd changed his clothes from the sweat-stained boxers he'd worn this morning to a black fishnet undershirt, black spandex shorts that didn't do much to hide Mr. Lumpy, two gold chains around his neck, and brand new Air Jordans that looked to be about a size 42.

'All dressed up,' I said to him.

'Gotta maintain the image. Don't like to disappoint the chicks.'

I handed him the decoded note. 'The next clue is in the red Dumpster.'

He walked to the Dumpster, stuck his head over the edge and recoiled.

'Pretty ripe,' I said. 'Maybe you want to put on some old clothes before you go in there.'

'What, are you nuts? I'm not wading through that shit.'

'It's your note.'

'Yeah, but I've hired *you*,' Eddie said.

'You didn't hire me to go Dumpster surfing.'

'I hired you to find her. That's all I want. I just want you to find her.'

He had two pagers clipped onto his spandex shorts.

One of them beeped and displayed a message. He read the message and sighed. 'Chicks,' he said. 'They never stop.'

Right. It was probably from his mother.

He went to his car and made a couple of calls on his car phone. He finished the calls and came back to me. 'Okay,' he said, 'it's all taken care of. All you have to do is stay here and wait for Carlos. I'd stay, but I got other things to do.'

I watched him leave, then I turned and squinted beyond the lot. 'Hey Maxine,' I yelled. 'You out there?' If it had been me I'd have wanted to see Kuntz slopping around in the garbage. 'Listen,' I said, 'it was a good idea, but it didn't work out. How about you let me buy you a couple pieces of chicken?'

Maxine didn't come forward, so I sat in my car and waited for Carlos. After about twenty minutes a flatbed truck pulled into the lot and unloaded a backhoe. The flatbed driver fired up the backhoe, rolled it to the Dumpster and put the bucket under the bin's bottom edge. The Dumpster tipped in slow motion and then crashed to the pavement and lay there like a big dead dinosaur. Garbage bags hit the ground and burst, and a glass jar clinked onto the blacktop, rolled between the bags and came to rest a few feet from where I was standing. Someone had used a Magic Marker to write 'clue' on the outside of the jar.

The backhoe driver looked over at me. 'You Stephanie?'

I was staring, transfixed, at the Dumpster and the mess in front of me, and my heart was beating with a sickening thud. 'Unh huh.'

'You want me to spread this garbage around some more?'

'No!'

People were standing in the doorways and staring through the windows of Cluck in a Bucket. Two high school kids dressed in yellow-and-red Cluck uniforms ran across the lot to the backhoe.

'What are you doing? What are you doing?' one of the kids yelled.

'Hey, don't get your undies in a bunch,' the driver said to the kid. 'Life's too short.' He motored the backhoe onto the flatbed, got behind the wheel, gave us a military salute and drove off.

We all stood there, momentarily speechless.

The kid turned to me. 'Do you know him?'

'Nope,' I said. 'Never saw him before in my life.'

I WAS LESS than a mile from my apartment, so I grabbed the jar, jumped into my car and headed for home. All the way, I kept looking over my shoulder, half expecting to be tracked down like a dog by the garbage police.

I unlocked my door and called to Rex. 'Another one of those days.'

Rex was asleep in his soup can and made no response, so I went into the kitchen and made myself a peanut butter and olive sandwich. I cracked open a beer and studied the new encrypted message while I ate. I looked for run-together words and extra letters, but it was all a big glob of nothing to me. Finally I gave up and called Sally. His phone rang three times and his machine kicked in. 'Sally and Sugar aren't home, but they'd just *loooooove* to talk to you, so leave a message.'

I left my name and number and went back to staring at the note. By three o'clock my eyes felt fried and there was no word from Sally, so I decided to go door-to-door to the seniors again. Mr. Kleinschmidt told me it wasn't a crossword. Lorraine told me it wasn't a jumble. Mr. Markowitz told me he was watching TV and didn't have time for such nonsense.

The light was blinking on my phone machine when I returned to my kitchen.

The first message was from Eddie Kuntz. 'So where is she?' That was it. That was the whole message.

'What a moolack,' I said to the answering machine.

The second message was from Ranger. 'Call me.'

Ranger is a man of few words. He's Cuban-American, former Special Forces, he makes a much better friend than an enemy, and he's Vinnie's numero uno bounty hunter. I dialed Ranger's number and waited to hear breathing. Sometimes that was all you got.

'Yo,' Ranger said.

'Yo yourself.'

'I need you to help me take down a skip.'

This meant Ranger either needed a good laugh or else he needed a white female to use as a decoy. If Ranger needed serious muscle he wouldn't call me. Ranger knew people who would take on the Terminator for a pack of Camels and the promise of a fun time.

'I need to get an FTA out of a building, and I haven't got what it takes,' Ranger said.

'And just exactly what is it that you're lacking?'

'Smooth white skin barely hidden behind a short skirt and tight sweater. Two days ago Sammy the Gimp bought the farm. He's laid out at Leoni's, and my man, Kenny Martin, is in there paying his respects.'

'So why don't you just wait until he comes out?'

'He's in there with his mother and his sister and his Uncle Vito. My guess is they'll leave together, and I don't want to wade through the whole Grizolli family to get at this guy.'

No kidding. The landfill was littered with the remains of people who tried to wade through Vito Grizolli.

'Actually, I had plans for tonight,' I said. 'They include living a little longer.'

'I just want you to get my man out the back door. I'll take it from there.'

I heard the disconnect, but I shouted into the phone anyway. *'What are you freaking nuts?'*

FIFTEEN MINUTES LATER I was dressed in four-inch FMPs (short for 'fuck-me pumps,' because when you walked around in them you looked like Whorehouse Wonder Bitch). I shimmied into a low-cut black knit dress that was bought with the intent of losing five pounds, gunked up my eyes with a lot of black mascara and beefed up my cleavage by stuffing Nerf balls into my bra.

Ranger was parked on Roebling, half a block from the funeral home. He didn't turn when I pulled to the curb, but I saw his eyes on me in the rearview mirror.

He was smiling when I slid in beside him. 'Nice dress you're almost wearing. You ever think about changing professions?'

'Constantly. I'm thinking about it now.'

Ranger handed me a photo. 'Kenny Martin. Age twenty-two. Minor league loser. Charged with armed robbery.' He glanced at the black leather bag I had draped on my shoulder. 'You carrying?'

'Yes.'

'Is it loaded?'

I stuck my hand in the bag and rooted around. 'I'm not sure, but I think I've got a few bullets in here somewhere . . .'

'Cuffs?'

'I definitely have cuffs.'

'Defense spray?'

'Yep. Got defense spray.'

'Go get 'em, tiger.'

I sashayed across the street and up the steps to Leoni's. A small knot of old Italian men stood smoking on the front porch. Conversation stopped when I approached, and the group parted to let me pass. There were more people in the vestibule. None of them was Kenny Martin. I went to room one, where Sammy the Gimp was on display, resting nicely in an ornate mahogany casket. There were lots of flowers and lots of old Italian women. No one seemed to be too upset about Sammy's demise. No heavily sedated widow. No wailing mother. No Kenny.

I said good-bye to Sammy and tottered down the hall in my heels. There was a small foyer at the end of the hall. The foyer opened to the back door, and Kenny Martin was standing in front of the door, sneaking a smoke. Beyond the door was a covered driveway, and somewhere beyond the driveway was Ranger.

I leaned against the wall across from Kenny and smiled. 'Hi.'

His eyes fixed onto my Nerf balls. 'Are you here to see Sammy?'

I shook my head no. 'Mrs. Kowalski in room two.'

'You don't look all broke up.'

I shrugged.

'If you was all broke up I could comfort you. I got lots of ways to comfort a woman.'

I raised an eyebrow. 'Hmm?'

He was 5'10" and a solid 190 pounds. He was dressed in a dark blue suit and white shirt with the top button popped open.

'What's your pleasure, dollie?' he asked.

I looked him up and down and smiled as if I liked what I saw. 'What's your name?'

'Kenny. Kenny "the Man" Martin.'

Kenny the Man. Unh! Mental head slap. I extended my hand. 'Stephanie.'

In lieu of a handshake he laced his fingers into mine and stepped closer. 'Pretty name.'

'I was going outside for some fresh air. Want to join me?'

'Yeah, sure. Nothing in here but dead people. Even the people who are alive are dead, you know what I mean?'

A little girl ran down the hall to us. 'Kenny, Mama says we have to go now.'

'Tell her I'll be there in a minute.'

'She said I'm supposed to bring you *now*!'

Kenny did palms-up. A gesture of the futility of arguing. Everyone knows you never win against an Italian mother. 'Maybe I could call you sometime?' Kenny said to me. 'Maybe we could get together later.'

Never underestimate the power of a Nerf ball. 'Sure. Why don't we go outside, and I'll write down my number. I really need some air.'

'Now!' the kid yelled.

Kenny made a lunge at the kid, and she whirled and ran back to Mama, shrieking at the top of her lungs.

'I gotta go,' Kenny said.

'One second. I'll give you my business card.' I had my head in my bag, scrounging for my defense spray. If I couldn't get him to walk through the door, I'd give him a shot of spray and drag him out.

I heard more footsteps on the carpet and looked up to find a woman striding toward us. She was slim and pretty with short blond hair. She was wearing a gray suit and heels, and her expression turned serious when she saw me with Kenny.

'Now I see the problem,' she said to Kenny. 'Your mother sent me to fetch you, but it looks like you've got a complication here.'

'No complication,' Kenny said. 'Just tell her to keep her shirt on.'

'Oh yeah,' the woman said. 'I'm going to tell your mother to keep her shirt on. That's like a death wish.' She looked to me, and then she looked to Kenny, and then she smiled. 'You don't know, do you?' she asked Kenny.

I was still searching for the spray. Hair brush, flashlight, travel pack of tampons. Damn it, where was the spray?

'Know what?' Kenny said. 'What are you talking about?'

'Don't you ever read the paper? This is Stephanie Plum. She blew up the funeral home last year. She's a bounty hunter.'

'You're shitting me!'

Oh boy.

CHAPTER THREE

Kenny gave me a shot to the shoulder that knocked me back a couple of feet. 'Is that true, what Terry said? Are you a bounty hunter?'

'Hey!' I said. 'Keep your hands off me.'

He gave me another whack that had me against the wall. 'Maybe you need to be taught a lesson not to mess with Kenny.'

'Maybe you need to be taught a lesson not to jump bail.' I had my hand in my bag, and I couldn't find the lousy defense spray, so I hauled out a can of extra-hold hair spray and let him have it square in the face.

'Yeow,' Kenny yelped, jumping back, hands to his face. 'You bitch, I'll get you for this. I'll . . .' He took his hands away. 'Hey, wait a minute. What is this shit?'

Terry's smile widened. 'You've been hair-sprayed, Kenny.'

The little girl and an older woman hustled down the hall.

'What's going on?' the woman wanted to know.

An old man appeared. Vito Grizolli, looking like he'd walked off the set of *The Godfather*.

'Kenny's been hair-sprayed,' Terry told everyone. 'He put up a pretty good fight, but he just didn't have the muscle to stand up to extra hold.'

The mother turned on me. 'You did this to my boy?'

I tried not to sigh, but one escaped anyway. Some days it doesn't pay to get out of bed. 'I'm a bond enforcement officer,' I told her. 'I work for Vincent Plum. Your son failed to appear in court, and now I need to bring him in to reschedule and have his case reviewed.'

Mrs. Martin sucked in air and faced-off at Kenny. 'You did that? You didn't go to court? What's the matter with you? Don't you know anything?'

'It's all bullshit,' Kenny said.

Mrs. Martin smacked him on the side of the head. 'You watch your language!'

'And how is this to dress?' she said to me. 'If you were my daughter I wouldn't let you out of the house.'

I scrambled away before she could smack me, too.

'Kids,' Vito Grizolli said. 'What's happening to this world?'

From a man who had people killed on a regular basis.

He shook his finger at Kenny. 'You should have kept your court date. You do this like a man. You go with her now, and you let the lawyers do their job.'

'I got hair spray in my eye,' Kenny said. 'It's watering. I need a doctor.'

I held the back door open for him. 'Don't be such a big baby,' I said. 'I get hair spray in my eyes all the time.'

Ranger was waiting under the canopy. He was dressed in a black T-shirt and black assault pants tucked into black boots. He had a body like Schwarzenegger, dark hair slicked back off his face and a two-hundred-watt smile. He was drop-dead sexy, he was as sane as Batman, and he was a primo bounty hunter.

He gave me all two hundred watts. 'Nice touch with the hair spray.'

'Don't start.'

MONDAY MORNING I woke up feeling restless. I wanted to move on Maxine Nowicki, but I was stalled on the clue. I looked at the note again and felt frustration gnawing at me. Sally Sweet hadn't returned my call. I was itching to call him again, but it was eight o'clock, and I thought it was possible drag queens weren't early risers.

I was on my second cup of coffee when the phone rang.

'It's me,' Sally said.

I read the note over the phone, letter by letter.

Silence.

'Sally?'

'I'm thinking. I'm thinking. I've been up all night, looking sexy, shaking my ass. It isn't easy, you know.'

I could hear yelling in the background. 'What's going on?'

'It's Sugar. He's got breakfast all made.'

'Sugar makes your breakfast?'

'I'm on the phone with Stephanie,' Sally yelled back.

'Boy, I don't have anyone make breakfast for me.'

'What you have to do is live with a gay guy,' Sally said. 'They're into this cooking shit.'

Something to think about.

'I don't want to rush your breakfast,' I said. 'I'll be home for another hour, then I'm going to the office. When you figure it out you can call me at the office, or you can leave a message on my machine.'

'Ten four, kemosabe.'

I took a shower and dressed for another scorcher day. I

gave Rex fresh water and some hamster food, which he didn't deem worthy to so much as sniff at.

I slung my black leather tote over my shoulder, locked up and took the stairs to the lobby. Outside, the blacktop was steaming, and the sun was beginning to throb in a murky sky. I played Savage Garden all the way to the office and arrived psyched because I'd had good traffic karma, sailing through the lights.

Connie was bent over a file when I walked in. Her black hair was teased high around her face like a movie set that was all facade. Everything up front and nothing in the back. Killer hair as long as she didn't turn around.

'If you want to talk to the man, he isn't in,' she said.

Lula popped up from behind a bank of file cabinets. 'He's doin' a nooner with a goat today. I saw it on his calendar.'

'So how's it going?' Connie asked. 'Any action on the Nowicki thing?'

I passed a copy of the note to Connie and Lula. 'I have a message from her that's written in some kind of code.'

'Lose me,' Lula said. 'Code isn't one of my specialties.'

Connie sunk two teeth into a heavily lipsticked lower lip. 'Maybe the numbers are really letters.'

'I thought of that, but I couldn't get it to work.'

We all stared at the note for a while.

'Might not mean anything,' Lula finally said. 'Might be a joke.'

I nodded. Joke note was a possibility.

'I helped Ranger with an apprehension yesterday,' I said. 'Kenny Martin.'

Connie gave a low laugh. 'Vito Grizolli's nephew? Bet that was fun.'

'There was a woman with him that I can't place. I

know I've seen her before, but it keeps slipping away from me.'

'What'd she look like?'

'Slim, pretty, short blond hair. He called her Terry.'

'Terry Gilman,' Connie said. 'Used to be Terry Grizolli. Was married to Billy Gilman for about six hours and kept his name.'

'Terry Grizolli! That was Terry Grizolli?' Terry Grizolli was two years older than me and had been linked with Joe Morelli all through high school. She'd been voted prom queen and had created a school scandal by choosing Joe as her escort. After graduation, she'd gone on to become a professional cheerleader for the New York Giants. 'I haven't seen her in years,' I said. 'What's she doing now? Is she still a cheerleader?'

'Rumor has it she's working for Vito. She has a lot of money and no discernible job.'

'You telling me she's like a wise guy?'

'Affirmative action,' Connie said.

The front door opened, and we all turned to look. Lula was the first to find her voice. 'Killer earring.'

It was a parrot swinging on a gold hoop that was looped through one of Sally's ears.

'Got it at the shore,' he said. 'You buy a pair of thong briefs and they throw in the earring.' He made a grab at his ass and hiked himself up. 'Christ, I don't know how they wear these thong things. They're giving me hemorrhoids.'

He was minus the Farrah wig, and his own hair was a mess of dark brown corkscrew strands. Sort of Rasta without the dreds. He was wearing cut-off denims, a white T-shirt, red clogs and was freshly manicured with silver polish.

'This is Sally Sweet,' I told Connie and Lula.

'I bet,' Lula said.

Sally handed me the translation of the coded message and looked around. 'I thought there'd be wanted posters on the walls and gun racks filled with shotguns.'

'This isn't Dodge City,' Lula said. 'We got some class here. We keep the guns in the back room with the pervert.'

I read the note. ' "One-thirty-two Howser Street. Under the bench." That's Maxine's mother's address.'

Sally slouched onto the couch. 'When I was a kid I watched reruns of Steve McQueen. Now *he* was a bounty hunter.'

'Damn skippy,' Lula said. 'He was the shit.'

'So now what?' Sally wanted to know. 'We going to Howser Street?'

Foreboding sliced into my stomach. We?

Lula slammed her file drawer shut. 'Hold on. You're not going off without me! Suppose something goes wrong? Suppose you need a big full-figure woman like me to help straighten things out?'

I like Lula a lot, but last time we worked together I gained seven pounds and almost got arrested for shooting a guy who was already dead.

'*I'm* going to Howser Street,' I said. 'Only me. One person. Steve McQueen worked alone.'

'I don't mean to be insulting,' Lula said, 'but you ain't no Steve McQueen. And something happens you'll be happy I'm around. Besides, this'll be fun . . . the two of us working on a case together again.'

'Three of us,' Sally said. 'I'm going, too.'

'Oh boy,' Lula said. 'The three muffkateers.'

*

49

LULA GAVE THE Nowicki house the once-over. 'Don't appear like Maxine's mama spends much time spiffing up the old homestead.'

We were in Lula's Firebird with Sally in the back seat doing air guitar to Lula's rap music. Lula cut the engine, the music stopped, and Sally snapped to attention.

'Looks kind of spooky,' Sally said. 'You guys have guns, right?'

'Wrong,' I said. 'We don't need guns to retrieve a clue.'

'Well, this is fucking disappointing. I figured you'd kick the door down and blast yourselves into the house. You know, rough up some people.'

'You want to cut down on the breakfast drugs,' Lula said to Sally. 'You keep going like this all your nose hairs are gonna fall out.'

I unbuckled my seat belt. 'There's a little wooden bench on the front porch. With any luck, we won't have to go in the house.'

We crossed the patchy lawn, and Lula tested the bottom porch step, pausing when it groaned under her weight. She moved to the next step and picked her way around floorboards that were obviously rotted.

Sally tiptoed behind her. *Clonk, clonk, clonk* with his clogs. Not exactly the stealth transvestite.

They each took an end of the bench and flipped it over.

No note stuck to the bottom.

'Maybe it blew away,' Lula said.

There wasn't a stray breath of air in all of Jersey, but we checked the surroundings anyway, the three of us fanning out, covering the yard.

No note.

'Hunh,' Lula said. 'We been given the runaround.'

There was a crawl space under the porch, enclosed with wooden lattice. I dropped to hands and knees and squinted through the lattice. 'The note said "under the bench." It could have meant under the porch, under the bench.' I jogged to the car and retrieved a flashlight from the glove compartment. I returned to the porch, scrunched low and flashed the beam around the dirt floor. Sure enough, there was a glass jar directly under the part of the porch that supported the bench.

Two yellow eyes caught in the light, held for a second, and skittered away.

'Do you see it?' Lula wanted to know.

'Yep.'

'Well?'

'There are eyes under there. Little beady yellow ones. And spiders. Lots of spiders.'

Lula gave an involuntary shiver.

Sally made another adjustment on his thong.

'I'd go get it, but a big woman like me wouldn't fit,' Lula said. 'Sure is a shame it isn't just a little roomier.'

'I think you'd fit.'

'Nope, unh ah, I know I wouldn't fit.'

I considered the spiders. 'I might not fit, either.'

'I'd fit,' Sally said, 'but I'm not doing it. I paid twenty bucks for this manicure, and I'm not fucking it up crawling under some rat-infested porch.'

I hunkered down for another look. 'Maybe we can stick a rake in there and pull the jar out.'

'Nuh ah,' Lula said. 'A rake isn't gonna be big enough. You gotta go in from the end here, and it's too far away. Where you gonna get a rake anyway?'

'We can ask Mrs. Nowicki.'

'Oh yeah,' Lula said. 'From the looks of this lawn she

does lots of gardening.' Lula stood on tiptoes and looked in a window on the side of the house. 'Probably not even home. Seems like she'd be out by now what with us up on her porch and all.' Lula moved to another window and pressed her nose to the glass. 'Uh oh.'

'What uh oh?' I hated uh oh.

'You'd better look at this.'

Sally and I trotted over and pressed our noses to the glass.

Mrs. Nowicki was stretched out on the kitchen floor. She had a bloody towel wrapped around the top of her head, and an empty bottle of Jim Beam was on the floor beside her. She was wearing a cotton nightgown, and her bare feet were splayed toes out.

'Looks to me like dead city,' Lula said. 'You want a rake, you better get it yourself.'

I knocked on the window. 'Mrs. Nowicki!'

Mrs. Nowicki didn't move a muscle.

'Think this must have just happened,' Lula said. 'If she'd laid there for any amount of time in this heat she'd be swelled up big as a beach ball. She'd have burst apart. There'd be guts and maggots all over the place.'

'I hate to miss seeing the guts and maggots,' Sally said. 'Maybe we should come back in a couple hours.'

I turned from the window and headed for the car. 'We need to call the police.'

Lula was on my heels. 'Hold the phone on the *we* part. Those police people give me the hives.'

'You're not a hooker anymore. You don't have to worry about the police.'

'One of them traumatic emotional things,' Lula said.

Ten minutes later, two blue-and-whites angled to the curb behind me. Carl Costanza emerged from the first car, looked at me and shook his head. I'd known Carl since grade school. He was always the skinny kid with the bad haircut and wise mouth. He'd bulked up some in the last few years, and he'd found a good barber. He still had the wise mouth, but under it all, he was a decent person and a pretty good cop.

'Another dead body?' Carl asked. 'What are you going for, a record? Most bodies found by an individual in the city of Trenton?'

'She's on the kitchen floor. We haven't been in the house. The door is locked.'

'How do you know she's on the floor if the door is locked?'

'I was sort of looking in the window, and . . .'

Carl held up his hand. 'Don't tell me. I don't want to hear this. Sorry I asked.'

The cop in the second car had gone to the side window and was standing there, hands on gun belt. 'She's on the floor all right,' he said, peering in. He rapped on the window. 'Hey, lady!' He turned to us and narrowed his eyes against the sun. 'Looks dead to me.'

Carl went to the front door and knocked. 'Mrs. Nowicki? It's the police.' He knocked louder. 'Mrs. Nowicki, we're coming in.' He gave the door a good shot with his fist, the rotted molding splintered off, and the door swung open.

I followed Carl into the kitchen and watched while he stooped over Mrs. Nowicki, feeling for a pulse, looking for a sign of life.

There were more bloody towels in the sink and a bloody paring knife on the counter. My first thought had been gunshot, but there were no guns in sight and no sign of struggle.

'You better call this in for the ME,' Carl said to the second cop. 'I don't know exactly what we've got here.'

Sally and Lula had taken positions against the wall.

'What do you think?' Lula asked Carl.

Carl shrugged. 'Nothing much. She looks pretty dead.'

Lula nodded. 'That what I thought, too. Soon as I saw her I said to myself, Hell, that woman's dead.'

The second cop disappeared to make the call, and Lula inched closer to Mrs. Nowicki. 'What do you think happened to her? I bet she fell and hit her head, and then she wrapped her head in a towel and croaked.'

That sounded reasonable to me . . . except for the paring knife with blood and pieces of hair stuck to it.

Lula bent at the waist and examined the towel, wrapped turban style. 'Must have been a good clonk she took. Lots of blood.'

Usually when people die their bodies evacuate and the smell gets bad fast. Mrs. Nowicki didn't smell dead. Mrs. Nowicki smelled like Jim Beam.

Carl and I were both registering this oddity, looking at each other sideways when Mrs. Nowicki opened one eye and fixed it on Lula.

'YOW!' Lula yelled, jumping back a foot, knocking into Sally. 'Her eye popped open!'

'The better to see you with,' Mrs. Nowicki rasped out, alto voiced, one pack short of lung cancer.

Carl stepped into Mrs. Nowicki's line of sight. 'We thought you were dead.'

'Not yet, honey,' Mrs. Nowicki said. 'But I'll tell you, I have one hell of a headache.' She raised a shaky hand and felt the towel. 'Oh, yeah, now I remember.'

'What happened?'

'It was an accident. I was trying to cut my hair, and my

hand slipped, and I gave myself a little nick. It was bleeding some, so I wrapped my head in a towel and took a few medicinal hits from the bottle.' She struggled to sit. 'Don't exactly know what happened after that.'

Lula had her hand on her hip. 'Looks to me like you drained the bottle and passed out. Think you took one too many of them medicinal hits.'

'Looks to me like she didn't take enough,' Sally murmured. 'I liked her better dead.'

'I need a cigarette,' Mrs. Nowicki said. 'Anybody got a cigarette?'

I could hear cars pulling up outside and footsteps in the front room. The second uniform came in, followed by a suit.

'She isn't dead,' Carl explained.

'Maybe she used to be,' Lula said. 'Maybe she's one of them *living* dead.'

'Maybe you're one of them *nut cases*,' Mrs. Nowicki said.

Lights from an EMS truck flashed outside, and two paramedics wandered into the kitchen.

I eased my way out the door, to the porch and onto the lawn. I didn't especially want to be there when they unwound the towel.

'I don't know about you,' Lula said, 'but I'm ready to leave this party.'

I didn't have a problem with that. Carl knew where to find me if there were questions. Didn't look like there was anything criminal here, anyway. Drunken lush slices scalp with a paring knife and passes out. Probably happens all the time.

We piled into the Firebird and hauled ass back to the office. I said good-bye to Lula and Sally, slid behind the wheel of my CRX and motored home. When things calmed down I'd go back with some sort of long-handled mechanism for retrieving the bottle. I didn't want to explain to the cops about the clues.

In the meantime, there were a few phone calls I could make. I'd only gotten partially through Eddie Kuntz's list. It wouldn't hurt to run through the rest of the names.

Mrs. Williams, one of my neighbors, was in the lobby when I swung through the doors. 'I've got a terrible ringing in my ears,' she said. 'And I'm having a dizzy spell.'

Another neighbor, Mrs. Balog, was standing next to Mrs. Williams, checking her mailbox. 'It's the hardening of the arteries. Evelyn Krutchka on the third floor has it something awful. I heard her arteries are just about turned to stone.'

Most of the people in my building were seniors. There were a couple of single mothers with babies, Ernie Wall and his girlfriend, May, and one other woman my age, who only spoke Spanish. We were the segment of society on fixed incomes or incomes of dubious reliability. We weren't interested in tennis or sitting at poolside. For the most part we were a quiet, peaceful group, armed to the teeth for no good reason, violent only when a premium parking slot was at stake.

I took the stairs to the second floor, hoping they'd have some effect on the pie I'd had for breakfast. I let myself into my apartment and made an instant left turn into the kitchen. I stuck my head in the refrigerator and pushed things around some, searching for the perfect lunch. After a few minutes of this I decided on a hard-boiled egg and a banana.

I sat at my dining room table, which is actually in a

little alcove off my living room, and I ate my egg and started on the list of names and businesses Kuntz had given me. I dialed Maxine's cleaner first. No, they hadn't seen her lately. No, she didn't have any clothes to pick up. I called my cousin Marion, who worked at Maxine's bank, and asked about recent transactions. No new postings, Marion said. The most recent transaction was two weeks ago when she withdrew three hundred dollars from the outside ATM.

Last name on the list was a 7-Eleven in north Trenton, a quarter mile from Eddie Kuntz and Mama Nowicki. The night manager had just come on when I called. She said a woman meeting Maxine's description had been in the night before. She remembered the woman because she was a regular. It had been late at night and store traffic had been slow. The woman had been chatty and had relieved the tedium.

I stuffed Maxine's photo into my shoulder bag and took off for the 7-Eleven to confirm the identification. I parked nose-in to the curb at the front of the store and stared beyond the plate glass windows to the register. There were four men in line. Three still in suits, looking rumpled from the heat and the workday. By the time I made my way through the door, there were two men left. I waited for them to complete their business before introducing myself to the woman behind the counter.

She extended her hand. 'Helen Badijian. I'm the night manager. We spoke on the phone.'

Her brown hair was plaited in a single braid that reached to her shoulder blades, and her face was devoid of makeup with the exception of eyes lined in smudgy black liner. 'I didn't get it straight on the phone,' Helen said. 'Are you with the police?'

I usually try to avoid answering that question directly. 'Bond enforcement,' I said, leaving Helen to believe whatever. Not that I would *lie* about police affiliation. Imitating a police officer isn't smart. Still, if someone misunderstood because they weren't paying attention . . . that wasn't my problem.

Helen looked at Maxine's photo and nodded her head. 'Yep, that's her. Only she's a lot more tan now.'

So I knew two things. Maxine was alive, and she had time to sit in the sun.

'She bought a couple packs of cigarettes,' Helen said. 'Menthol. And a large Coke. Said she had a long drive ahead of her. I asked her if she was going to buy a lottery ticket because that's what she always did . . . bought a ticket every week. She said no. Said she didn't need to win the lottery anymore.'

'Anything else?'

'That was it.'

'You notice the car she was driving?'

'Sorry. I didn't notice.'

I left my card and asked Helen to call if Maxine returned. I expected the card would go in the trash the moment I pulled out of the lot, but I left one anyway. For the most part, people would talk to me when confronted face-to-face but were unwilling to take a more aggressive step like initiating a phone call. Initiating a phone call felt like snitching, and snitching wasn't cool.

I rolled out of the lot and drove past the hot spots . . . Margie's house, Maxine's apartment, Kuntz's house, Mama Nowicki's house and the diner. Nothing seemed suspicious. I was itching to get the next clue, but there were people out on Howser Street. Mrs. Nowicki's neighbor was watering his lawn. A couple of kids were

FOUR TO SCORE

doing curb jumps on skateboards. Better to wait until dark, I thought. Two more hours and the sun would go down and everyone would move inside. Then I could skulk around in the shadows and, I hoped, not have to answer any questions.

I returned to my apartment and found Joe Morelli sitting on the floor in my hall, back to the wall, long legs stretched in front of him, crossed at the ankles. He had a brown paper bag next to him, and the entire hall smelled like meatballs and marinara.

I gave him the silent question look.

'Stopped by to say hello,' Morelli said, getting to his feet.

My gaze dropped to the bag.

Morelli grinned. 'Dinner.'

'Smells good.'

'Meatball subs from Pino's. They're still hot. I just got here.'

Ordinarily I wouldn't let Morelli into my apartment, but it would be a sin against everything holy to turn away Pino's meatballs.

I unlocked the door, and Morelli followed me in. I dumped my shoulder bag on the small hall table and swung into the kitchen. I took two plates from the wall cabinet and set them on the counter. 'I'm having a hard time believing this is entirely social.'

'Maybe not entirely,' Morelli said, close enough for me to feel his breath on the back of my neck. 'I thought you might want a medical update on Maxine Nowicki's mother.'

I put the subs on plates and divided up the tub of coleslaw. 'Is it going to ruin my appetite?'

Morelli moved off to the fridge in search of beer. 'She

was scalped. Like in the old cowboy and Indian movies. Only in this case, not enough was removed to kill her.'

'That's sick! Who would do such a thing?'

'Good question. Nowicki isn't saying.'

I took the plates to the table. 'What about prints on the knife?'

'None.'

'Not even Mrs. Nowicki's?'

'Correct. Not even Mrs. Nowicki's.'

I ate my sub and thought about this latest turn of events. Scalped. Yuk.

'You're looking for her daughter,' Morelli said. Statement, not question.

'Yep.'

'Think there could be a tie-in?'

'Two days ago I interviewed one of Maxine's friends from the diner. She had a big bandage on her hand. Said she'd whacked her finger off in a kitchen accident.'

'What's this friend's name?'

'Margie something. Lives on Barnet. Works the dinner shift at the Silver Dollar.'

'Any other mutilations I should know about?'

I tried some of the coleslaw. 'Nope. That's it. It's been a slow week.'

Morelli watched me. 'You're holding something back.'

'What makes you say that?'

'I can tell.'

'You can tell nothing.'

'You're still mad at me for not calling.'

'I am *not mad*!' I slammed my fist down on the table, making my beer bottle jump in place.

'I *meant* to call,' Morelli said.

I stood and gathered the empty plates and the

silverware. *CRASH, clang, clang*! 'You are a dysfunctional human being.'

'Oh yeah? Well, you're fucking frightening.'

'Are you saying you're afraid of me?'

'Any man in his right mind would be afraid of you. You know that scarlet letter thing? You should have a tattoo on your forehead that says "Dangerous Woman. Stand Back!" '

I stormed into the kitchen and slapped the dishes onto the countertop. 'I happen to be a very nice person.' I turned on him and narrowed my eyes. 'What's so dangerous about me?'

'Lots of things. You have that look. Like you want to pick out kitchen curtains.'

'I do *not* have that look!' I shouted. 'And if I did it would *not* be for *your* kitchen curtains!'

Morelli backed me into the refrigerator. 'And then there's the way you make my heart beat fast when you get excited like this.' He leaned into me and kissed the curve of my ear. 'And your hair . . . I love your hair.' He kissed me again. 'Dangerous hair, babe.'

Oh boy.

His hands were at my waist and his knee slid between mine. 'Dangerous body.' His lips skimmed my mouth. 'Dangerous lips.'

This wasn't supposed to be happening. I had decided against this. 'Listen, Morelli, I appreciate the meatball sub and all, but . . .'

'Shut-up, Stephanie.'

And then he kissed me. His tongue touched mine, and I thought, Well, what the hell, maybe I am dangerous. Maybe this isn't such a bad idea. After all, there was a time when I'd wanted nothing more than a Morelliinduced orgasm. Well, here was my chance. It wasn't as if we were strangers. It wasn't as if I didn't *deserve* it.

'Maybe we should go into the bedroom,' I said. Get away from sharp knives in case something goes wrong and I'm tempted to stab him.

Morelli was wearing jeans with a navy T-shirt. Under the drape of the T-shirt he was wearing a pager and a .38. He unclipped his pager and put it in the refrigerator. He threw the bolt on the front door and kicked his shoes off in the hall.

'What about the gun?' I asked.

'The gun stays. Nothing's stopping me this time. You change your mind, and I'll shoot you.'

'Um, there's the issue of safety.'

He had his hand on his zipper. 'Okay, I'll leave it on the nightstand.'

'I wasn't talking about the gun.'

Morelli stopped the progress of the zipper. 'You're not on the pill?'

'No.' I didn't think sex once a millennium warranted it.

'What about . . .'

'I haven't got any of them, either.'

'Shit,' Morelli said.

'Nothing in your wallet?'

'You're going to find this hard to believe, but cops aren't required to carry emergency condoms.'

'Yes, but . . .'

'I'm not eighteen years old. I no longer score with nine out of ten women I meet.'

That was encouraging. 'I don't suppose you'd want to tell me the current ratio?'

'Right now, it's zero for zero.'

'We could try a plastic sandwich bag.'

Morelli grinned. 'You want me bad.'

'Temporary insanity.'

The grin widened. 'I don't think so. You've wanted me for years. You've never gotten over having me touch you when you were six.'

I felt my mouth drop open and instantly closed it with a snap, leaning forward, hands fisted to keep from strangling him. 'You are such a jerk!'

'I know,' Morelli said. 'It's genetic. Good thing I'm so cute.'

Morelli was many things. Cute wasn't one of them. Cocker spaniels were cute. Baby shoes were cute. Morelli wasn't cute. Morelli could look at water and make it boil. Cute was much too mild an adjective to describe Morelli.

He reached out and tugged at my hair. 'I'd run to the store, but I'm guessing your door would be locked when I got back.'

'It's a good possibility.'

'Well, then I guess there's only one thing to do.'

I braced myself.

CHAPTER FOUR

MORELLI PADDED INTO the living room and picked up the channel changer. 'We can watch the ball game. The Yankees are playing. You got any ice cream?'

It took me a full sixty seconds to find my voice. 'Raspberry Popsicles.'

'Perfect.'

I'd been replaced by a raspberry Popsicle, and Morelli didn't look all that unhappy. I, on the other hand, wanted to smash something. Morelli was right . . . I wanted him bad. He might have been right about the curtains too, but I didn't want to dwell on the curtains. Lust I could manage, but the very thought of wanting a relationship with Morelli made my blood run cold.

I handed him his Popsicle and sat in the overstuffed armchair, not trusting myself to share the couch, half afraid I'd go after his leg like a dog in heat.

Around nine-thirty I started looking at my watch. I was thinking about the clue under Mrs. Nowicki's porch, and I was wondering how I was going to get it. I could borrow a rake from my parents. Then I could extend the handle with something. I'd probably have to use a flashlight, and I'd have to work fast because people were bound to see the light. If I waited until two in the morning chances of someone's being up to see me were greatly reduced. On the other hand, a flashlight beam at two in the morning was much more suspicious than a flashlight beam at ten at night.

'Okay,' Morelli said, 'what's going on? Why do you keep looking at your watch?'

I yawned and stretched. 'Getting late.'

'It's nine-thirty.'

'I go to bed early.'

Morelli made tsk, tsk, tsk sounds. 'You shouldn't fib to a cop.'

'I have things to do.'

'What sort of things?'

'Nothing special. Just . . . things.'

There was a knock at the door, and we both glanced in the direction of the sound.

Morelli looked at me speculatively. 'You expecting someone?'

'It's probably old Mrs. Bestler from the third floor. Sometimes she forgets where she lives.' I put my eye to the security peephole. 'Nope. Not Mrs. Bestler.' Mrs. Bestler didn't have big red hair like Little Orphan Annie. Mrs. Bestler didn't wear skin-tight black leather. Mrs. Bestler's breasts weren't in the shape of ice-cream cones.

I turned back to Morelli. 'I don't suppose I could get you to wait in the bedroom for a moment or two . . .'

'Not on your life,' Morelli said. 'I wouldn't miss this for anything.'

I threw the bolt and opened the door.

'I don't know why I'm doing this,' Sally said. 'I'm like sucked into this bounty hunter trip.'

'The excitement of the chase,' I said.

'Yeah. That's it. It's the fucking chase.' He held a jar out to me. 'I went back and got the clue. Borrowed one of those long-handled duster things. I decoded the note, but I don't know what it means.'

'Weren't there people around, wondering what you were doing?'

'When you look like this nobody asks. They're all happy as shit I'm not close-dancing on their front lawn with Uncle Fred.' He lifted his chin a fraction of an inch and gave Joe the once-over. 'Who's this?'

'This is Joe Morelli. He was just leaving.'

'No I wasn't,' Morelli said.

Sally stepped forward. 'If she says you're leaving then I think you're leaving.'

Morelli rocked back on his heels and grinned. 'You gonna make me?'

'You think I can't?'

'I think somebody should help you pick out a bra. This year the rounded look is in.'

Sally looked down at his ice-cream cones. 'They're my trademark. I'm making a fucking fortune off these babies.' He looked up and sucker-punched Morelli in the gut.

'Oof,' Morelli said. Then he narrowed his eyes and lunged at Sally.

'No!' I yelped, jumping between them.

There was some close-in scuffling. I got clipped on the chin and went down like a sack of sand. Both men stooped to pick me up.

'Back off,' I yelled, slapping them away. 'Don't either of you touch me. I don't need help from you two infantile morons.'

'He insulted my breasts,' Sally said.

'That's what happens when you have breasts,' I shouted. 'People insult them. Get used to it.'

Joe glared at Sally. 'Who are you? And what's with this jar?'

Sally extended his hand. 'Sally Sweet.'

Joe took the offered hand. 'Joe Morelli.'

They stood like that for a moment or two, and I saw a red flush begin to creep into Sally's cheeks. The cords in Morelli's neck grew prominent. Their hands remained clasped and their bodies jerked in rigid struggle. The morons were arm wrestling.

'That does it,' I said. 'I'm getting my gun. And I'm going to shoot the winner.'

Eyes slid in my direction.

'Actually, I've gotta run,' Sally said. 'I've got a gig at the shore tonight, and Sugar's waiting in the car.'

'He's a musician,' I told Morelli.

Morelli took a step backward. 'It's always a treat to meet Stephanie's friends.'

'Yeah,' Sally said, 'my fucking pleasure.'

Morelli was grinning when I closed and locked the door. 'You never disappoint me,' he said.

'What was that wrestling match about?'

'We were playing.' He glanced down at the jar. 'Tell me about this.'

'Maxine Nowicki has been leaving clues for Eddie Kuntz. Sort of a revenge-driven scavenger hunt. The clues are always in code. That's where Sally comes in. He's good at cracking codes.' I opened the jar, removed the paper and read the message. ' "Our spot. Wednesday at three." '

'They have a spot,' Morelli said. 'Makes me feel all romantic again. Maybe I should make a fast run to the drugstore.'

'Suppose you went to the drugstore. How many would

you buy? Would you buy one? Would you buy a month's worth? Would you buy a whole case?'

'Oh, boy,' Morelli said. 'This is about curtains, isn't it?'

'Just want to get the rules straight.'

'How about we live one day at a time.'

'One day at a time is okay,' I said. I suppose.

'So if I go to the drugstore you'll let me back in?'

'No. I'm not in the mood.' In fact, I was suddenly feeling damn cranky. And for some unknown reason the image of Terry Gilman kept popping up in my mind.

Morelli ran a playful finger along my jawbone. 'Bet I could change your mood.'

I crossed my arms over my chest and looked at him slitty eyed. 'I don't think so.'

'Hmmm,' Morelli said, 'maybe not.' He stretched, and then he sauntered into the kitchen and retrieved his pager from the refrigerator. 'You're in a bad mood because I wouldn't commit to a case.'

'Am not! I absolutely would *not* want a case commitment!'

'You're cute when you lie.'

I pointed stiff-armed to the door. 'Out!'

THE FOLLOWING MORNING, I could have called Eddie Kuntz and told him the newest message, but I wanted to talk to him face-to-face. Maxine Nowicki's apartment had been ransacked, and two people connected to her had been mutilated. I was thinking maybe someone wanted to find her for something other than love letters. And maybe that someone was Eddie Kuntz.

Kuntz was washing his car when I drove up. He had a

boom box on the curb, and he was listening to shock jock radio. He stopped when he saw me and shut the radio off.

'You find her?'

I gave him the note with the translation. 'I found another message.'

He read the message and made a disgusted sound. ' "Our spot," ' he said. 'What's that supposed to mean?'

'You didn't know you had a spot?'

'We had lots of spots. How am I supposed to know which spot she's talking about?'

'Think about it.'

Eddie Kuntz stared at me, and I thought I caught a hint of rubber burning.

'She's probably talking about the bench,' he said. 'The first time we met was in the park, and she was sitting on a bench, looking at the water. She was always talking about that bench like it was some kind of shrine or something.'

'Go figure.'

Kuntz gave me a hands-up. 'Women.'

A Lincoln Town Car eased to the curb. Navy exterior, tinted windows, half a block long.

'Aunt Betty and Uncle Leo,' Eddie said.

'Big car.'

'Yeah. I borrow it sometimes to pick up a few extra bucks.'

I wasn't sure if he meant driving people around or running people over. 'I have your occupation listed as cook, but you seem to be home a lot.'

'That's because I'm between jobs.'

'When was your last job as a cook?'

'I dunno. This morning. I toasted a waffle. What's it to you?'

'Curious.'

'Try being curious about Maxine.'

Aunt Betty and Uncle Leo walked up to us.

'Hello,' Aunt Betty said. 'Are you Eddie's new girlfriend?'

'Acquaintance,' I told her.

'Well, I hope you turn into a girlfriend. You're Italian, right?'

'Half Italian. Half Hungarian.'

'Well, nobody's perfect,' she said. 'Come in and have some cake. I got a nice pound cake at the bakery.'

'Gonna be another scorcher today,' Uncle Leo said. 'Good thing we got air.'

'You got air,' Kuntz said. 'My half doesn't have air. My half's hotter'n hell.'

'I gotta get in,' Uncle Leo said. 'This heat is murder.'

'Don't forget about the cake,' Betty said, following Leo up the steps. 'There's cake any time you want it.'

'So you're doing other stuff to find Maxine, right?' Kuntz asked. 'I mean, you're not just waiting for these clues, are you?'

'I've been going through the list of names and businesses you gave me. The manager of the 7-Eleven said Maxine stopped by Sunday night. So far, no one else has seen her.'

'Christ, she's here all the time leaving these stupid clues. Why doesn't someone see her? What is she, the freaking Phantom?'

'The manager of the 7-Eleven said something that stuck in my mind. She said Maxine always used to buy a lottery ticket, but this time she said she didn't need to win the lottery anymore.'

The line of Kuntz's mouth tightened. 'Maxine's a lunatic. Who knows what she's thinking.'

I suspected Eddie Kuntz knew exactly what Maxine was thinking.

'You need to be on that bench tomorrow at three,' I told Kuntz. 'I'll call you in the morning and make the final arrangements.'

'I don't know if I like this. She pitched a rock into my window. There's no telling what she might do. Suppose she wants to snuff me?'

'Throwing a rock through a window doesn't equate with killing someone.' I stared at him for a moment. 'Does she have a reason for wanting to kill you?'

'I pressed charges against her. Is that a reason?'

'It wouldn't be for me.' This loser wasn't worth doing time for. 'Hard to say about Maxine.'

I LEFT KUNTZ fiddling with his boom box. I'm not sure why I'd felt compelled to see him in person. I suppose I wanted to look him in the eye and learn if he'd scalped Maxine's mother. Unfortunately, in my experience, eyes are vastly overrated as pathways to the soul. The only thing I saw in Eddie Kuntz's eyes was last night's booze tally, which I could sum up as being too much.

I looped past Mrs. Nowicki's house and saw no sign of life. Her windows were closed shut. Shades were drawn. I parked the car and went to the door. No one answered my knock. 'Mrs. Nowicki,' I called out. 'It's Stephanie Plum.' I knocked again and was about to leave when the door opened a crack.

'Now what?' Mrs. Nowicki said.

'I'd like to talk.'

'Lucky me.'

'Can I come in?'

'No.'

The entire top of her head was bandaged. She was without makeup and cigarette, and she looked old beyond her years.

'How's your head?' I asked.

'Been worse.'

'I mean from the cut.'

She rolled her eyes up. 'Oh, that . . .'

'I need to know who did it.'

'I did it.'

'I saw the blood. And I saw the knife. And I know you didn't do this to yourself. Someone came looking for Maxine. And you ended up getting hurt.'

'You want my statement? Go read it from the cops.'

'Did you know someone visited Maxine's friend, Marjorie, and chopped off her finger?'

'And you think the same guy did both of us.'

'It seems reasonable. And I think it would be better for Maxine if I found her before he does.'

'Life is a bitch,' Mrs. Nowicki said. 'Poor Maxie. I don't know what she did. And I don't know where she is. What I know is that she's in a lot of trouble.'

'And the man?'

'He said if I talked he'd come back and kill me. And I believe him.'

'This is all in confidence.'

'It don't matter. There's nothing I can tell you. There were two of them. I turned around and there they were in my kitchen. Average height. Average build. Wearing coveralls and stocking masks. Even had on those disposable rubber gloves like they wear in the hospital.'

'How about their voices?'

'Only one spoke, and there wasn't anything to remember about it. Not old. Not young.'

'Would you recognize the voice if you heard it again?'

'I don't know. Like I said, there wasn't anything to remember.'

'And you don't know where Maxine is staying?'

'Sorry. I just don't know.'

'Let's try it from another direction. If Maxine wasn't living in her apartment and didn't have to go to work every day . . . where would she go?'

'That's easy. She'd go to the shore. She'd go to get some ocean air and play the games on the boardwalk.'

'Seaside or Point Pleasant?'

'Point Pleasant. She always goes to Point Pleasant.'

This made sense. It accounted for the tan and the fact that she wasn't conducting business in Trenton.

I gave Mrs. Nowicki my card. 'Call me if you hear from Maxine or think of anything that might be helpful. Keep your doors locked and don't talk to strangers.'

'Actually, I've been thinking of going to stay with my sister in Virginia.'

'That sounds like a good idea.'

I TURNED LEFT onto Olden and caught a glimpse of a black Jeep Cherokee in my rearview mirror. Black Cherokees are popular in Jersey. They're not a car I'd ordinarily notice, but from somewhere in the recesses of my subconscious a mental abacus clicked in and told me I'd seen this car one time too many. I took Olden to Hamilton and Hamilton to St. James. I parked in my lot and looked around for the Cherokee, but it had disappeared. Coincidence, I said. Overactive imagination.

I ran up to my apartment, checked my answering machine, changed into my swimsuit, stuffed a towel, a T-shirt and some sunscreen into a canvas tote, pulled on a pair of shorts and took off for the shore.

The hole in my muffler was getting bigger, so I punched up the volume on Metallica. I reached Point Pleasant in less than an hour, then spent twenty minutes looking for cheap parking on the street. I finally found a space two blocks back from the boardwalk, locked up and hooked the tote bag over my shoulder.

When you live in Jersey a beach isn't enough. People have energy in Jersey. They need things to do. They need a beach with a boardwalk. And the boardwalk has to be filled with rides and games and crappy food. Add some miniature golf. Throw in a bunch of stores selling T-shirts with offensive pictures. Life doesn't get much better than this.

And the best part is the smell. I've been told there are places where the ocean smells wild and briny. In Jersey the ocean smells of coconut-scented suntan lotion and Italian sausage smothered in fried onions and peppers. It smells like deep-fried zeppoles and chili hot dogs. The scent is intoxicating and exotic as it expands in the heat rising from crowds of sunbaked bodies strolling the boardwalk.

Surf surges onto the beach and the sound is mingled with the rhythmic *tick, tick, tick* of the spinning game wheels and the high-pitched *Eeeeeeee* of thrill seekers being hurtled down the log flume.

Rock stars, pickpockets, homies, pimps, pushers, pregnant women in bikinis, future astronauts, politicians, geeks, ghouls, and droves of families who buy American and eat Italian all come to the Jersey shore.

When I was a little girl, my sister and I rode the

carousel and the whip and ate cotton candy and frozen custard. I had a stomach like iron, but Valerie always got sick on the way home and threw up in the car. When I was older, the shore was a place to meet boys. And now I find myself here on a manhunt. Who would have thought?

I stopped at a frozen custard stand and flashed Maxine's photo. 'Have you seen her?'

No one could say for sure.

I worked my way down the boardwalk, showing the picture, distributing my cards. I ate some french fries, a piece of pizza, two chunks of fudge, a glass of lemonade and a vanilla-and-orange-swirl ice-cream cone. Halfway down the boardwalk I felt the pull of the white sand beach and gave up the manhunt in favor of perfecting my tan.

You have to love a job that lets you lie on the beach for the better part of the afternoon.

THE LIGHT WAS frantically blinking on my answering machine when I got home. If I had more than three messages my machine always went hyper. Blink, blink, blink, blink—faster than Rex could twitch his whiskers.

I accessed the messages and all were blank. 'No big deal,' I said to Rex. 'If it's important, they'll call back.'

Rex stopped running on his wheel and looked at me. Rex went nuts over blank messages. Rex had no patience to wait for people to call back. Rex had a problem with curiosity.

The phone rang, and I snatched it up. 'Hello.'

'Is this Stephanie?'

'Yes.'

'This is Sugar. I don't suppose Sally is with you.'

'No. I haven't seen Sally all day.'

'He's late for dinner. He told me he'd be home, but he isn't here. I thought maybe he was off doing some bounty hunter thing since that's all he talks about anymore.'

'Nope. I worked alone today.'

I OPENED THE curtains in my bedroom and looked out across the parking lot. It was mid-morning and already the heat was shimmering on the blacktop. A dog barked on Stiller Street, behind the lot. A screen door banged open and closed. I squinted in the direction of the barking dog and spotted a black Jeep Cherokee parked two houses down on Stiller.

No big deal, I said to myself, lots of people drive black Jeep Cherokees. Still, I'd never seen a Cherokee there before. And it really did remind me of the car that had been tailing me. Best to check it out.

I was wearing cut-off jeans and a green Big Dog T-shirt. I stuck my .38 into the waistband of the jeans and pulled the shirt over the gun. I walked around like this for a few minutes, trying to get used to the idea of carrying, but I felt like an idiot. So I took the gun out and returned it to its place in the brown bear cookie jar.

I rode the elevator to the small lobby, exited from the front entrance and walked one block down St. James. I hung a left at the corner, continued on for two blocks, turned and came up behind the Cherokee. The windows were tinted, but I could see a shadowy form at the wheel. I crept closer and knocked on the driver's-side window. The window rolled down and Joyce Barnhardt smiled out at me.

'*Ciao*,' Joyce said.

'What the hell do you think you're doing?'

'I'm staking you out. What does it look like I'm doing?'

'I suppose there's a reason?'

Joyce shrugged. 'We're both after the same person. I thought it wouldn't hurt to see what pathetic attempts you've made to find her . . . before I take over and get the job done.'

'We aren't after the same person. That simply isn't done. Vinnie would never give the same case to two different agents.'

'A lot you know.'

I narrowed my eyes.

'Vinnie didn't think you were making any progress, so he gave Maxine Nowicki to me.'

'I don't believe you.'

Joyce held her contract up for me to see. 'Authorized by the Vincent Plum Agency to apprehend Maxine Nowicki . . .' she read.

'We'll see about this!'

Joyce made a pouty kissy face.

'And stop following me!'

'It's a free country,' Joyce said. 'I can follow you if I want to.'

I huffed off, back to my building. I stomped upstairs, got my keys and my shoulder bag, stomped back downstairs and gunned the CRX out of the lot . . . with Joyce close on my back bumper.

I didn't bother to lose her. I turned onto Hamilton and in less than five minutes was at the office. Joyce parked half a block back and stayed in her car while I stormed through the front door.

'Where is he? Where is that miserable little worm?'

'Oh oh,' Lula said. 'Been there, done that.'

'Now what?' Connie said.

'Joyce Barnhardt, that's what. She showed me a contract authorizing her to bring in Maxine Nowicki.'

'That's impossible,' Connie said. 'I issue all the contracts, and I don't know anything about it. And besides, Vinnie never gives out an FTA to two different agents.'

'Yeah, but remember that Joyce person came in real early on Tuesday morning,' Lula said. 'And she and Vinnie were locked in his office together for almost an hour, and they were making those weird barnyard sounds.'

'I forgot my gun again,' I said.

'I got a gun,' Connie said, 'but it isn't going to do you any good. Vinnie went to North Carolina yesterday to pick up a jumper. He should be back the end of the week.'

'I can't work like this,' I said. 'She's in my way. She's following me around.'

'I can fix that,' Lula said. 'Where is she? I'll go talk to her.'

'She's in the black Cherokee, but I don't think that's a good idea.'

'Don't worry about nothing,' Lula said, swinging through the door. 'I'll be real diplomatic. You wait here.'

Lula, diplomatic?

'Lula,' I yelled, 'come back here. I'll take care of Joyce Barnhardt.'

She reached the car and was standing by the curbside rear quarter panel. 'This the one?' she called to me.

'Yes, but . . .'

Lula pulled a gun out from under her T-shirt and—BANG! She blew a cantaloupe-sized hole in Joyce's back tire. She had the gun back under the shirt by the time Joyce got out of the car.

Joyce saw the tire and her mouth dropped open.

'Did you see that?' Lula asked Joyce. 'A guy came by here and shot up your tire. And then fast as anything, he ran away. I don't know what this world is coming to.'

Joyce looked from Lula to the tire and from Lula to the tire, all the while her mouth still open but no words coming out.

'Well, I gotta get back to work,' Lula said, turning her back on Joyce, walking back to the office.

'I can't believe you did that!' I said to Lula. 'You can't just go around shooting out people's tires!'

'Look again,' Lula said.

Connie was at her desk. 'Anybody want to go to Mannie's for lunch today? I'm in a pasta mood.'

'I have to follow up on a lead,' I told her.

'What kind of lead?' Lula wanted to know. 'There gonna be action? If there is, I want to go along, because I'm in an action mood now.'

Truth is, I could use another person to keep an eye out for Maxine. I'd have preferred Ranger, but that was going to be awkward with Lula standing in front of me, hankering after action.

'No action,' I said. 'This is a boring lead. Very boring.'

'It's about Maxine, isn't it? Oh boy, this is gonna be great. That body we found last time was almost dead. Maybe this time we'll hit the jackpot.'

'We'll need to take your car,' I said to Lula. 'If there's a takedown we can't all fit in my CRX.'

'Fine by me,' Lula said, retrieving her purse from a file drawer. 'I got air in my car. And another advantage, my car's parked out back, so we don't have to put on our sympathy face to Joyce, being that she's got a flat tire and we don't. Where we going anyway?'

'Muffet Street. North Trenton.'

'I STILL DON'T like this,' Kuntz said. 'Maxine is crazy. Who knows what she'll do. I'm gonna feel like a sitting duck out there.'

Lula was standing behind me on Kuntz's porch. 'Probably just another dumb-ass note taped to the bottom of the bench. Think you should stop your whining,' she said to Kuntz, 'on account of it makes you look like a wiener. And with a name like Kuntz you gotta be careful what you look like.'

Eddie cut his eyes to Lula. 'Who's this?'

'I'm her partner,' Lula said. 'Just like Starsky and Hutch, Cagney and Lacey, the Lone Ranger and What's-his-name.'

Truth is, we were more like Laurel and Hardy, but I didn't want to share that information with Kuntz.

'We'll be in place ahead of time,' I said. 'Don't worry if you don't see us. We'll be there. All you have to do is show up and go sit on the bench and wait.'

'What if there's trouble?'

'Wave your arms if you need help. We won't be that far away.'

'You know which bench, right?'

'The bench next to the flagpole.'

'Yeah. That's the one.'

Betty stuck her head out next door. 'Hello, dear. Isn't it a lovely day? Are you young people planning some sort of activity? If I was your age I'd go on a picnic today.'

'We're working today,' Lula said. 'We got a big lead to follow up on.'

'Betty,' Leo yelled from deep in the house, 'where's my coffee cake? I thought you were bringing me a piece of coffee cake.'

Betty pulled her head in and closed the door, shutting off the flow of cold air.

'Nosy old bag,' Kuntz said. 'You can't do nothing around here without her knowing it.'

'Why do you stay if you dislike it so much?'

'Cheap rent. I get a break because I'm family. Betty's my mother's sister.'

'YOU KNOW WHAT we need?' Lula said, sliding behind the wheel, buckling herself in. 'We need some disguises. I bet Maxine knows what you look like by now. And the way I remember that part of the park, there aren't a lot of places to hide. We're gonna have to hide out in the open. We're gonna need some disguises.'

I'd been thinking similar thoughts. Not that we needed disguises but that we were going to have a hard time making ourselves invisible.

'I know just the place to get a good disguise, too,' Lula said. 'I know where we can get wigs and everything.'

Twenty minutes later we were standing outside the door to Sally's condo.

'This feels a little weird,' I said.

'You know someone else who's got wigs?'

'I don't need a wig. I can stuff my hair up under a ball cap.'

Lula rolled her eyes. 'Oh yeah, that's gonna fool a lot of people.'

The door opened and Sally looked out at us. His eyes were bloodshot, and his hair was standing on end.

'Yikes,' Lula said.

'What's the matter? This the first time you've seen a hung-over transvestite?'

'Not me,' Lula said. 'I've seen lots of 'em.'

Lula and I followed him into the living room. 'We have a strange sort of favor to ask,' I said. 'We need to go on a stakeout this afternoon, and I'm worried about being recognized. I thought you could help me with a disguise.'

'Who do you want to be . . . Barbarella, Batgirl, the fucking slut next door?'

CHAPTER FIVE

'MAYBE I COULD just borrow a wig,' I said to Sally. He ambled off to the bedroom. 'What do you want? Farrah? Orphan Annie? Elvira?'

'Something that won't attract attention.'

He returned with a blond wig and held it out for approval. 'This is from my Marilyn collection. Very popular with older men who like to be spanked.'

I was thinking *Yuk*, but Lula looked like she was filing it away in case she decided to return to her former profession.

Sally pinned my hair back and tugged the wig on. 'Needs something.'

'Needs Marilyn lips,' Lula said. 'Can't have Marilyn hair without Marilyn lips.'

'I don't know how to do lips,' Sally said. 'Sugar always does my lips. And Sugar isn't here. We sort of had a fight, and he went off in a snit.'

'You two fight a lot?' Lula asked.

'Nope. Never. Sugar's real easy to live with. He's just a little nerdy, you know. Like, he thinks I shouldn't be hanging out with you because it's too dangerous. That's what we had the fight about.'

'Jeez,' I said. 'I don't want to come between you and your roommate.'

'No problem, man. Sugar's cool. He's just one of those worry-wart motherfuckers.' Sally opened a professional-size makeup case. 'Here's lots of shit if you know how to use it.'

I chose candy-apple-pink lip gloss and made big, glossy, pouty lips.

Sally and Lula stood back and did the take-a-look thing.

'Gotta lose the shoes,' Lula said. 'Never gonna get away with those lips and that hair and those shoes.'

Sally agreed. 'The shoes aren't Marilyn.'

'I saw these great shoes at Macy's,' Lula said. 'They'd be perfect.'

'No! I'm not going to Macy's. I want to get to the park early, so we can hang out and watch for Maxine.'

'Only take a minute,' Lula said. 'You'd go bonkers over these shoes.'

'No. And that's final.'

'Just let me put some lip gloss on and I'll be ready to go,' Sally said.

Lula and I sent each other a look that said, Uh oh.

Sally paused with lip gloss in hand. 'You didn't think you were going to leave me here, did you?'

'Well, yeah,' I said.

'This is bounty hunter shit,' Lula said. 'And you don't know any bounty hunter shit.'

'I know other kinds of shit. And besides, I don't think you know a big fucking bunch of bounty hunter shit, either.'

I was staring at the wall, and I was thinking it might feel good to run full tilt and bash my head against it. 'Stop! We'll *all* go. We'll *all* pretend to be bounty hunters.'

Sally turned to the hall mirror and smeared lip gloss on his lips. 'Sugar gave me this cool cherry-tasting shit to use on my lips. He says I've got to keep my lips from getting chapped so my lipstick goes on nice and smooth. I'm telling you, this woman stuff is complicated.'

He was wearing leather sandals, cut-offs that were so short he had cheek showing, a sleeveless T-shirt top and a two-day beard.

'Not sure you totally got the hang of this woman stuff,' Lula said. 'Think maybe you'd do better shaving your ass than worrying about lip gloss.'

IT WAS A little after one when we got to the park.

'Those shoes make all the difference,' Lula said, staring down at my new shoes. 'Didn't I tell you those shoes were the shit?'

'Slut shoes,' Sally said. 'Retro fucking slut.'

Great. Just what I needed, another pair of retro slut shoes—and an extra $74 on my Macy's charge card.

We were sitting in the parking lot, and directly in front of us was a large man-made lake. A jogging path circled the lake, sometimes snaking through patches of trees. A snack bar and rest rooms were in a cinder-block building to our right. To the left was an open field with swing sets and wooden structures for climbing. Benches had been placed at the water's edge but were empty at this time of day. The park saw more use in early evening when the temperature dropped. Seniors came to watch the sunset and families came to feed the ducks and play children's games.

'Kuntz will be sitting on the bench by the flagpole,' I said. 'Instructions were that he should be there at three.'

'I bet she pops him,' Sally said. 'Why else would you set someone up like that?'

I didn't think there was much chance that Maxine would pop him. The bench was too exposed. And there were no good escape routes. I didn't suppose Maxine was a rocket scientist, but I didn't think she was entirely stupid, either. It looked to me like Maxine was playing with Eddie Kuntz. And it looked to me like she was the only one who thought the game was funny.

I passed the photo of Maxine around. 'This is what she looks like,' I said. 'If you see her, grab her and bring her to me. I'll be covering the area between the snack bar and the car. Lula, you take the playground. Sally, I want you to sit on the bench by the boat ramp. Keep your eye out for snipers.' I did a mental eye roll on this one. 'And watch that no one rushes Kuntz after he sits down.'

Not only had Sally and Lula talked me into buying platform sandals with strappy tie things halfway up my calf, they'd also managed to get me to trade my shorts for a black stretch miniskirt. It was an excellent disguise except for the fact that I couldn't run, sit or bend.

At two o'clock a couple of women arrived and took off jogging. Not Maxine. I walked down to the snack bar and bought a bag of popcorn to feed to the ducks. Two older men did the same. A few more joggers showed up. Men, this time. I fed the ducks and waited. Still no sign of Maxine. Lula was sitting on a swing, filing her nails. Sally had stretched out on the ground behind his bench and appeared to be sleeping. Do I have a team, or what?

For as long as I'd been there, no one had approached the bench by the pole. I'd inspected it from top to bottom when I'd first arrived and found nothing unusual. One of the joggers had returned from his run and sat two benches down, unlacing his shoes and drinking from a water bottle.

Kuntz arrived at 2:55 and went straight to the bench.

Lula looked up from her filing, but Sally didn't move a muscle. Kuntz stood at the bench for a moment. He paced away from it. Nervous. Didn't want to sit down. He looked around, spotted me at the snack bar and silently mouthed something that looked like 'Holy shit.'

I had a short panic attack, fearing he'd come over to me, but then he turned and slouched onto the bench.

A black Jeep Cherokee rolled into the lot and parked next to Kuntz's Blazer. I didn't need a crystal ball to figure this one out. Joyce had followed Kuntz. Not much I could do about that now. I watched the car for a while but there was no action. Joyce was sitting tight.

Ten minutes ticked by. Fifteen minutes. Twenty. Nothing was happening. The park population had increased, but no one was approaching Kuntz, and I didn't see Maxine. Two guys carrying a cooler chest walked toward the water. They stopped and spoke to the jogger who was still sitting on the bench near Kuntz. I saw the jogger shake his head no. The two guys exchanged glances. There was a brief discussion between them. Then one of the guys opened the chest, took out a pie and smushed it into the jogger's face.

The jogger jumped to his feet. 'Jesus Christ!' he shrieked. 'What are you nuts?'

Lula was off the swing and moving in. Joyce ran down from the parking lot. Kuntz edged off his bench. Even Sally was on his feet.

Everyone converged on the jogger, who had one of the pie guys by the shirt. People were yelling 'Break it up' and 'Stop' and trying to untangle the two men.

'I was only doing my job!' the pie guy was saying. 'Some lady told me to get the guy sitting on the bench by the fountain.'

I glared at Eddie Kuntz. 'You dunce! You were on the wrong bench!'

'The fountain, the flagpole . . . how am I supposed to keep track of these things?'

The aluminum pie plate and globs of chocolate cream pie were lying ignored on the ground. I fingered through the remains and found the scrap of paper, tucked into a plastic bag. I stuffed the bag, chocolate globs and all, into my purse.

'What's that?' Joyce said. 'What did you just put in your purse?'

'Pie crust. I'm taking it home for my hamster.'

She grabbed at my shoulder strap. 'I want to see it.'

'Let go of that strap!'

'Not until I see what you put in your purse!'

'What's going on here?' Lula asked.

'Stay out of this, fatso,' Joyce said.

'Fatso,' Lula said, eyes narrowed. 'Who you calling fatso?'

'I'm calling *you* fatso, you big tub of lard.'

Lula reached out to Joyce, Joyce made a squeak, her eyes went blank, and she crashed to the ground.

Everyone turned to Joyce.

'Must have fainted,' Lula said to the crowd. 'Guess she's one of those women can't stand to see men fighting.'

'I saw that!' I said to Lula, keeping my voice low. 'You zapped her with your stun gun!'

'Who me?'

'You can't do that! You can't zap someone just because they call you fatso!'

'Oh, excuse me,' Lula said. 'Guess I didn't understand that.'

Joyce was coming around, making feeble movements in her arms and legs. 'What happened?' she murmured. 'Was I struck by lightning?'

Kuntz sidled up to me. 'Like your disguise. Want to go out for a drink later?'

'No!'

'Try *me*,' Sally said to Kuntz. 'It's *my* wig. And I wouldn't look bad in that skirt, either.'

'Jesus,' Kuntz said to me. 'Is he with you?'

'Damn right, I'm with her,' Sally said. 'I'm the fucking cryptographer. I'm part of the team.'

'Some team,' Kuntz said. 'A fruit and a fatso.'

Lula leaned forward. 'First off, let me tell you something. I'm not a fatso. I happen to be a big woman.' She reached into her purse and came out with the stun gun. 'Second, how'd you like to have your brain scrambled, you dumb, over-developed gorilla?'

'No!' I said. 'No more brain scrambling.'

'He called us names,' Lula said. 'He called Sally a fruit.'

'Well, okay,' I said. 'Just this once, but then no more scrambling.'

Lula looked at her stun gun. 'Damn. I used all my juice. I got a low battery here.'

Kuntz made a hands-in-the-air, I-give-up, I-hired-a-loser gesture and walked away. Several bystanders helped Joyce to her feet. And Lula and Sally and I retreated to the car.

'So what was it you and Joyce were squabbling about?' Lula wanted to know.

'I got another clue. As soon as I saw the pie I knew it

was supposed to be for Eddie Kuntz, and I figured there was a clue in it. Joyce saw me pick the clue up off the ground.' I pulled the plastic bag from my purse. 'Ta dah!' I sang.

'Hot dang!' Lula said. 'You are *so* good.'

'We're like the A-team,' Sally said.

'Yeah, only the A-team didn't have no drag queen,' Lula said.

'Mr. T. liked jewelry,' Sally said. 'I could be Mr. T.'

'Nuh uh. I want to be Mr. T. on account of he was big and black like me.'

Sally had taken the note out of the bag and was reading it. 'This is interesting. She keeps changing the code. This is much more sophisticated than the others.'

'Can you read it?'

'Hey, I'm the fucking code master. Just give me some time.'

I PARKED IN the lot to my apartment building and took the stairs to the second floor. Mrs. Delgado, Mr. Weinstein, Mrs. Karwatt and Leanne Kokoska were standing, staring at my door.

'Now what?' I asked.

'Someone left you a message,' Mrs. Karwatt said. 'I was going out with the garbage when I noticed it.'

'It's a pip, too,' Mrs. Delgado said. 'Must be from one of them hoodlums you're out to get.'

I stepped up and looked at the door. The message was scribbled in black marker: 'I hate you! And I'll get even!'

'Who do you suppose did this?' Leanne asked. 'Are you on a real dangerous case? You after a murderer or something?'

Truth is, I had no idea anymore who I was after.

'Permanent marker,' Mr. Weinstein said. 'Gonna be the devil to get off. Probably gonna have to paint over it.'

'I'll call Dillon,' I told them, shoving the key in the lock. 'Dillon will fix it for me.'

Dillon Ruddick was the super, and Dillon would fix anything for a smile and a beer.

I let myself into my apartment, and my neighbors went off looking for a new adventure. I slipped the safety chain into place, bolted my door and headed for the kitchen. The light was blinking on my answering machine. One message.

I punched Replay. 'This is Helen Badijian, the manager at the 7-Eleven.' There was a pause and some fumbling. 'You left your card here and said I should call if I had information about Miss Nowicki.'

I dialed the 7-Eleven and Helen answered.

'I'm very busy now,' she said. 'If you could drop by later, maybe around ten, I think I might have something for you.'

This was turning into a halfway decent day. Sally was working on the clue, and the 7-Eleven woman had a potential lead.

'We need to celebrate,' I told Rex, trying to overlook the fact that I was actually very creeped out by the message on my door. 'Pop-Tarts for everyone.'

I looked in my cupboard, but there were no Pop-Tarts. No cookies, no cereal, no cans of spaghetti, no soup, no extra jars of peanut butter. A piece of paper was taped to the cupboard door. It was a shopping list. It said, 'buy everything.'

I took the note down and shoved it into my bag so I wouldn't forget what I needed and slung the bag over my shoulder. I had my hand on the doorknob when the phone rang.

It was Kuntz. 'So, about that drink?'

'No. No drink.'

'Your loss,' he said. 'I saw you fingering the pie on the ground. You find another note?'

'Yes.'

'And?'

'And I'm working on it.'

'Looks to me like we're not making much progress with the note crappola. All we ever get are more notes.'

'There might be more. The manager at the 7-Eleven called and said she had something for me. I'm going to stop around later tonight.'

'Why later? Why don't you go now? Cripes, can't you move faster on this? I need those letters.'

'Maybe you should tell me what this is really about. I'm having a hard time believing you're in this much of a sweat about a couple of love letters.'

'I told you they could be embarrassing.'

'Yeah, right.'

I LOOKED IN my shopping cart and wondered if I had everything. Ritz crackers and peanut butter for when I felt fancy and wanted to make hors d'oeuvres, Entenmann's coffee cake for PMS mornings, Pop-Tarts for Rex, salsa so I could tell my mother I was eating vegetables, frosted flakes in case I had to go on a stakeout, corn chips for the salsa.

I was in the middle of my inventory when a cart crashed nose to nose into mine. I looked up and found Grandma Mazur driving and my mother one step behind.

My mother closed her eyes. 'Why me?' she said.

'Dang,' Grandma Mazur said.

I was still in the wig and the little skirt. 'I can explain.'

'Where did I go wrong?' my mother wanted to know.

'I'm in disguise.'

Mrs. Crandle rattled her cart down the aisle. 'Hello, Stephanie, dear. How are you today?'

'I'm fine, Mrs. Crandle.'

'Some disguise,' my mother said. 'Everybody knows you. And why do you have to be disguised as a tramp? Why can't you ever be disguised as a normal person?' She looked into my cart. 'Jars of spaghetti sauce. The checkout clerk will think you don't cook.'

My left eye had started to twitch. 'I have to go now.'

'I bet this is a good getup for meeting men,' Grandma said. 'You look just like Marilyn Monroe. Is that a wig? Maybe I could borrow it sometime. I wouldn't mind meeting some men.'

'You loan her that wig and anything happens, I'm holding you responsible,' my mother said.

I UNPACKED MY groceries, replaced the wig with a Rangers hat, traded the skirt in for a pair of shorts and resigned the retro slut shoes to a back corner of my closet. I shared a Pop-Tart with Rex and cracked a beer open for myself. I called Dillon to tell him about my door, and then I went out the bedroom window to my fire escape to think. The air was still and sultry, the horizon dusky. The parking lot was filled with cars. The seniors were all home at this time of day. If they went out to eat it was for the early bird special at the diner, and even if they went to the park to sit for a half hour they were home by six. If they were eating in it was at five o'clock so as not to interfere with *Wheel of Fortune* and *Jeopardy.*

Most cases I get from Vinnie are routine. Usually I go to the people who put up the bond and explain to them that they'll lose their house if the skip isn't found. Ninety percent of the time they know where the skip is and help me catch him. Ninety percent of the time I have a handle on the sort of person I'm dealing with. This case didn't fall into the ninety percent. And even worse, this case was weird. A friend had lost a finger, and a mother had been scalped. Maxine's treasure hunt seemed playful by comparison. And then there was the message on my door. 'I hate you.' Who would do such a thing? The list was long.

A pickup pulled away from the curb half a block away, exposing a black Jeep Cherokee which had been parked behind the pickup. Joyce.

I allowed myself the luxury of a sigh and drained the beer bottle. You had to respect Joyce's tenacity, if nothing else. I raised my bottle in a salute to her, but there was no response.

The problem with being a bounty hunter is it's all on-the-job training. Ranger is helpful, but Ranger isn't always around. So most of the time when something new comes up I end up doing it wrong before I figure out how to do it right. Joyce, for instance. Clearly, I don't know how to get rid of Joyce.

I crawled back through the window, got another bottle of beer and another Pop-Tart, stuffed the portable phone under my arm and went back to the fire escape. I ate the Pop-Tart and washed it down with beer and all the while I watched the black Cherokee. When I finished the second bottle of beer I called Ranger.

'Talk,' Ranger said.

'I have a problem.'

'So what's your point?'

I explained the situation to Ranger, including the tire and the park episode. There was a silence where I sensed he was smiling, and finally he said, 'Sit tight, and I'll see what I can do.'

Half an hour later, Ranger's $98,000 BMW rolled to a stop in my parking lot. Ranger got out of the car and stood for a moment staring at me on my fire escape. He was wearing an olive-drab T-shirt that looked like it had been painted on him, GI Joe camouflage pants and shades. Just a normal Jersey guy.

I gave him a thumbs-up.

Ranger smiled and turned and walked across the lot and across the street to the black Cherokee. He walked to the passenger-side door, opened the door and got in the car. Just like that. If it had been me in the car, the door would have been locked, and no one looking like Ranger would get in. But this is me, and that was Joyce.

Five minutes later, Ranger exited the car and returned to my lot. I dove through my window, rushed out the door, down the stairs and skidded to a stop in front of Ranger.

'Well?'

'How bad do you want to get rid of her? You want me to shoot her? Break a bone?'

'No!'

Ranger shrugged. 'Then she's gonna stick.'

There was the sound of a car engine catching and headlights flashed on across the street. We both turned to watch Joyce pull away and disappear around the corner.

'She'll be back,' Ranger said. 'But not tonight.'

'How'd you get her to leave?'

'Told her I was gonna spend the next twelve hours ruining you for all other men, and so she might as well go home.'

I could feel the heat rush to my face.

Ranger gave me the wolf smile. 'I lied about it being tonight,' he said.

AT LEAST JOYCE was gone for a while, and I didn't have to worry about her following me to the 7-Eleven. I trudged upstairs to my apartment, made myself a peanut butter and Marshmallow Fluff sandwich on worthless white bread and channel surfed until it was time to go see Helen Badijian.

Most of the time I enjoyed my aloneness, relishing the selfish luxury of unshared space and ritual. Only *my* hand held the television remote, and there was no compromise on toilet paper brand or climate control. And even more, there was a tentative, hopeful feeling that I might be an adult. And that the worst of childhood was safely behind me. You see, I said to the world, I have my own apartment. That's good, right?

Tonight my satisfaction with the solitary life was tempered by a bizarre message still scrawled on my door. Tonight my aloneness felt lonely, and maybe even a little frightening. Tonight I made sure my windows were closed and locked when I left my apartment.

En route to Olden I did a two-block detour, checking my mirror for headlights. There'd been no sign of Joyce, but better to be safe than sorry. I had a feeling this was a good lead, and I didn't want to pass it on to the enemy.

I reached the 7-Eleven a few minutes before ten. I sat in my car a while to see if Joyce would miraculously appear. At 10:05 there was no Joyce, but from what I could see through the store's plate glass windows there was also no Helen Badijian. A young guy was behind the register, talking to an older man. The older man was waving his arms, looking royally pissed off. The young guy was shaking his head, yes, yes, yes.

I entered the store and caught the end of the conversation.

'Irresponsible,' the older man was saying. 'No excuse for it.'

I wandered to the back and looked around. Sure enough. Helen wasn't here.

'Excuse me,' I said to the clerk. 'I thought Helen Badijian would be working tonight.'

The clerk nervously looked from me to the man. 'She had to leave early.'

'It's important that I speak to her. Do you know where she can be reached?'

'Girlie, that's the hundred-dollar question,' the older man said.

I extended my hand. 'Stephanie Plum.'

'Arnold Kyle. I own this place. I got a call about an hour ago from the cops telling me my store was unattended. Your friend Helen just walked out of here. No notice. No nothing. Didn't even have the decency to lock up. Some guy came in to buy cigarettes and called the cops when he figured out there was no one here.'

I had a real bad feeling in my stomach. 'Was Helen unhappy with her job?'

'Never said anything to me,' Arnold said.

'Maybe she got sick and didn't have time to leave a note.'

'I called her house. Nobody's seen her. I called the hospital. She isn't there.'

'Have you looked everywhere in the store? A storage room? The cellar? Bathroom?'

'Checked all that out.'

'Does she drive to work? Is her car still here?'

Arnold looked to the young guy.

'It's still here,' the young guy said. 'I parked next to it when I came in. It's a blue Nova.'

'Must have gone off with one of her friends,' Arnold said. 'You can't trust anyone these days. No sense of responsibility. A good time comes along, and they kiss you good-bye.'

I turned my attention to the clerk. 'Any money missing?'

He shook his head no.

'Any sign of struggle? Anything knocked over?'

'I got here first,' Arnold said. 'And there wasn't anything. It looked like she just waltzed out of here.'

I gave them my card and explained my relationship with Helen. We did a brief behind-the-counter search for a possible note, but nothing turned up. I thanked Arnold and the clerk and asked them to call if they heard from Helen. I had my hands on the counter, and I looked down and saw it. A book of matches from the Parrot Bar in Point Pleasant.

'Are these yours?' I asked the clerk.

'Nope,' he said. 'I don't smoke.'

I looked at Arnold. 'Not mine,' he said.

'Do you mind if I snitch them?'

'Knock yourself out,' Arnold said.

At the risk of seeming paranoid I checked my rearview mirror about sixty times on the way home. Not so much for Joyce, but for the guys who might have spooked or snatched Helen Badijian. A week ago, I'd have drawn the same conclusion as Arnold . . . that Helen took off. Now that I knew about chopped-off fingers and scalpings I took a more extreme view of events.

I parked in my lot, did a fast look around, inhaled a deep breath and bolted from my car. Across the lot, through the rear entrance, up the stairs to my apartment. The hate message was still on my door. I was breathing hard, and my hand was shaking so that it took concentration to get the key in the lock.

This is stupid, I told myself. Get a grip! But I didn't have a grip, so I locked myself in and checked under the bed, in the closets and behind the shower curtain. When I was convinced I was safe I ate the Entenmann's coffee cake to calm myself down.

When I was done with the cake I called Morelli and told him about Helen and asked him to check on her.

'Just exactly what did you have in mind?'

'I don't know. Maybe you could see if she's in the morgue. Or in the hospital, getting some missing body part sewed back on. Maybe you could ask some of your friends to keep an eye out for her.'

'Probably Arnold's right,' Morelli said. 'Probably she's at a bar with a couple friends.'

'You really think so?'

'No,' Morelli said. 'I was just saying that to get you off the phone. I'm watching a ball game.'

'There's something that really bothers me here that I didn't tell you.'

'Oh boy.'

'Eddie Kuntz was the only one who knew I was going to see Helen Badijian.'

'And you think he got to her first.'

'It's crossed my mind.'

'You know there was a time when I'd say to myself . . . How does she do it? How does she get mixed up with these weirdos? But now I don't even question it. In fact, I've come to expect such things of you.'

'So are you going to help me, or what?'

CHAPTER SIX

I DIDN'T LIKE the idea that I might be responsible for Helen's disappearance. Morelli had agreed to make a few phone calls, but I still felt unsatisfied. I pulled the Parrot Bar matches out of my pocket and examined them. No hastily scribbled messages on the inside flap. For that matter, nothing to identify them as Maxine's. Nevertheless, first thing in the morning, I'd be on my way to Point Pleasant.

I went to the phone book and looked up Badijian. Three of them. No Helen. Two were in Hamilton Township. One was in Trenton. I called the Trenton number. A woman answered and told me Helen wasn't home from work yet. Easy. But not the right answer. I wanted Helen to be home.

Okay, I thought, maybe what I needed to do was go see for myself. Take a look in Kuntz's windows and see if he had Helen tied to a kitchen chair. I strapped on my black web utility belt and filled the pockets. Pepper spray, stun gun, handcuffs, flashlight, .38 Special. I thought about loading the .38 and decided against it. Guns creeped me out.

I shrugged into a navy windbreaker and scooped my hair up under my hat.

Mrs. Zuppa was coming in from bingo just as I was

leaving the building. 'Looks like you're going to work,' she said, leaning heavily on her cane. 'What are you packin'?'

'A thirty-eight.'

'I like a nine-millimeter myself.'

'A nine's good.'

'Easier to use a semiautomatic after you've had hip replacement and you walk with a cane,' she said.

One of those useful pieces of information to file away and resurrect when I turn eighty-three.

Traffic was light at this time of night. A few cars on Olden. No cars on Muffet. I parked around the corner on Cherry Street, a block down from Kuntz, and walked to his house. Downstairs lights were on in both halves. Shades were up. I stood on the sidewalk and snooped. Leo and Betty were feet up in side-by-side recliners watching Bruce Willis bleed on TV.

Next door, Eddie was talking on the phone. It was a portable, and I could see him pacing in his kitchen in the back of the house.

Neighboring houses were dark. Lights were on across the street, but there was no activity. I slipped between the houses, avoiding the squares of light thrown onto the grass from open windows, and crept in shadow to the back of Kuntz's house. Snatches of conversation drifted out to me. Yes, he loved her, Kuntz said. And yes, he thought she was sexy. I stood in deep shade and looked through the window. His back was to me. He was alone, and there were no whacked-off body parts lying on his kitchen table. No Helen chained to the stove. No unearthly screams coming from his cellar. The whole thing was damn disappointing.

Of course, Jeffrey Dahmer kept his trophies in his

refrigerator. Maybe what I should do was go around front, knock on the door, tell Kuntz I was in the neighborhood and thought I'd stop in for that drink. Then I could look in his refrigerator when he went for ice.

I was debating this plan when a hand clamped over my mouth and I was dragged backward and pressed hard into the side of the house. I kicked out with my feet, and my heart was pounding in my chest. I got a hand loose and went for the pepper spray, and I heard a familiar voice whisper in my ear.

'If you're looking to grab something, I can do better than pepper spray.'

'Morelli!'

'What the hell do you think you're doing?'

'I'm investigating. What does it look like I'm doing?'

'It looks like you're invading Eddie Kuntz's privacy.' He pushed my jacket aside and stared down at my gun belt. 'No grenades?'

'Very funny.'

'You need to get out of here.'

'I'm not done.'

'Yes, you are,' Morelli said. 'You're done. I found Helen.'

'Tell me.'

'Not here.' He took my hand and tugged me forward, toward the street.

The light over Eddie's back stoop went on, and the back screen door creaked open. 'Somebody out here?'

Morelli and I froze against the side of the house.

A second door opened. 'What is it?' Leo said. 'What's going on?'

'Somebody's creeping around the house. I heard voices.'

'Betty,' Leo yelled, 'bring the flashlight. Turn on the porch light.'

Morelli gave me a shove. 'Go for your car.'

Keeping to the shadows, I ran around the neighboring duplex, cut back through the driveway and scuttled across yards, heading for Cherry. I scrambled over a four-foot-high chain-link fence, caught my foot on the cross section and sprawled facedown on the grass.

Morelli hoisted me up by my gun belt and set me in motion.

His pickup was directly behind my CRX. We both jumped in our cars and sped away. I didn't stop until I was safely in my own parking lot.

I slid from behind the wheel, locked my car and assumed what I hoped was a casual pose, leaning against the CRX, ignoring the fact that my knees were scraped and I had grass stains the entire length of my body.

Morelli sauntered over and stood back on his heels, hands in his pockets. 'People like you give cops nightmares,' he said.

'What about Helen?'

'Dead.'

My breath caught in my chest. 'That's terrible!'

'She was found in an alley four blocks from the 7-Eleven. I don't know much except it looks like there was a struggle.'

'How was she killed?'

'Won't know for sure until they do the autopsy, but there were bruises on her neck.'

'Someone choked her to death?'

'That's what it sounds like.' Morelli paused. 'There's something else. And this is not public information. I'm telling you this so you'll be careful. Someone chopped her finger off.'

Nausea rolled through my stomach, and I tried to pull in some oxygen. There was a monster out there . . . someone with a sick, twisted mind. And I'd unleashed him on Helen Badijian by involving her in my case.

'I hate this job,' I said to Morelli. 'I hate the bad people, and the ugly crimes, and the human suffering they cause. And I hate the fear. In the beginning, I was too stupid to be afraid. Now it seems like I'm always afraid. And if all that isn't bad enough, I've killed Helen Badijian.'

'You didn't kill Helen Badijian,' Morelli said. 'You can't hold yourself responsible for that.'

'How do you get through it? How do you go to work every day, dealing with all the bottom feeders?'

'Most people are good. I keep that in front of me so I don't lose perspective. It's like having a basket of peaches. Somewhere in the middle of the basket is a rotten peach. You find it and remove it. And you think to yourself, Well, that's just the way it is with peaches . . . good thing I was around to stop the rot from spreading.'

'What about the fear?'

'Concentrate on doing the job, not on the fear.'

Easy to say, hard to do, I thought. 'I assume you came to Kuntz's house looking for me?'

'I called to give you the news,' Morelli said, 'and you weren't home. I asked myself if you'd be dumb enough to go after Kuntz, and the answer was yes.'

'You think Kuntz killed Helen?'

'Hard to say. He's clean. Has no record. The fact that he knew you were seeing Helen might have no bearing on this at all. There could be someone out there working entirely independently, turning up the same leads you're turning up.'

'Whoever they are, they're ahead of me now. They got to Helen.'

'Helen might not have known much.'

That was possible. Maybe all she had were the matches.

Morelli locked eyes with me. 'You aren't going back after Kuntz, are you?'

'Not tonight.'

SALLY CALLED WHILE I was waiting for my morning coffee to finish dripping.

'The code was fun, but the message is boring,' Sally said. ' "The next clue is in a box marked with a big red X." '

'That's it? No directions to find the box?'

'Just what I read. You want the paper? It's sort of a mess. Sugar tidied the kitchen this morning and accidentally tossed the clue in the trash masher. I was lucky to find it.'

'Is he still mad?'

'No. He's on one of his cleaning, cooking, interior decorating benders. He got up this morning and made scratch waffles, sausage patties, fresh squeezed orange juice, a mushroom omelet, put a coffee cake in the oven, scoured the kitchen to within an inch of its life and took off to buy new throw cushions for the couch.'

'Dang. I was afraid he might be upset because I borrowed the wig.'

'Nope. He was all Mr. Congeniality this morning. Said you could borrow the wig anytime you wanted.'

'What a guy.'

'Yeah, and he makes a bitchin' waffle. I have rehearsal at ten in Hamilton Township. I can stop on my way and give you the clue.'

I poured a mug of coffee and called Eddie Kuntz.

'She was here,' he said. 'The bitch was spying on me last night. I was on the phone, and I heard someone talking outside, so I ran out to look, but she got away. There were two of them. Maxine and someone else. Probably one of her wacky girlfriends.'

'You sure it was Maxine?'

'Who else would it be?'

Me, that's who, you big dumb jerk. 'I got the pie clue worked out. The next clue is coming in a box with a big red X on it. You have any boxes like that sitting on your lawn?'

'No. I'm looking out my front window, and I don't see any boxes.'

'How about in back?'

'This is stupid. Clues and boxes and . . . Shit, I found the box. It's on my back stoop. What should I do?'

'Open the box.'

'No way. I'm not opening this box. There could be a bomb in it.'

'There's no bomb.'

'How do you know?'

'It's not Maxine's style.'

'Let me tell you about Maxine. Maxine has no style. Maxine's a nut case. You feel so confident about this box, you come over and open it.'

'Fine. I'll come over and open it. Just leave it where it is, and I'll be there as soon as I can.'

I finished my coffee and gave Rex some Cheerios for

breakfast. 'Plan for the day,' I said to Rex. 'Wait for Sally to drop off the note. Next thing I drive over to Kuntz's house to open the box. Then I spend the rest of the day in Point Pleasant looking for Maxine. Is that a plan, or what?'

Rex rushed out of his soup can, stuffed all the Cheerios into his cheeks and rushed back into the soup can. So much for Rex.

I was debating if a second cup of coffee would give me heart palpitations when someone knocked on my door. I answered the knock and stared out at a flower delivery person, just about hidden behind a huge flower spray.

'Stephanie Plum?'

'Yes!'

'For you.'

Wow. Flowers. I love getting flowers. I took the flowers and stepped back. And the flower person stepped forward into my apartment and leveled a gun at me. It was Maxine.

'Tsk, tsk, tsk,' she said. 'Fell for the old flower delivery routine. What'd you just get off the banana boat?'

'I knew it was you. I just wanted to talk to you, so I didn't let on.'

'Yeah, right.' She kicked the door closed and looked around. 'Put the flowers on the kitchen counter and then stand facing the refrigerator, hands on the refrigerator door.'

I did as she said, and she cuffed me to the fridge door handle.

'Now we're going to talk,' she said. 'This is the deal. Stop being such a pain in the ass and I'll let you live.'

'Would you really shoot me?'

'In a heartbeat.'

'I don't think so.'

'Miss Know-it-all.'

'What's with these clues?'

'The clues are for the jerk. I wanted to make him jump like he made me jump. But you had to come along, and now you do all his dirty work for him. What is it with this guy and women? How does he manage?'

'Well, I can't speak for anyone else, but I'm doing it for the money.'

'I'm so stupid,' she said. 'I did it for free.'

'There's something else going on here,' I said. 'Something serious. Do you know about your apartment being ransacked? Do you know about Margie and your mother?'

'I don't want to get into that. There's nothing I can do now. But I can tell you one thing. I'm going to get what's coming to me from that son of a bitch Eddie Kuntz. He's going to pay for everything he did.'

'You mean like scalping your mother?'

'I mean like breaking my nose. I mean like all the times he got drunk and smacked me around. All the times he cheated on me. All the times he took my paycheck. And the lies about getting married. That's what he's going to pay for.'

'He said you took some love letters that belong to him.'

Maxine tipped her head back and laughed. It was a nice honest throaty laugh that would have been contagious if I hadn't been chained to my refrigerator. 'That's what he told you? Boy, that's good. Eddie Kuntz writing love letters. You probably own stock in the Brooklyn Bridge, too.'

'Listen, I'm just trying to do a job.'

'Yeah, and I'm trying to have a life. This is my advice

to you. Forget about trying to find me because it isn't going to happen. I'm only hanging around to have some fun with the jerk and then I'm out of here. Soon as I'm done yanking Kuntz's chain I'm gone.'

'You have money to make you disappear?'

'More than God has apples. Now I'm going to tell you something about that box. It's filled with dog doody. I spent all day in the park, filling a plastic bag. The clue is in the doody in the plastic bag. I want the jerk to paw through that doody. And trust me, he wants to find me bad enough to do it. So back off and don't help him out.'

I felt my lip involuntarily curl back. Dog doody. Ugh.

'That's all I have to say to you,' Maxine said. 'Go look for somebody else and stop helping the jerk.'

'Are you the one who wrote on my door?'

She turned to leave. 'No, but it's a pretty cool message.'

'You're going to leave the key to the cuffs, aren't you?'

She looked at me and winked and waltzed away, closing the door behind her.

Damn! 'I'm not the only one after you!' I yelled. 'Watch out for that bitch Joyce Barnhardt!' Shit. She was getting away. I yanked at the cuffs, but they were secure. No knives or helpful kitchen utensils within reach. Phone too far away. I could yell until doomsday and Mr. Wolensky, across the hall, wouldn't hear me over his TV. Think, Stephanie. Think! 'Help!' I yelled. 'Help!'

No one came to help. After about five minutes of yelling and fuming I started to feel a headache coming on. So I stopped yelling, and I looked in the refrigerator for something that would stop a headache. Banana cream pie. There was some left from Sunday. I ate the pie and washed it down with milk. I was still hungry, so I ate some peanut butter and a bag of baby carrots. I was finishing up with the carrots when there was another knock at my door.

I went back to the yelling 'Help!' routine.

The door swung open and Sally stuck his head in. 'Fucking kinky,' he said. 'Who cuffed you to the fridge?'

'I had a little scuffle with Maxine.'

'Looks like you lost.'

'Don't suppose you saw her hanging out in the parking lot?'

'Nope.'

My biggest fear was that she'd gotten away, never to be found. My second biggest fear was that Joyce had nabbed her. 'Go down to the basement and get Dillon, the super, and ask him to come up with his hacksaw.'

Twenty minutes later I was still wearing a bracelet, but at least I was free of the refrigerator. Sally had left for rehearsal. Dillon was on his way downstairs with a six-pack under his arm. And I was late for an appointment with a box full of dog shit.

I barreled down the stairs and out the door. I started toward my car but pulled up short when Joyce rolled into the parking lot.

'Joyce,' I said, 'long time, no see.' I peeked into her car, looking for Maxine. 'You still following me?'

'Hell no. I have better things to do than to sit around all day waiting for someone to get hit with a pie. I came by to tell you good-bye.'

'Giving up?'

'Getting smart. I don't need you to find Maxine.'

'Oh yeah? Why is that?'

'I know where she's hiding. I have a contact who knows all about Maxine's transactions. Too bad you were never in retail like me. I made a lot of connections.'

The driver's-side window rolled up, and Joyce roared out of the lot, down the street.

Great. Joyce has connections.

I crossed to the CRX and noticed that someone had left a note under my windshield wiper.

'*I said I'd get even and I meant it. I've been watching you and I know he was here. This is your last warning. Leave my boyfriend alone! Next time I soak something with gasoline I'll strike a match to it.*'

This was about somebody's boyfriend. And only one person came to mind. Morelli. Ugh! To think I almost went to bed with him. I squeezed my eyes shut. I fell for all that talk about no condoms and no sex. What was I thinking? I should have known better than to believe anything Morelli told me. And it wasn't hard to guess the girlfriend's name. Terry Gilman. This threat had mob written all over it. And Connie had said Terry was connected.

I sniffed at my car. Gasoline. I put my finger to the hood. It was still wet. Morelli's unhinged girlfriend must have just been here. Probably did this while I was chained to the refrigerator. No big deal, I thought. I'd run the CRX through a car wash.

I stuck the key in the door lock more out of force of habit than actual thought. The key didn't go through the usual turn, which meant the door wasn't locked. I looked closer and saw the scratches made next to the window. Someone had used a jimmy bar to pop the lock.

I had a premonition of bad news.

I did a fast peek in the window. Nothing seemed stolen. The radio looked intact. I opened the driver's-side door and the gasoline smell almost knocked me to my knees. I put my hand to the seat. It was soaked. The floor mats were soaked. The dash was soaked. Gasoline pooled in nooks and crannies.

Shit! Goddamn Morelli. I was more angry at him than I was at Terry. I looked around the lot. No one there but me.

I whipped out my cell phone and started dialing. No answer at Morelli's house. No answer at his office number. No answer on his car phone. I kicked a tire and did some inventive swearing.

I was parked in a back corner of the lot with no cars in the immediate vicinity. It seemed to me the safest thing to do right now was to leave the car parked and let some of the gas evaporate away. I opened the windows wide, went back to the apartment building and called Lula at the office.

'I need a ride,' I told Lula. 'Car problems.'

'OKAY, SO TELL me again about this box,' Lula said, lining the Firebird up with the curb in front of Kuntz's house.

'Maxine says it's filled with dog doody, so we shouldn't touch it.'

'You believe Maxine? Suppose it's a bomb?'

'I don't think it's a bomb.'

'Yeah, but are you sure?'

'Well, no.'

'I tell you what. I'm staying on the front porch while you open that box. I don't want to be anywhere near that box.'

I walked around to the back of the house, Lula following anyway, and sure enough, there was the box, sitting on the stoop. The box was about a foot square. It was heavy cardboard, sealed up with tape, marked with a red X.

Kuntz was at the screen door. 'Took you long enough.'

'You're lucky we came at all,' Lula said. 'And if you don't change your attitude we're gonna leave. So what do you think of that?'

I crouched down and examined the box. Nothing ticking. Didn't smell like dog shit. No warning labels that said Dangerous Explosives. Truth is, anything could be in the box. Anything. Could be cooties left over from Desert Storm. 'Looks okay to me,' I said to Kuntz. 'Go ahead and open it.'

'You're sure it's safe?'

'Hey,' Lula said, 'we're trained professionals. We know about these things. Right, Stephanie?'

'Right.'

Kuntz stared at the box. He cracked his knuckles and pulled his lips tight against his teeth. 'Damn that Maxine.' He took a Swiss army knife out of his pocket and bent to the box.

Lula and I discreetly stepped away from the stoop.

'You're sure?' he asked again, knife poised.

'Oh yeah.' Another step backward.

Kuntz slit the tape, parted the flaps and peeked into the box. Nothing exploded, but Lula and I kept our distance all the same.

'What the hell?' Kuntz said, looking more closely. 'What is this? Looks like a plastic bag sealed with one of those twisty tie things and filled with chocolate pudding.'

Lula and I exchanged glances.

'I suppose the clue's in the bag,' Kuntz said. He poked at the bag, his face contorted, and he uttered something that sounded like 'Ulk.'

'Something wrong?' Lula asked.

'This isn't pudding.'

'Well, look on the bright side,' Lula said. 'It didn't explode, did it?'

'Gosh, look at the time,' I said, tapping my watch. 'I'm going to have to run.'

'Yeah, me too,' Lula said. 'I got things to do.'

The color had drained from Kuntz's face. 'What about the clue?'

'You can call me later, or you can leave it on the machine. Just read the letters off to me.'

'But . . .'

Lula and I were gone. Around the side of the house. Into the Firebird. Down the street.

'Now what?' Lula said. 'Gonna be hard to top that for excitement. Not every day I get to see a box full of poop.'

'I need to look for Maxine. I'm not the only one to figure out she's in Point Pleasant. Unfortunately, I've got a vandalized car sitting in my parking lot, and I'm going to have to take care of that first.'

I tried Morelli on the cell phone again, and got him in his car.

'Your girlfriend visited me,' I said.

'I don't have a girlfriend.'

'Bull*shit*!'

I read him the note and told him about my door and my car.

'Why do you think it's my girlfriend?' Morelli wanted to know.

'I can't think of anyone else who would make a woman so totally deranged.'

'I appreciate the compliment,' Morelli said. 'But I'm not involved with anyone. I haven't been for a long time.'

'What about Terry Gilman?'

'Terry Gilman wouldn't pour gasoline on your car. Terry Gilman would politely knock on your door, and when you answered she'd gouge your eyes out.'

'When was the last time you saw Terry?'

'About a week ago. I ran into her in Fiorello's Deli. She was wearing a little denim skirt, and she looked very fine, but she's not the woman in my life right now.'

I narrowed my eyes. 'So who *is* the woman in your life now?'

'You.'

'Oh. Then what is this boyfriend stuff all about?'

'Maybe it's Maxine. You said it happened after she chained you to the refrigerator.'

'And she's talking about Kuntz? I don't know. It doesn't feel right.'

LULA PARKED NEXT to the CRX, and we got out to assess the damage.

'I don't know how you get rid of this much gasoline,' Lula said. 'It's everywhere. It's even spilled on the outside. You got gas puddles here.'

I needed to call the police and get a report on file, and then I needed to call my insurance company. The car needed to be professionally cleaned. I probably had a deductible, but I couldn't remember the amount. Not that it mattered. I couldn't drive the car like this.

'I'm going inside to make a couple phone calls,' I told Lula. 'If I hustle I might be done with this in time to go to Point Pleasant and look for Maxine.'

'You know what I love about Point Pleasant? I love those half-orange and half-vanilla swirly frozen custard cones. Maybe I'll have to go with you. Maybe you could use a bodyguard.'

A blue Fairlane swung into the lot and skidded to a stop behind us.

'Holy cats,' Lula said. 'It's old lady Nowicki, driving half in the bag.'

Mrs. Nowicki lurched out of the car and swayed over. 'I heard that, and I'm not half in the bag. If I was half in the bag I'd be a lot happier.'

She was dressed in poison-green spandex. She'd troweled on full face makeup, a cigarette was stuck in the corner of her mouth and wisps of orange frizz framed a poison-green turban . . . which I knew hid a freshly scalped head.

She looked at my car and gave a bark of laughter. 'This yours?'

'Yeah.'

'Didn't anybody tell you the gasoline's supposed to go in the tank?'

'Something you want to see me about?'

'I'm leaving town,' Mrs. Nowicki said. 'And I have some news for you. Maxine would be real mad if she knew I told you this, but I think you were right about it being better you found her than . . . you know.'

'You've heard from her?'

'She brought her car around for me. Said she didn't need it anymore.'

'Where is she?'

'Well, she used to be in Point Pleasant, like I thought. But she said people got wind of that so she's moved to Atlantic City. She wouldn't give me an address, but I know she likes to play at Bally's Park Place. Thinks the odds are better there.'

'You're sure?'

'Well, pretty sure.' She took a deep drag on the cigarette which just about wore it down to the filter. Blue smoke filtered out her nose, and she flicked the butt away. It hit the pavement, rolled under my car and . . . *phunff!* The car ignited.

'YIKES!' Lula and I yelped, jumping back.

The car was engulfed in a big yellow fireball.

'FIRE! FIRE!' Lula and I hollered.

Mrs. Nowicki turned to look. 'What?'

KABOOM! There was an explosion, Mrs. Nowicki got knocked on her ass, and a second fireball erupted. Lula's Firebird!

'My car! My baby!' Lula yelled. 'Do something! Do something!'

People were pouring out of the building, and sirens wailed in the distance. Lula and I stooped over Mrs. Nowicki, who was stretched out on the pavement, face up, eyes wide.

'Uh oh,' Lula said. 'You aren't gonna be dead again, are you?'

'I need a cigarette,' Mrs. Nowicki said. 'Light me up.'

A squad car slid into the lot, lights flashing. Carl Costanza got out of the car and walked over to me. 'Pretty good,' he said. 'Looks like you blew up two cars this time.'

'One was Lula's.'

'We gonna have to look for body parts? Last time you blew up a car we found body parts a block away.'

'You only found one single foot a block away. Most of the parts were right here in the lot. Personally, I think Mrs. Burlew's dog carried the foot there.'

'So what about this time? We gotta go looking for feet?'

'Both cars were unoccupied. Mrs. Nowicki got shook up, but I think she's okay.'

'She's so okay, she left,' Lula said. 'She could do that on account of her piece-of-junk car didn't get cooked.'

'She left?' My voice sounded like Minnie Mouse's. I couldn't believe she left after causing the accident.

'Just this second,' Lula said. 'Saw her just leave the lot.'

I looked out to St. James, and an unsettling thought flashed into my head. 'You don't suppose she did this on purpose, do you?'

'Blew up both our cars so we couldn't go off looking for her daughter? You think she's smart enough to think of something like that?'

THE FIRE TRUCKS left first, then the police, then the tow trucks. And now all that was left was a charred, sanded spot on the blacktop.

'Oh well,' Lula said. 'Easy come, easy go.'

'You don't seem very upset. I thought you loved that car.'

'Well the radio wasn't working right, and it got a ding on the side of the door at the supermarket. I can go out and get a new one now. Soon as I get the paperwork done I'm going car shopping. Nothing I like better than car shopping.'

Nothing I *hated* more than car shopping. I'd rather have a mammogram than go car shopping. I never had enough money to get a car I really liked. And then there were the car salesmen . . . second only to dentists in their ability to inflict pain. Ick. An involuntary shiver gripped my spine.

'See, I'm one of those positive type people,' Lula went on. 'My glass isn't half empty. Nuh uh. My glass is always half full. That's why I'm making something of myself. And anyway, there's people lots worse off than me. I didn't spend *my* afternoon looking for a note in a box full of dog poop.'

'Do you think Mrs. Nowicki was telling the truth about Atlantic City? She could have been trying to throw us off the trail.'

'Only one way to find out.'

'We need wheels.'

We looked at each other and did a double grimace. We both knew where there was an available car. My father had a powder-blue-and-white '53 Buick sitting in his garage. From time to time I'd been desperate enough to borrow the beast.

'No, no, no,' Lula said. 'I'm not going down to Atlantic City in that big blue pimpmobile.'

'Where's your positive attitude? What about all that cup-is-half-full stuff?'

'Fuck the cup is half full. I can't be cool in that car. And I don't ride in no uncool car. I got a reputation at stake. You see a big black woman sliding across the seat in that car, and you think one thing. Twenty-five dollars for a blow job. I'm telling you, if you aren't Jay Leno you got no business being in that car.'

'Okay, let me get this straight. If I decide to go to Atlantic City, and the only car I can come up with is Big Blue . . . you don't want to go with me.'

'Well, since you put it that way . . .'

I called Lula a cab, and then I trudged up the stairs to my apartment. I let myself in and went straight to the refrigerator for a beer. 'I have to tell you,' I said to Rex. 'I'm getting discouraged.'

I checked my answering machine and received a terse message from Eddie Kuntz. 'I got it.'

Kuntz didn't sound any happier when I called him back. He read the letters out to me. Fifty-three in all. And he hung up. No inquiring as to my health. No suggestion to have a nice day.

I dialed Sally and transferred the burden onto him. 'By the way,' I said. 'What kind of car do you have?'

'Porsche.'

Figures. 'Two seater?'

'Is there any other kind?'

Room for me. No room for Lula. She'd understand. After all, this was business, right? And the fact that her car just got blown up, that was business too, right? 'It wasn't my fault,' I said. 'I wasn't the one who tossed the cigarette.'

'I must have been beamed up for a minute there,' Sally said. 'I think I just got a couple sentences from the other side.'

I explained about the cars' catching fire and about the lead from Mrs. Nowicki.

'Sounds like we need to go to Atlantic City,' Sally said.

'You think we could squash Lula into the Porsche with us?'

'Not even if we greased her.'

I gave an internal sigh of regret and told Sally we'd go in my car and I'd pick him up at seven. No way was I going to be able to cut Lula out of this caper.

CHAPTER SEVEN

'OTHER MOTHERS HAVE daughters who get married and have children,' my mother said. 'I have a daughter who blows up cars. How did this happen? This doesn't come from *my* side of the family.'

We were at the table, eating dinner, and my father had his head bent over his plate, and his shoulders were shaking.

'What?' my mother said to him.

'I don't know. It just struck me funny. Some men could go a lifetime and never have their kid blow up a car, but I have a daughter who's knocked off three cars and burned down a funeral home. Maybe that's some kind of record.'

Everyone sat in shocked silence because that was the longest speech my father had made in fifteen years.

'Your Uncle Lou used to blow up cars,' my father said to me. 'You don't know that, but it's true. When Louie was young he worked for Joey the Squid. Joey owned car lots back then, and he was in a war with the Grinaldi brothers, who also owned car lots. And Joey would pay Louie to blow up Grinaldi cars. Louie got paid by the car. Fifty dollars a car. That was big money in those days.'

'You've been to the lodge, drinking,' my mother said

to my father. 'I thought you were supposed to be out with the cab?'

My father forked in some potatoes. 'Nobody wanted to take a cab. Slow day.'

'Did Uncle Lou ever get caught?'

'Never. Lou was good. The Grinaldi brothers never suspected Lou. They thought Joey was sending out Willy Fuchs. One day they clipped Willy, and then Lou stopped blowing up Grinaldi cars.'

'Ommigod.'

'Worked out okay,' my father said. 'Lou went into the wholesale fruit business after that and did pretty good.'

'Funky bracelet you got on your arm,' Grandma said. 'Is it new?'

'Actually, it's half of a pair of cuffs. I accidentally locked myself into them and then couldn't find the key. So I had to hacksaw one of them off. I need to go to a locksmith to get this half opened, but I haven't had the time.'

'Muriel Slickowsky's son is a locksmith,' my mother said. 'I could call Muriel.'

'Maybe tomorrow. I have to go to Atlantic City tonight. I'm checking out a lead on Maxine.'

'I should go along,' Grandma said, jumping out of her chair, heading for the stairs. 'I could help. I blend right in there. Atlantic City's full of old babes like me. Let me change my dress. I'll be ready in a jiffy!'

'Wait! I don't think . . .'

'Wasn't nothing good on TV tonight anyway,' Grandma called from the second floor. 'And don't worry, I'll come prepared.'

That brought me out of my seat. 'No guns!' I looked

over at my mother. 'She doesn't still have that forty-five, does she?'

'I looked all over in her room, and I couldn't find it.'

'I want her strip-searched before she gets in my car.'

'Not enough money in the universe,' my father said. 'Not under threat of death would I look at that woman naked.'

LULA, GRANDMA MAZUR and I stood in the hall, waiting for Sally to answer his doorbell. I was wearing a short denim skirt, white T-shirt and sandals. Grandma was wearing a red-and-blue print dress with white sneakers. Lula was wearing a low-cut red knit dress that hiked up about three inches below her ass, red-tinted hose and red satin sling-back heels.

And Sally opened the door in full drag. Black bitch queen wig, skin-tight silver-sequined sheath that stopped three inches below *his* ass, and strappy silver platform heels that put him at a startling 6′ 8″ without the hair.

Sally gave me the once-over. 'I thought we were supposed to be in disguise.'

'I'm disguised as a fox,' Lula said.

'Yeah, and I'm disguised as an old lady,' Grandma said.

'My mother wouldn't let me go if I was disguised as somebody,' I said.

Sally tugged at his dress. 'I'm disguised as Sheba.'

'Girlfriend,' Lula said to him, 'you are the shit.'

'Sally's a drag queen,' I explained to Grandma.

'No kidding,' Grandma said. 'I always wanted to meet a drag queen. I always wanted to know what you do with your dingdong when you wear girl's clothes.'

'You're supposed to wear special underpants that tuck you under.'

We all looked down at the crotch-level bulge in the front of Sally's dress.

'So sue me,' Sally said. 'They give me a rash.'

Lula tipped her nose in the air. 'What's that smell? Mmmmmm, I smell something baking.'

Sally rolled his eyes. 'It's Sugar. He's in a fucking frenzy. He must have gone through ten pounds of flour in the last two hours.'

Lula muscled past Sally into the kitchen. 'Lord,' she said, 'will you look at this . . . cakes as far as the eye could see.'

Sugar was at the counter, kneading bread dough. He looked up when we came in and gave us an embarrassed smile. 'You probably think I'm weird to be doing all this baking.'

'Honey, I think you're cute as a button,' Lula said. 'You ever want a new roommate you give me a call.'

'I like the way it smells when you have something in the oven,' Sugar said. 'Like home.'

'We're going to Atlantic City,' I said to Sugar. 'Would you like to join us?'

'Thanks, but I have a pie ready to go in, and this dough has to rise, and then I have some ironing . . .'

'Damn,' Lula said, 'you sound like Cinderella.'

Sugar poked at his dough. 'I'm not much of a gambler.'

We each took a cookie from a plate on the counter and herded ourselves out of the kitchen, down the hall and into the elevator.

'What a sad little guy,' Lula said. 'He don't look like he has much fun.'

'He's a lot more fun when he's in a dress,' Sally said. 'You put him in a dress and his whole personality changes.'

'Then why don't he always wear a dress?' Lula wanted to know.

Sally shrugged. 'I don't know. Guess that doesn't feel right, either.'

We crossed the sleek marble lobby and walked the flower-bordered path to the lot.

'Over here,' I said to Sally. 'The blue-and-white Buick.'

Sally's mascared lashes snapped open. 'The Buick? Holy shit, is this *your* car? It's got portholes. Fucking portholes! What's under the hood?'

'A V-8.'

'Yow! A V-8! A fucking V-8!'

'Good thing he don't have them tuck underpants on,' Lula said. 'He'd rupture himself.'

The Buick was a man thing. Women hated it. Men loved it. I thought it must have something to do with the size of the tires. Or maybe it was the bulbous, egglike shape . . . sort of like a Porsche on steroids.

'We'd better get going,' I said to Sally.

He took the keys out of my hand and slid behind the wheel.

'Excuse me,' I said. 'This is *my* car. I get to drive.'

'You need someone with balls to drive this car,' Sally said.

Lula stood hip stuck out, hand on hip. 'Hah! And you think we don't have balls? Look again, Tiny Tim.'

Sally held tight to the wheel. 'Okay, what'll it take? I'll give you fifty bucks if you let me drive.'

'I don't want money,' I said. 'If you want to drive the car, all you have to do is ask.'

'Yeah, you just don't go pulling this macho shit on us,' Lula said. 'We don't stand for none of that. We don't take that bus.'

'This is gonna be great,' Sally said. 'I always wanted to drive one of these.'

Grandma and Lula piled in back, and I got in front.

Sally pulled a slip of paper from his purse. 'Before I forget, here's the latest clue.'

I read it aloud. ' "Last clue. Last chance. Blue Moon Bar. Saturday at nine." '

Maxine was getting ready to bolt. She was setting Eddie up one last time. And what about me? I thought she might be setting me up one last time, too, by sending me on a wildgoose chase to Atlantic City.

THE FIRST THING I always notice about Atlantic City is that it's not Las Vegas. Vegas is all splash from the outside to the inside. Atlantic City is not so much about neon lights as about good parking. The casinos are built on the boardwalk, but truth is, nobody gives a damn about the boardwalk. A.C. is not about ocean. A.C. is about letting it ride. And if you're a senior citizen, so much the better. This is the Last Chance Saloon.

The city's slums sit butt-flush with the casinos' back doors. Since Jersey is not about perfection this isn't a problem. For me, Jersey is about finding the brass ring and grabbing hold, and if you have to go through some slums to get to the slots . . . fuck it. Crank up your car window, lock your door and roll past the pushers and pimps to valet parking.

It's all very exhilarating.

And while it's not Vegas, it's also not Monte Carlo. You don't see a lot of Versace gowns in Atlantic City. There are always some guys at the craps table with slicked-back hair and pinkie rings. And there are always some women dressed up like bar singers standing next to the oily, pinkie ring guys. But mostly what you see in Atlantic City is sixty-five-year-old women wearing polyester warm-up suits, toting buckets of quarters, heading for the poker machines.

I could go to New York or Vegas with Lula and Sally and never be noticed. In Atlantic City it was like trying to blend in with Sigfried and Roy and five of their tigers.

We came onto the floor, four abreast, letting the noise wash over us, taking it all in . . . the mirrored ceiling, the 3-D carpet, the flashing lights, and hustling, swirling crowds of people. We moved through the room and old men walked into walls, pit bosses turned silent, waitresses stopped in their tracks, chips were dropped on the floor and women stared with the sort of open-mouthed curiosity usually reserved for train wrecks. As if they'd never seen a seven-foot transvestite and two-hundred-pound black woman with blond baloney curls all dressed up like Cher on a bad day.

Do I know how to conduct an undercover operation, or what?

'Good thing I got my Social Security check yesterday,' Grandma said, eyeing the slots. 'I feel lucky.'

'Pick your poison,' Lula said to Sally.

'Blackjack!'

And off they all went.

'Keep your eyes open for Maxine,' I said to their departing backs.

I walked the room for an hour, lost $40 shooting craps, but got a free beer for a $5 tip. I hadn't run across Maxine, but then that wasn't a surprise. I found a sectional with good visibility and settled in to watch the people.

At eleven-thirty Grandma appeared and sank down next to me. 'Won twenty bucks on my first machine, and then it turned on me,' she said. 'Bad luck all night after that.'

'Got any money left?'

'None. Still, it wasn't all wasted. I met a real looker. He picked me up at the two-dollar poker machines, so you know he's no cheapskate.'

I raised my eyebrows.

'You should have stayed with me. I could have gotten you fixed up, too.'

Oh boy.

A small white-haired man approached us. 'Here's your Manhattan,' he said to Grandma, handing her a drink. 'And who's this?' he asked, turning to me. 'This must be your granddaughter.'

'This here's Harry Meaker,' Grandma said to me. 'Harry's from Mercerville, and he had bum luck tonight, too.'

'I always got bum luck,' Harry said. 'Had bum luck all my life. Been married two times, and both wives died. Had a double bypass last year, and now I'm clogging up again. I can feel it. And look at this. See this red scaly patch on my nose? Skin cancer. Gonna have it cut out next week.'

'Harry came down on the bus,' Grandma said.

'Prostate problems,' Harry said. 'Need a bus with a toilet on it.' He looked at his watch. 'I gotta go. Bus leaves in a half hour. Don't want to miss it.'

Grandma watched him walk away. 'What do you think? He's a live one, huh? For a while, anyway.'

Lula and Sally trudged over and plopped down on the couch next to me.

'Didn't hear no gunfire, so I guess no one saw Maxine,' Lula said.

'Maxine was the smart one,' Sally said. 'She stayed home.'

I looked at him. 'Not a good night?'

'Cleaned me out. I'm going to have to do my own nails this week.'

'I could do them for you,' Lula said. 'I'm real good at nails. See those little palm trees on my nails? I put them on myself.'

'Hold it,' I said, getting to my feet. 'Look at that woman in the turquoise slacks by the craps table. The one with all the yellow hair . . .'

The woman had her back to me, but she'd turned a moment ago, giving me a good look at her face. And she looked a lot like Maxine.

I started walking toward her when she turned again and stared directly at me. Recognition registered simultaneously for both of us. She pivoted on her heel and disappeared into a crush of people at the far side of the table.

'I see her!' Lula said, one step behind me. 'Don't lose sight!'

But I had lost sight. The room was crowded, and Maxine wasn't dressed in red spangles like Lula. Maxine blended right in.

'I got my eye on her,' Grandma yelled. 'She's going for the boardwalk.'

Grandma had climbed onto a blackjack table and was

standing, sneakered feet planted wide. The dealer made a grab for her, and Grandma hit him on the head with her purse. 'Don't be rude,' she said to the dealer. 'I just come up here to get a good look on account of the osteoporosis shrunk me and now I'm too short.'

I took off at a run for the boardwalk entrance, weaving between clusters of gamblers, trying not to mow anyone over. In two heartbeats I was out of the game room, into the wide hallway leading to the door. I caught a glimpse of big straw hair in front of me, saw it bob through the wide glass door. I was pushing people away and yelling 'Excuse me' and I was breathing heavy. Too many dough-nuts, not enough exercise.

I swung through the door and saw Maxine ahead of me, running for all she was worth. I kicked it up a notch, and I heard Lula and Sally clattering and swearing half a block back.

Maxine made a sharp turn, off the boardwalk, down a side street. I made the same turn just as a car door slammed and an engine caught. I ran to the car, reached it just as its wheels spun. And then the car was gone. And since Maxine was nowhere to be seen, I supposed Maxine was gone, too.

Sally slid to a stop and bent at the waist to catch his breath. 'That's it for me, man. From now on fuck the heels.'

Lula crashed into him. 'Heart attack. Heart attack.'

We were all walking around, gasping for breath, and Grandma trotted up. 'What happened? What'd I miss? Where is she?'

'Got away,' I said.

'Dang!'

Three guys came out of the shadows at us. They looked

to be late teens, wearing baggy homey pants and unlaced court shoes.

'Hey, momma,' one said. 'What's happening?'

'Give me a break,' Sally said.

'Whoa,' the kid said. 'Big bitch!'

Sally straightened his wig. 'Thanks.'

The kid pulled a Buck knife out of his pants pocket. 'How about giving me your purse, bitch?'

Sally hiked up his skirt, reached into his briefs and pulled out a Glock. 'How about using that knife to slice off your balls?'

Lula whipped a gun out of her red satin purse and Grandma hauled out her .45 long-barrel.

'Day my make, punk,' Grandma said.

'Hey, I don't want any trouble,' the kid said. 'We were just having some fun.'

'I want to shoot him,' Sally said. 'Nobody'll tell, right?'

'No fair,' Lula said. 'I want to shoot him.'

'Okay,' Grandma said. 'On the count of three, we'll all shoot him.'

'No shooting!' I said.

'Then how about if I kick the shit out of him?' Sally said.

'You're all nuts,' the kid said, backing away. 'What kind of women are you?' His friends took off, and he ran after them.

Sally put his gun back in his pants. 'Guess I flunked the estrogen test.'

We all stared at his crotch, and Grandma said what Lula and I were thinking.

'I thought that bulge was your dingdong,' Grandma said.

'Jesus,' Sally said, 'who do you think I am, Thunder the Wonder Horse? My gun wouldn't fit in my purse.'

'You need to get a smaller gun,' Lula said. 'Ruins your lines with that big old Glock in your drawers.'

GRANDMA, LULA AND Sally were asleep fifteen minutes out of Atlantic City. I drove the big car in the dark and the quiet, thinking about Maxine. I still wasn't convinced this was anything other than a wild-goose chase. True, I'd seen Maxine, just as her mother had said, but she'd gotten away a little too easily. And she hadn't looked all that surprised to see me. Her car had been parked on a dark side street. Not the sort of thing a lone woman would do. It was safer and more convenient to park in the parking garage. She'd taken off in a black Acura. And while I didn't actually see her get in the car, I suspected she wasn't driving. It had all been too fast. The motor had caught the instant I heard the car door slam shut.

So I was thinking maybe she wanted to throw me off. Maybe she was still in Point Pleasant. Maybe she'd paid her rent for the month and didn't want to move. So when she discovered her mother had informed on her, she concocted this scenario to keep me away from Point Pleasant. Or maybe this was another game. Maybe Eddie Kuntz had been right about Maxine's fascination with James Bond.

I dropped Sally off first, then Lula, and Grandma last.

'Mom thinks you've gotten rid of that gun,' I said to Grandma.

'Hunh,' Grandma said. 'Imagine that.'

My mother was at the front door, standing arms crossed, looking out at us. If I was a good daughter I'd go in and have some cookies. But I wasn't that good a daughter. I loved my mother, but love only goes so far when you're trying to explain how your grandmother ended up standing on a blackjack table in a packed casino.

I waited for Grandma to successfully negotiate the steps, then I waved good-bye and drove away in the big blue car. I made every light on Hamilton, turned at St. James and felt a nervous flutter in my stomach at the sight of emergency vehicles at the corner. Cop cars, fire trucks, EMTs. The parking lot to my building was filled with them. Lights were blazing, and the squawk of loudspeakers carried back to me. Sooty water ran in the gutter, and people dressed in bathrobes and hastily put together outfits milled about on the sidewalks. Whatever it was, it seemed to be over. Firefighters were packing up. Some of the curious were dispersing.

Fear arrowed into me. *Next time I'll strike a match*.

The street was blocked, so I parked where I was and ran across the small patch of grass that bordered the lot. I shielded my eyes from the glare of the lights and squinted through a haze of smoke and diesel fumes, counting windows to locate the fire. Second floor, two apartments over. The fire was in my apartment. The window glass was broken and the surrounding brick was blackened. No other apartment showed any damage.

My only coherent thought was of Rex. Rex was trapped in a glass aquarium in the middle of all that ruin. I stumbled to the building's back door, begging for a miracle, not sure if I was screaming or crying, focused only on Rex. I was dragging in air that felt thick and unbreathable. Like swimming through Jell-O. Vision and sound distorted. Hands pulling at me as I struggled to cross the crowded lobby. I heard my name being called.

'Here!' Mr. Kleinschmidt shouted. 'Over here!'

He was with Mrs. Karwatt, and Mrs. Karwatt had both arms wrapped around Rex's glass aquarium.

I shoved my way through to them, barely able to believe Rex had been saved. 'Is he okay? Is Rex okay?' I asked, raising the lid to see for myself, tilting the soup can to look at a startled Rex.

Probably it's silly to feel so much affection for a hamster, but Rex is my roommate. Rex keeps my apartment from feeling empty. And besides that, he likes me. I'm almost sure of it.

'He's fine,' Mrs. Karwatt said. 'We got him out right away. Thank goodness you gave me a key to your apartment. I heard the explosion and went right in. Lucky the fire started in your bedroom.'

'Was anyone hurt?'

'No one was hurt. It was all in your apartment. Mrs. Stinkowski below you has some water damage, and we all smell smoky, but that's it.'

'This must be a doozy of a case you're on,' Mr. Kleinschmidt said. 'Someone blew up your car and your apartment all in one day.'

Kenny Zale clomped over to me. I went to grade school with Kenny, and for a while in high school dated his older brother, Mickey. Kenny was a fireman now. He was dressed in boots and black bunker pants, and his face was grimy with sweat and soot.

'Looks like you visited my apartment,' I said to Kenny.

'Maybe you should think about getting a different job.'

'How bad is it?'

'The bedroom's gone. That's where it started. Looks to me like someone pitched a firebomb through your window. The bathroom is salvageable. The living room is pretty much trashed. The kitchen will probably be okay when it gets cleaned up. You'll need new flooring. Probably have to paint. There's a lot of water damage.'

'Can I get in?'

'Yeah. This would be a good time. The fire marshal's up there now. He'll probably walk you through to let you get what you can, and then he'll seal it until the investigation's over and he's sure it's safe.'

'John Petrucci still the fire marshal?'

'Yeah. You're probably on intimate terms.'

'We've spent some time together. I wouldn't say we were intimate.'

He grinned and ruffled my hair. 'I'm glad you weren't in bed when this happened. You'd be toast.'

I left Rex with Mrs. Karwatt, ran the stairs and worked my way through the crush of people in the hall. The area around my apartment was water soaked and sooty. The air was acrid. I looked through the door and my heart contracted. The destruction was numbing. The walls were black, the windows broken, the furniture unrecognizable as anything other than drenched, charred rubble.

I'm a firm believer in denial. My reasoning is why deal with unpleasantness today when you could get hit by a bus tomorrow. And if you procrastinate long enough, maybe the issue will go away. Unfortunately, this issue wasn't going away. This issue was beyond denial. This issue was fucking depressing.

'Shit!' I shrieked. 'Shit, shit, shit, shit!'

Everyone on the floor stopped what they were doing and stared at me.

'Okay,' I said. 'I feel better now.' It was a lie, of course, but it felt good to say.

Petrucci walked over. 'You got any idea who did this?'

'No. Do you?' Another lie. I had a few ideas.

'Somebody with a pretty good arm.'

That could be Maxine. The softball star. But it still felt wrong. It felt more like mob . . . like Joe's pal, Terry.

I gingerly stepped into the kitchen. The brown bear cookie jar was untouched. The phone looked okay. The soot and water were pervasive and depressing. I bit down hard on my lip. I wasn't going to cry. Rex was safe. Everything else was replaceable, I told myself.

We went room by room, and not much was salvageable. A few cosmetics that had been in the bathroom and a hair dryer. I put them in a bag from the kitchen.

'Well, this isn't so bad,' I said to Petrucci. 'I've been wanting to redecorate. I just wish the bathroom had gone.'

'What, you don't like orange and brown?'

'Do you think it's too late to burn the bathroom?'

Petrucci looked pained. Like I'd asked him to fart in public. 'You have insurance for all your stuff?'

'Yes.' Maybe.

Mrs. Karwatt was waiting in the hall with Rex. 'Are you okay? Do you have some place to stay? You could sleep on my couch tonight.'

I took the cage from her. 'That's nice of you to offer, but I'll probably go home to my parents. They have a spare bedroom.'

Old Mrs. Bestler was in the elevator. 'Going down,' she said, leaning on her walker. 'First floor, ladies' handbags.'

The doors opened to the lobby, and the first person I saw was Dillon in his superintendent coveralls.

'I was just going up to take a look,' he said. 'Guess I'll have to get the paintbrush out.'

'Gonna take a lot of paint.' My lip was trembling again.

'Hey, don't worry about it. Remember when Mrs. Baumgarten set fire to her Christmas tree? The whole apartment was burned to a crisp. Nothing left but ashes. And now look . . . good as new.'

'It's worth a case of Guinness for you to take a sledge-hammer to the bathroom.'

'What, you don't like orange and brown?'

I WAS GLAD I'd parked the Buick on the street, out of sight of the fire-blackened building. Out of sight, out of mind. Sort of. The Buick was quiet and womblike. Nice and insulating against the outside world. The doors were locked, and the activity was all in front of me, half a block away.

Rex and I sat in the car and tried to collect our thoughts. After a while Rex started running on his wheel, and I assumed his thoughts were all collected. My thoughts were taking longer to come together. My thoughts were running in frightening directions. Some-one wanted me scared and maybe dead. There was a remote possibility it was the same someone who was chop-ping off fingers and whacking off scalps, and I didn't like the idea that this was in my future.

I rested my head on the steering wheel. I was exhausted, and I was on the brink of tears. And I was afraid if I started crying I wouldn't stop for a long, long time.

I looked at my watch. It was two A.M. I needed to get some sleep. Where? The most obvious solution was to go home to my parents, but I didn't want to put their lives in jeopardy. I didn't want the next target for a firebomb to be their house on High Street. So where could I go? A hotel? There are no hotels in Trenton. There are some in Princeton, but they were forty minutes away, and I was reluctant to spend the money. I could call Ranger, but no one knows where Ranger lives. If Ranger took me in for the night, he'd probably have to kill me in the morning to make sure his secret was safe. Lula? That was sort of a scary idea. Better to face the scalper than sleep with Lula. There was my best friend, Mary Lou, and there was my sister, Valerie, but I didn't want to endanger them, either. I needed someone who was expendable. Someone I didn't have to worry about. Someone who had extra room.

'Oh boy,' I said to Rex. 'Are you thinking what I'm thinking?'

I sat for another five minutes, but I couldn't come up with a better solution to my problem, so I turned the key in the ignition and slowly drove past the lone fire truck at the end of the street. I tried not to look at my apartment, but I caught a glance of the fire escape from the corner of my eye. My chest gave a painful constriction. My poor apartment.

I took a deep breath. I didn't want to die. And I didn't want someone to hate me. And I absolutely did *not* want to cry.

'Don't worry about a thing,' I said to Rex. 'This will all work out. We've had bad times before, right?'

I took Hamilton to Chambers and followed Chambers to Slater. Two blocks down Slater I found the house I was looking for. It was a modest brown-shingled row house. All lights were off. I closed my eyes. I was dog tired, and I didn't want to do this.

'Maybe we should sleep in the car tonight,' I said to

Rex. 'Then tomorrow we can get something more permanent.'

Rex was doing a four-minute mile on the wheel. He blinked at me once, and that was it. The mental message was, You're on your own, kid.

Truth is, I didn't want to stay in my car. The crazy person could come and get me while I slept. He could jimmy the window, and he could cut off all my fingers. I looked at the house again. This was the one place I could feel safe and not be completely freaked out if the house was destroyed. This house belonged to Joe Morelli.

I hauled my cell phone out of my bag and dialed.

The phone rang six times before Joe answered with a mumbled hello.

'Joe?' I said. 'It's Stephanie.'

'Does this involve death?'

'Not yet.'

'Does it involve sex?'

'Not yet.'

'I can't imagine why else you'd be calling me.'

'Someone firebombed my apartment tonight, and I need a place to stay.'

'Where are you?'

'In front of your house.'

An upstairs curtain was pulled aside.

'I'll be right down,' Joe said. 'Don't get out of your car until I open my door.'

CHAPTER EIGHT

I HAULED REX'S cage off the front seat. 'Now remember,' I said, 'no sniveling over the fact that our life
is sucky. And no getting all mushy because Morelli is so
hot. And no crying. We don't want Morelli thinking we're
losers.'

Morelli was on his small cement front porch. The door
was open behind him, and I could see light from the
upstairs hall. He was barefoot, dressed in cut-offs that
rode his hips. His hair was tousled from sleep, and he had
a gun in his hand, hanging loose at his side. 'You talking
to someone?'

'Rex. He's a little nervous about all this.'

Morelli took the cage from me, kicked his door shut
and carried Rex into the kitchen. He put the cage on the
counter and flipped the overhead light on. It was an old-
fashioned kitchen with dated appliances and Formica
counters. Cupboards had been recently painted with
cream enamel, and there was new linoleum on the floor. A
pot sat soaking in the sink. Looked like Morelli'd had
spaghetti for supper.

Morelli put a quart of cold milk and a bag of Oreo's on
the small wood table that pressed against one kitchen
wall. He took two glasses from the dish drain, sat down at
the table and poured out two glasses of milk.

'So,' he said, 'you want to talk about it?'

'I was in Atlantic City looking for Maxine tonight, and while I was gone someone pitched a firebomb through my bedroom window. The whole apartment went up. Fortunately, Mrs. Karwatt had a key and managed to rescue Rex.'

Morelli stared at me for a beat with his unreadable cop face. 'Remember those purple shoes you bought last year?'

'Reduced to ashes.'

'Damn. I had plans for those shoes. I've spent a few sleepless nights thinking about you wearing those shoes and nothing else.'

I helped myself to a cookie. 'You need a life.'

'Tell me about it. I spent last weekend laying linoleum.' He took a second cookie. 'I notice you're driving the Buick. What happened to the CRX?'

'Remember I told you about how someone soaked it with gasoline? Well, it sort of exploded.'

'It exploded?'

'Actually, it caught fire first. Then it exploded.'

'Hmm,' Morelli said, eating the top half of the Oreo.

A tear slid down my cheek.

Morelli stopped eating. 'Wait a minute. Is this for real? You aren't making this up?'

'Of course this is for real. Why else do you think I'm here?'

'Well, I thought . . .'

I jumped up, and my chair crashed to the floor. 'You thought I made this up so I could come over here in the middle of the night and crawl into your bed!'

The line to Morelli's mouth tightened. 'Let me get this straight. Yesterday, someone actually blew up your car and your apartment. And now you want to move in with me?

What, do you hate me? You're a walking disaster! You're Calamity Jane in fucking spandex!'

'I am *not* a walking disaster!' But he was right. I was a walking disaster. I was an accident waiting to happen. And I was going to cry. My chest ached and my throat felt like I'd swallowed a baseball and tears gushed out of my eyes. 'Shit,' I said, swiping the tears away.

Morelli grimaced and reached out to me. 'Listen, I'm sorry. I didn't mean—'

'Don't touch me!' I shrieked. 'You're right. I'm a disaster. Look at me. I'm homeless. I'm carless. And I'm hysterical. What kind of a bounty hunter gets hysterical? A loser bounty hunter, that's what kind. A l-l-loser.'

'Maybe milk wasn't the right choice here,' Morelli said. 'Maybe you could use some brandy.'

'And there's more,' I sobbed. 'I lost forty bucks on craps, and I was the only one who didn't have a gun tonight!'

Morelli pulled me into his arms and held me close to him. 'That's okay, Steph. Forty dollars isn't so much. And lots of people don't have guns.'

'Not in New Jersey. Not bounty hunters.'

'There are some people in Jersey who don't have a gun.'

'Oh yeah? Name one.'

He held me at arm's length and grinned. 'I think we should get you up to bed. You'll feel better in the morning.'

'About the bed . . .'

He pushed me toward the stairs. 'I have a spare bedroom made up.'

'Thanks.'

'And I'll leave my door open in case you get lonely.'
And I'd lock my door in case I got weak.

I AWOKE DISORIENTED, staring at a ceiling that wasn't mine. The walls were covered with faded green paper patterned with barely discernible viney flowers. Comforting in an old-fashioned way. Morelli had inherited this house from his Aunt Rose and hadn't changed much. My guess was the simple white curtains that hung on the windows had been chosen by Rose. It was a small room with a queen-size bed and a single chest of drawers. The floors were wood, and Morelli had placed a rag throw rug beside the bed. It was a sunny room and much quieter than my own bedroom, which faced out to the parking lot. I was sleeping in one of Morelli's T-shirts, and I was now faced with grim reality. I had no clothes. No clean underwear, no shorts, no shoes, no nothing. First thing would be a trip to Macy's for an emergency wardrobe.

There was a clock radio on the chest of drawers. It was nine o'clock. The day had started without me. I opened my door and peeked into the hall. All was silent. No sign of Morelli. A piece of paper had been taped to my door. It said Morelli had gone off to work and I should make myself at home. It said there was an extra key for me on the kitchen table and towels laid out in the bathroom.

I showered and dressed and went downstairs in search of breakfast. I poured myself a glass of orange juice and looked in at Rex.

'No doubt about it, I made an idiot out of myself last night,' I said.

Rex was sleeping in his soup can and didn't show a lot of concern. Rex had seen me in my idiot state before.

I ate a bowl of cereal and took a look at the house. It was clean and orderly. The food in the cupboard was basic. The pots were second generation. Six glasses. Six dishes. Six bowls. Shelf paper left from Aunt Rose. He had a coffeemaker, but he hadn't made coffee, nor had he made breakfast. No dirty dishes. No new dishes in the dish drain. Morelli would stop on the way to work for coffee and whatever. Cops weren't known for their excellent diets.

I remembered Morelli's living room furniture from his apartment. Utilitarian. Comfort without style. It seemed off in the row house. The row house needed overstuffing with magazines on the coffee table and pictures on the walls.

Rooms were shotgunned. Living room, dining room, kitchen. Because Morelli lived in the middle of the block, there were no windows in the dining room. Not that it mattered. I couldn't see Morelli using the dining room. In the beginning, when Morelli had first moved here, I couldn't see him in the house at all. Now it suited him. Not that Morelli had turned domestic. It was more that the house had assumed independence. As if Morelli and the house had reached an agreement to coexist and leave it at that.

I called my mother and told her there'd been a fire and I was staying with Morelli.

'What do you mean, you're staying with Morelli? Ommigod, you're married!'

'It's not like that. Morelli has an extra bedroom. I'm going to pay him rent.'

'We have an extra bedroom. You could stay here.'

'I've tried that before, and it doesn't work. Too many people using one bathroom.' Too many homicidal maniacs wanting to kill me.

'Angie Morelli is gonna have a fit.'

Angie Morelli was Joe's mother. A woman both revered and feared in the burg.

'Angie Morelli's a good Catholic woman, and she's not as open-minded as I am,' my mother said.

The Morelli women were good Catholics. The men broke every commandment. The men played Monday night poker with the Antichrist.

'I have to go,' I said. 'I just wanted you to know I was okay.'

'Why don't you and Joe come over for dinner tonight? I'm making meat loaf.'

'We're not a couple! And I have things to do.'

'What things?'

'Things.'

My next phone call was to the office. 'My apartment got firebombed,' I told Connie. 'I'm staying with Morelli for a while.'

'Good move,' Connie said. 'You on the pill?'

I straightened the kitchen, pocketed the key and took off for the mall. Two hours later I had a week's worth of clothes and a maxed-out charge card.

It was noon when I got to the office. Connie and Lula were at Connie's desk eating Chinese.

'Help yourself,' Lula said, nudging a cardboard carton. 'We got lots. We got fried rice, shrimp clumps and Kung Fu something.'

I picked at a shrimp clump. 'Heard from Vinnie yet?'

'Not a word,' Connie said.

'How about Joyce? Heard from her?'

'Nope. And she hasn't brought Maxine in, either.'

'I been thinking about Maxine,' Lula said. 'I think she's in Point Pleasant. And I wouldn't be surprised if her mama was there, too. That Atlantic City thing was a big phony wild-goose chase to keep us away from Point Pleasant. Her getaway don't feel right. That car was sitting there waiting for her to come out and take off. I think her mama set us up.'

I tried some of the Kung Fu stuff. 'I've been thinking the same thing.'

LULA AND I stood in the middle of the boardwalk, across from the Parrot Bar, and clipped our pagers onto our shorts. I was wearing Day-Glo orange running shorts that had been on sale at Foot Locker, and Lula was wearing yellow-and-black tiger-striped spandex. She'd had her yellow ringlets beaded so that all over her head were four-inch strands of fluorescent pink, poison-green and bright yellow beads. It was ninety-six in the shade, the ocean was millpond calm, the sky was a cloudless azure, and you could fry an egg on the sand. We were here to find Maxine, but already I could see Lula getting distracted by the frozen custard stand.

'This is the plan,' I said to Lula. 'You're going to hang out here and keep your eye on the Parrot Bar, and I'm going to canvass the beach and the boardwalk. Page me if you see Maxine or anyone associated with her.'

'Don't worry, nobody'll get by me. I'd just like to see that bony-ass mother. I'll grab her by what little hair she's got left, and I'll—'

'No! No grabbing, no shooting, no gassing, no stungunning! If you spot someone just stick with them until I get to you.'

'Suppose it's self-defense?'

'There will be no self-defense. Don't let anyone see you. Try to blend in.'

'I need an ice cream to blend in,' Lula said, her hair beads jumping around, clacking every time she moved her head. 'You give me an ice cream and I'll look like everybody else here.'

Well hell, Tallulah, then go get an ice cream.

I walked north first. I'd brought a pair of mini-binoculars that I trained on the beach since Maxine seemed like the sunbather type. I went slowly and methodically, wandering through the arcades and bars. I walked beyond the amusement area to where the boardwalk was plain old boardwalk. After an hour of this I turned and headed back to Lula.

'Haven't seen anybody I know,' Lula said when I reached her. 'No Maxine. No Maxine's mama. No Joyce. No Travolta.'

I stared into the bar across the way, and I didn't see any of those people, either. I took a brush and an elastic scrunchy out of my bag and pulled my hair back, off my neck, into a ponytail. I had a real desire to jump in the ocean, but I decided to settle for a lemonade. I was down to the wire with Maxine. I didn't have time to waste on such frivolity as lowering my body temperature.

I left Lula on the bench, got a lemonade and continued to walk and to scan the south end of the beach. I walked past a series of spin-the-wheel games and came to an arcade. I stepped into the cool shade and moseyed past the claw machines and the skillo ramps. I looked over at the wall where the prizes were displayed and stopped in my tracks. A woman stood at the wall, surveying the prizes. Five pieces of Farberware for 40,000 points. Wooden lighthouse for 9,450. Looney Tunes watch, 8,450. Dirt Devil, 40,100. Boom box, 98,450 points. The woman seemed to be counting the tickets she held in her hand. One hand held the tickets. And the other hand was heavily bandaged. She had brown hair, slim body.

I stepped farther back in the room and waited to see her face. She stood there for a moment longer, turned and walked to the redemption desk. It was Margie. I scooted past the desk, behind Margie's back, out to the boardwalk and paged Lula. She was just a short distance away. She looked up when the pager went off. I caught her eye and gave her a 'come here' wave.

Margie was still at the desk when Lula trotted up.

'What's going on?' Lula asked.

'You remember I told you about Maxine's friend, Margie?'

'The one had her finger chopped off.'

'Yes. That's her at the redemption desk.'

'Point Pleasant sure is a popular place.'

Margie took a large box from an arcade employee and moved to the side door that opened to the street. She passed through the door and turned right, away from the boardwalk. Lula and I watched her walk to the end of the block and cross the street. We followed after her, Lula a little less than a block away and me behind Lula. Margie crossed another street, continued on and went into a house in the middle of the next block.

We held our positions and watched for a while, but Margie didn't come out. The house was a single-story bungalow with a small front porch. Surrounding houses were similar. Lots were small. Cars were parked on both sides of the street.

We weren't in a good position to conduct any kind of surveillance. We'd driven to Point Pleasant in a car that drew attention. My only consolation was that even if we had a more generic car, there were no parking places open.

'So I take it you think this Margie is with Maxine. And maybe Maxine's mama is there, too,' Lula said.

'Yeah. Problem is, I don't know if Maxine's in the house right now.'

'I could be the Avon lady,' Lula said. 'Ding dong, Avon calling.'

'If Maxine's mother is in there she'll recognize you.'

'Think maybe we be recognized standing on the street like this, too,' Lula said.

Very true. 'Okay, this is what we'll do. We'll go see if Maxine's in the house. If she isn't at home, we'll sit down with Margie and watch some TV until Maxine shows up.'

'Sounds like a plan to me. You want the back door or the front door?'

'Front door.'

'And you probably don't want me to shoot anybody.'

'Shooting isn't my favorite thing.'

Lula walked along the side of the house to the back, and I went to the front door. I knocked twice and Margie answered.

Her eyes opened wide in surprise. 'Oh!'

'Hi,' I said. 'I'm looking for Maxine.'

'Maxine isn't here.'

'You wouldn't mind if I came in and looked for myself?'

Maxine's mother swayed into view. 'Who is it?' She took a long drag on her cigarette and let the smoke curl from her nose, dragon style. 'Christ, it's you. You know, you're getting to be a real pain in the ass.'

Lula came in from the kitchen. 'Hope nobody minds my coming in. The back door wasn't locked.'

'Oh God,' Mrs. Nowicki said. 'Tweedledum.'

There was an empty box in the middle of the floor with a lamp sitting beside it.

'You win this lamp at the arcade?' Lula asked Margie.

'It's for my bedroom,' Margie said. 'Twenty-seven thousand points. Yesterday, Maxine won a deep fat fryer.'

'Hell, we won just about everything in this house,' Mrs. Nowicki said.

'Where's Maxine now?' I asked.

'She had some errands to run.'

Lula sat down on the couch and picked up the channel changer for the TV. 'Guess we'll be waiting then. You don't mind if I watch TV, do you?'

'You can't do this,' Mrs. Nowicki said. 'You can't just waltz in here and make yourself at home.'

''Course we can,' Lula said. 'We're bounty hunters. We can do anything we want. We're protected by a dumb-ass law made back in 1869 when people didn't know any better.'

'Is that true?' Mrs. Nowicki wanted to know.

'Well, actually the law doesn't cover control of the channel changer,' I said. 'But it does give us a lot of rights when it comes to the pursuit and capture of a felon.'

There was the sound of gravel crunching in the driveway between houses, and Margie and Mrs. Nowicki exchanged glances.

'That's Maxine, isn't it?' I asked.

'You're going to ruin everything for us,' Mrs. Nowicki

said. 'We had this all planned out, and now you're screwing it up.'

'I'm screwing it up? Look at you two. You've been scalped and had your finger chopped off. Back in Trenton there's a dead store clerk. And you're still playing this stupid treasure hunt game.'

'It isn't that simple,' Margie said. 'We can't leave yet. They have to pay the price.'

A car door slammed and Mrs. Nowicki gave a start. 'Maxie!' she yelled.

Lula gave Mrs. Nowicki a bump with her hip. Mrs. Nowicki lost her balance and flopped onto the couch, and Lula sat on her. 'I know I'll get hollered at if I shoot you,' Lula said. 'So I'll just sit on you until you be quiet.'

'I can't breathe,' Mrs. Nowicki said. 'You ever think about cutting back on the helpings?'

Margie had a trapped animal look, like she couldn't decide whether to shout a warning or bolt for the door herself.

'Sit,' I told her, pulling an industrial-size can of pepper spray out of my bag, shaking the can to make sure it was active. 'Don't go running around confusing things.'

I was hidden by the door when Maxine came in, but Lula was in full view, sitting on Mrs. Nowicki.

'Lo,' Lula said to Maxine.

'Shit,' Maxine said. Then she did an about-face and lunged for the door.

I kicked the door closed and aimed the spray at her. 'Stop! Don't make me use this.'

Maxine took a step back and raised her hands.

'Now get off me, you big load of blubber,' Mrs. Nowicki said to Lula.

I had a pair of cuffs stuck into the waistband of my

shorts. I handed the cuffs to Lula and told her to secure Maxine.

'Sorry to have to do this,' I said to Maxine. 'The charges against you are minimal. If you cooperate you might not even get jail time.'

'It's not jail time I'm worried about,' Maxine said. 'It's dead time.'

Lula reached out to snap the cuffs, and without warning the front and back doors crashed open. Joyce Barnhardt, dressed in swat black with 'bounty hunter' emblazoned on her T-shirt, charged into the room with guns drawn. There were three other women with her, all dressed like Joyce, all armed like Rambo on rampage, all yelling 'Freeze' at the top of their lungs and doing those squatting cop stances you see in the movies.

Margie's new lamp got knocked over and crashed on the floor, and Margie and Mrs. Nowicki and Maxine started yelling and running around, trying to protect their stuff. They were yelling 'Oh no!' and 'Help!' and 'Don't shoot!' Lula dove behind the couch and made herself as small as anyone weighing two hundred pounds could make herself. And I was yelling at everyone to stop yelling.

There was a lot of confusion and a lot of people in that one small room, and it suddenly occurred to me that Maxine wasn't one of them. I heard gravel fly against the house and looked out the window to see Maxine gun the car out of the driveway and take off down the road.

I didn't have a car, so there wasn't much point in my rushing out. And I sure as hell wasn't going to help Joyce catch Maxine, so I didn't say anything. I just backed off and sat down in a big, overstuffed chair and waited for things to calm down. What I really wanted to do was to wade in and beat Joyce to a bloody pulp, but I didn't want to set a bad example for Lula.

Joyce had recruited her cousin Karen Ruzinski and Marlene Cwik to help with the takedown. I didn't know the third woman. Karen had two little kids, and I guess she was happy to get out of the house and do something different.

'Hey Karen,' I said, 'where are the kids? Day care?'

'They're with my mother. She's got a pool in her yard. One of those big ones with the deck around it.' Karen set her gun down on the coffee table and pulled her wallet out of one of the pockets in her swat pants. 'Look here,' she said. 'This is Susan Elizabeth. She starts school this year.'

Mrs. Nowicki picked up Karen's gun, squeezed a shot off, and a chunk of plaster fell out of the ceiling onto the television set. Everyone stopped dead in their tracks and stared at Mrs. Nowicki.

Mrs. Nowicki leveled the gun at Joyce. 'Party's over.'

'You're in big trouble,' Joyce said. 'You're harboring a fugitive.'

A humorless smile slashed Mrs. Nowicki's face. 'Honey, I'm not harboring anything. Look around. You see a fugitive?'

Understanding registered in Joyce's eyes. 'Where's Maxine?'

Now I was smiling with Mrs. Nowicki. 'Maxine left,' I said.

'You deliberately let her get away!'

'Not me,' I said. 'I wouldn't do such a thing. Lula, would I do such a thing?'

'Hell no,' Lula said. 'You're a professional. Although, I gotta say, you haven't got no cool bounty hunter shirt like they do.'

'She can't have gone far,' Joyce said. 'Everybody out to the car.'

Mrs. Nowicki searched through her pockets, found a cigarette and stuck it in her mouth. 'Maxie's long gone. They'll never find her.'

'Just out of morbid curiosity,' I said. 'What's this all about?'

'It's about money,' Mrs. Nowicki said. Then she and Margie laughed. Like that was a good joke.

MORELLI WAS SLOUCHED in front of the television when I got back to the house. He was watching *Jeopardy*, and there were three empty beer bottles alongside his chair.

'Bad day?' I asked.

'To begin with . . . you were telling the truth about your apartment. I checked. It's a big black cinder. Ditto for your car. Following along in the same vein, word has gotten out that we're living together, and my mother expects us for dinner tomorrow at six.'

'No!'

'Yes.'

'Anything else?'

'The case I've been working on for the last four months collapsed.'

'I'm sorry.'

Morelli made a disgusted gesture. 'It happens.'

'Have you had anything to eat?'

An eyebrow raised, and he looked at me sideways. 'What did you have in mind?'

'Food.'

'No. I haven't had any of that.'

I went to the kitchen and said hello to Rex, who was sitting on a small mound of assorted dinner treats. Compliments of Morelli, Rex was feasting on a grape, a miniature marshmallow, a crouton, and a beer nut. I removed the marshmallow and ate it, so Rex wouldn't run the risk of requiring a filling in his fang.

'So what do you want?' I asked Morelli.

'Steak, mashed potatoes, green beans.'

'How about a peanut butter sandwich?'

'That would be my second choice.'

I made two peanut butter sandwiches and brought them into the living room.

Morelli looked at his sandwich. 'What are these lumps?'

'Olives.'

He opened the sandwich and looked inside. 'Where's the jelly?'

'No jelly.'

'I think I need another beer.'

'Just eat it!' I yelled. 'What do I look like, Betty Crocker? I didn't have a great day, either, you know. Not that anybody asked me about my day!'

Morelli grinned. 'What about your day?'

I slumped onto the couch. 'Found Maxine. Lost Maxine.'

'Happens,' Morelli said. 'You'll find her again. You're the bounty hunter from hell.'

'I'm afraid she's getting ready to bolt big time.'

'Can't blame her. There are some scary guys out there.'

'I asked her mother what this was all about, and she said it was about money. Then she laughed.'

'You saw her mother?'

I filled Morelli in on the details, and he didn't look happy when I was done.

'Something has to be done about Barnhardt,' he said.

'Any ideas?'

'Nothing that wouldn't get my shield taken away.'

There was a moment of silence between us.

'So,' I said, 'how well do you know Joyce?'

The grin returned. 'What do you mean?'

'You know what I mean.'

'You want a full accounting of my sex life up to this moment?'

'That would probably take days.'

Morelli slouched a little lower in his chair, his legs stretched in front of him, his lips curved into a smile, his eyes dark and dreamy. 'I don't know Joyce as well as I know you.'

The phone rang, and we both gave a start. Morelli had the cordless on the table beside him. He answered and mouthed 'Your mother.'

I was making no, no, no signals, but Morelli continued to smile and handed the phone over to me.

'I saw Ed Crandle this afternoon,' my mother said. 'He said don't worry, he'll take care of everything. He's going to drop the forms off here.'

Ed Crandle lived across the street from my mother, and he sold insurance. I guessed this meant that I had some. Ordinarily I could look in my desk drawer to check. That wasn't possible now that my desk drawer and everything in it was smoke.

'And that nice superintendent, Dillon Ruddick, called and said your apartment was sealed for security right now, so you can't get in. But he said he was going to start work on it next week. Also, a woman named Sally would like you to call her back.'

I thanked my mother and again declined dinner and the use of my room. I hung up and called Sally.

'Shit,' Sally said, 'I just heard about your apartment. Hey, I'm really sorry. Is there anything I can do? You need a place to crash?'

I told him I was staying with Morelli.

'I would have fucking wrestled him into the ground if I wasn't wearing heels,' Sally said.

When I got off the phone Morelli had pulled the plug on *Jeopardy* and was watching a ball game. I felt gritty from sweat, the back of my neck was scratchy with sunburn, and I could see my nose glowing. Should have used sunblock.

'I'm going to take a shower,' I said to Morelli. 'It's been a long day.'

'Is this a sexual shower?'

'No. This is an I've-been-sweating-all-day-at-the-shore shower.'

'Just checking,' Morelli said.

The bathroom, like the rest of the house, was faded but clean. It was smaller than my apartment bathroom, and the fixtures were older. But the era of construction was more graceful. Morelli had stacked towels on a shelf above the toilet. His toothbrush, toothpaste and razor took up the left side of the sink vanity. I'd placed my toothbrush and toothpaste on the right. His and hers. I gave myself a mental shake. Get a grip, Stephanie . . . this isn't a romance novel. This is the result of a firebombing. There was an over-the-sink medicine cabinet, but I couldn't bring myself to open the door. It seemed like prying, and I was sort of afraid what I might find.

I showered and brushed my teeth and was toweling my hair dry when Morelli knocked on the door.

'Eddie Kuntz's on the phone,' Morelli said. 'You want him to call back?'

I wrapped the big bath towel around myself, cracked the door, and stuck my hand out. 'I'll take it.'

Morelli handed me the phone, and his eyes locked on my towel. 'Shit,' he whispered.

I tried to close the door, but he was still holding on to the phone. I was holding the towel with one hand, and the phone with the other, and I was nudging the door closed with my knee. I saw his eyes darken and soften, like liquid chocolate. I knew the look. I'd seen it before, and it had never turned out well for me.

'This isn't good,' Morelli said, his gaze now wandering the length of the three-inch opening between door and jamb, from the towel to my legs and back to the towel.

'Hello?' Kuntz said at the other end of the line. 'Stephanie?'

I tried to twist the phone out of Morelli's hand, but he was holding fast. My heart was going *ka-thunk, ka-thunk* in my chest, and I was starting to sweat in unusual places.

'Tell him you'll call him back,' Morelli said.

CHAPTER NINE

I CLENCHED MY teeth. 'Let go of the phone!'
Morelli relinquished the phone but kept his foot in the doorway.

'What?' I said to Kuntz.

'I want a progress report.'

'The report is that there's no progress.'

'You'd tell me, right?'

'Yeah, sure. And by the way, someone soaked my car with gasoline and firebombed my apartment. You wouldn't happen to know who that someone was, would you?'

'Jeez. No. You think it was Maxine?'

'Why would Maxine firebomb my apartment?'

'I don't know. Because you're working for me?'

Morelli reached in and took the phone. 'Later,' he said to Kuntz. Then he disconnected and tossed the phone in the sink.

'This isn't a good idea,' I said. But I was thinking, Why not? My legs were shaved. I didn't hardly have any clothes on so that awkward step was eliminated. And after everything I'd been through, I deserved an orgasm. I mean, it was the least I could do for myself.

Morelli moved in and nuzzled my bare shoulder. 'I know,' he said. 'This is a terrible idea.' His mouth brushed just below my earlobe. We locked eyes for a heartbeat, and Morelli kissed me. His mouth was gentle, and the kiss lingered. When I was in high school my best friend, Mary Lou, told me she heard Morelli had fast hands. Actually, just the opposite was true. Morelli knew how to go slow. Morelli knew how to drive a woman crazy.

He kissed me again, our tongues touched, and the kiss deepened. His hands were at my waist and then at my back pressing me into him, and either he had one hell of an erection or else his night stick was rammed into my stomach. I was pretty sure it was an erection, and I thought if I could just get that nice big, stiff, magical thing deep inside me all my worries would fade away.

'I've got some,' Morelli said.

'Some what?'

'Some condoms. I've got a carton. Serious investment. Top of the line.'

The way I was feeling I figured that carton wouldn't take us to Sunday.

And then his mouth was on me again, kissing my neck, my collarbone, the swell of my breast at the top of the towel. And then the towel was gone and Morelli took his mouth to my nipple and fire flashed through me. His hands were everywhere, exploring, caressing . . . teasing. His mouth dropped lower, trailing a string of kisses to my navel, my belly, my . . . OMMIGOD!

Mary Lou had also told me she'd heard Morelli had a tongue like a lizard, and now I knew firsthand the accuracy of that rumor. God bless the wild kingdom, I thought with a new appreciation for reptiles. I had my fingers tangled in his hair, and my bare ass pressed against the sink, and I was thinking, *Oh, yum*! I was on the brink.

I could feel it coming . . . the delicious pressure, the heat and mind-emptying need for release.

And then he moved his mouth half an inch to the left.

'Go back!' I gasped. 'Go back. GO BACK!'

Morelli kissed my inner thigh. 'Not yet.'

I was feeling frantic. I was so close! 'What do you mean, not yet!'

'Too soon,' Morelli said.

'Are you kidding me? It's not too soon! It's been years!'

Morelli stood, scooped me up, carried me into his bedroom, and dropped me onto his bed. He stripped off his T-shirt and shorts, all the while watching me with dilated eyes, all black pupil beneath the black fringe of his lashes. His hands were steady, but his breathing was ragged. And then his briefs were gone and he was naked. And I wasn't sure anymore if this was going to work. It had been a long time, and he looked awfully big. Bigger than I'd remembered. Bigger than he'd felt through his clothes. He took a condom out of the box, and I scooted up to the headboard. 'On second thought . . .' I said.

Morelli grabbed me by the ankles, pulled me down flat on my back and pushed my legs apart. 'No second thoughts,' he said, kissing me. And then he put his finger on me in precisely *that* spot. He moved the finger a little, and now I was thinking he was looking just right. Not really too big at all. Now I was thinking I had to find a way to get the damn thing inside me. It wasn't bad to look at, but it wasn't really doing all that much for me bobbing around on its own.

I grabbed hold and tried to direct it, but Morelli moved out of reach. 'Not yet,' he said.

What was with this not yet all the time! 'I think I'm ready.'

'Not nearly,' Morelli said, dropping lower, doing some more of the terrific tongue torture.

Well okay, if this was what he really wanted to do it was fine by me because I actually liked this a lot. In fact, I was almost there. Another thirty seconds and I was going to fly off into the great beyond, shrieking like a banshee.

And then he moved a half inch to the left . . . again.

'Bastard,' I said . . . in a loving sort of way. I reached out and stroked him, heard his breath catch at my touch. I drew my fingertip across the little slit at the top, and Morelli went very still. I had his attention. I dipped my head down and gave him a lick.

'Christ,' Morelli gasped, 'don't do that. I'm not Superman!'

Had me fooled. I went on a much more extensive tasting expedition, and suddenly Morelli was galvanized into action. In an instant, I was on my back and Morelli was poised over me.

'Not yet,' I said. 'It's not time.'

He snapped the condom on. 'The hell it isn't.'

Heh, heh, heh, I thought.

THE FOLLOWING MORNING I awoke in a tangle of damp sheets and warm Morelli. We'd made a respectable dent in the condom supply, and I was feeling very relaxed. Morelli stirred beside me, and I cuddled into him.

'Mmm,' he said.

Two hours later there were a few less condoms in the box and Morelli and I were both lying facedown and slack limbed on the bed. I was thinking that sex was an excellent thing, but I probably didn't need any more now for ten or fifteen years. I eyeballed the distance between the bed and the bathroom and wondered if I could walk that far. The phone rang, and Morelli passed it over to me.

'I was wondering what I should wear tonight,' Sally said. 'Do you think I should be a man or a woman?'

'Doesn't matter to me,' I said. 'Lula and I are going to be women. You want to meet us there, or you want me to pick you up?'

'I'll meet you there.'

'Okeydokey.'

I turned to Morelli. 'Are you working today?'

'Half day, maybe. I need to talk to a couple people.'

'Me too.' I dragged myself off the bed. 'About dinner tonight . . .'

'Don't even think about standing me up,' Morelli said. 'I'll track you down and find you and make your life a living hell.'

I did a mental grimace and managed to get myself into the bathroom without hardly grunting or whimpering. The sex goddess was a trifle sore this morning, feeling a little like a human wishbone.

I took a shower, dressed and ambled down to the kitchen. I'd never seen Morelli in the morning, and I'm not sure what I'd expected, but it wasn't the half-man, half-beast that was reading the paper and drinking coffee. Morelli was wearing a misshapen T-shirt and rumpled tan shorts. He was sixteen hours beyond a five o'clock shadow, and he hadn't combed his hair, which was multiple weeks beyond needing a haircut.

It had been sexy last night. This morning it was downright frightening. I poured out coffee and a bowl of cereal and sat across from him at the small table. The back door was open, and the morning air coming through it was cool. In another hour it would turn hot and steamy.

Already the cicadas were singing. I thought about my own kitchen and sad charred apartment and my throat closed over. Remember what Morelli told you, I thought. Concentrate on the positive. The apartment will be okay. Brand-new carpet and paint. Better than before. And what had he said about the fear? Concentrate on doing the job, not on the fear. Okay, I thought, I can do that. Especially when I was sitting across from the man of my dreams.

Morelli drained his coffee cup and continued to read the paper.

I found myself wanting to refill the cup. And I didn't want to stop there. I wanted to make breakfast for Morelli. Hotcakes and bacon and fresh squeezed orange juice. Then I wanted to do his laundry and put fresh sheets on the bed. I looked around. The kitchen wasn't bad, but it could be cozier. Fresh flowers, maybe. A cookie jar.

'Uh oh,' Morelli said.

'What uh oh?'

'You have that look . . . like you're redesigning my kitchen.'

'You don't have a cookie jar.'

Morelli looked at me like I was from Mars. 'That's what you were thinking?'

'Well, yeah.'

Morelli considered that for a moment. 'I've never actually seen the purpose for a cookie jar,' he finally said. 'I open the box. I eat the cookies. I throw the box away.'

'Yes, but a cookie jar makes a kitchen homey.'

I got another one of those Mars looks.

'I keep my gun in my cookie jar,' I said by way of further explanation.

'Honey, a man can't keep his gun in a cookie jar. It just isn't done.'

'Rockford did it.'

He got up and gave me a kiss on the top of my head. 'I'm gonna take a shower. If you leave before I'm out, promise me you'll be home by five.'

So much for the man of my dreams. I gave him one of my favorite Italian hand gestures, which he didn't see because he was already out of the room. 'Fuck the cookie jar,' I said to Rex. 'And he can do his own goddamn laundry, too.' I finished my cereal, rinsed the bowl and put it in the dishwasher. I slung my black leather tote over my shoulder and took off for the office.

'OMMIGOD,' CONNIE SAID when I walked into the office. 'You did it!'

'Excuse me?'

'How was it? I want details.'

Lula looked up from the stack of files she was sorting. 'Yep,' she said, 'you did the deed all right.'

I felt my eyes go wide. 'How do you know?' I sniffed at myself. 'Do I smell?'

'You just got that look like you've been totally fucked,' Lula said. 'Sort of relaxed.'

'Yeah,' Connie said. 'Satisfied.'

'It was the shower,' I said. 'I took a really long relaxing shower this morning.'

'Wish I had a shower like that,' Lula said.

'Is Vinnie in?'

'Yeah, he got back late last night. Hey, Vinnie,' Connie yelled. 'Stephanie's here!'

We heard him mumble 'Oh Christ' from deep inside his office, and then his door opened. 'What?'

'Joyce Barnhardt, that's what.'

'So I gave her a job.' Vinnie squinted at me. 'Jesus, you just get laid?'

'I don't believe this,' I said, hands in the air. 'I took a shower. I did my hair. I put on makeup, new clothes. I had breakfast. I brushed my goddamn teeth. How does everyone know I got laid?'

'You look different,' Vinnie said.

'Satisfied,' Connie said.

'Relaxed,' Lula added.

'I don't want to talk about it,' I shouted. 'I want to talk about Joyce Barnhardt. You gave her Maxine Nowicki. How could you do that? Nowicki is my case.'

'You weren't having any luck with it, so I figured what the hell, let Joyce take a shot at it, too.'

'I know how Joyce got that case,' I said. 'And I'm going to tell your wife.'

'You tell my wife, and she'll tell her father, and I'll be dead. And then you know where you'll be? Unemployed.'

'He got a point there,' Lula said. 'We all be unemployed.'

'I want her off the case. Lula and I had Maxine in custody, and Joyce barged in with the slut troop and screwed everything up.'

'Okay, okay,' Vinnie said. 'I'll talk to her.'

'You're going to take Nowicki away from her.'

'Yeah.'

'Sally called and said he was going to the bar tonight,' I told Lula. 'Do you want to come, too?'

'Sure, I don't want to miss any of the fun.'

'Need a ride?'

'Not me,' Lula said. 'I got a new car.' Her eyes slid past me to the front door. 'What I need now is a man to put in it. He got a name on him, too.'

Connie and I swiveled to look. It was Ranger, dressed in black, hair slicked into a ponytail, small gold hoop earring shining like the sun.

'Yo,' Ranger said. He stared at me for a moment and smiled. He raised his eyebrows. 'Morelli?'

'Shit,' I said. 'This is embarrassing.'

'Came by to get the papers on Thompson,' Ranger said to Connie.

Connie handed him a folder. 'Good luck.'

'Who's Thompson?'

'Norvil Thompson,' Ranger said. 'Stuck up a liquor store. Took four hundred dollars and change and a quart of Wild Turkey. Started celebrating in the parking lot where he parked his car, passed out and was found by a parking attendant who called the police. Didn't show up for his court date.'

'Like always,' Connie said.

'He's done this before?'

'Twice.'

Ranger signed his part of the contract, passed it back to Connie and looked over at me. 'Want to help me round up this cowboy?'

'He isn't going to shoot at me, is he?'

'Ah,' Ranger said, 'if only it was that simple.'

Ranger was driving a new black Range Rover. Ranger's cars were always black. They were always new. They were always expensive. And they were always of dubious origin. I never asked Ranger where he got his cars. And he never asked me my weight.

We cut through center city and turned right onto Stark Street. Ranger cruised past the auto body and the gym into a neighborhood of blighted row houses. It was midday, and welfare mothers and kids were on the stoops, looking for relief from the sweltering interiors of their airless rooms.

I leafed through the file to familiarize myself with Thompson. Black male, 5'9", 175 pounds, age sixty-four. Respiratory problems. That meant we couldn't use pepper spray.

Ranger parked in front of a three-story brick building. Gang slogans were spray-painted on the stoop and under the two first-floor windows. Fast-food flotsam had banked against the curb and crumpled wrappers littered the sidewalk. The entire neighborhood smelled like a big bean burrito.

'This guy isn't as dangerous as he looks on the sheet,' Ranger said. 'Mostly he's a pain in the ass. He's always drunk, so it doesn't do any good to threaten him with a gun. He's got asthma, so we can't spray him. And he's old, so you look like a fool if you beat him to a pulp. What we want to do is cuff him and carry him out. That's why you're along. Takes two to carry him out.'

Wonderful.

Two women were sitting two doors down. 'You coming after old Norvil?' the one asked. 'He run his bail again?'

Ranger raised his arm in acknowledgment. 'Hey, Regina, how's it going?'

'Picking up now that you're here.' She swiveled her head to the ground-level open window. 'Yo, Deborah,' she hollered. 'Ranger's here. Gonna give us some entertainment.'

Ranger moved into the building and started climbing the stairs. 'Third floor,' he said.

I was getting an uncomfortable feeling about this apprehension. 'What did she mean . . . entertainment?'

Ranger was on the second-floor landing. 'There are two tenants on the third floor. Thompson is on the left. One room and bath. Only one way out. He should be at home at this time of day. Regina would have told me if she'd seen him leave.'

'I get the feeling there's something else I should know about this guy.'

Ranger was halfway up the third flight of stairs. 'Only that he's freaking nuts. And if he whips his dick out to take a leak, stand back. He tagged Hanson once, and Hanson swears he was fifteen feet away.'

Hanson was another bounty hunter. Mostly worked for Gold Star Bail Bonds on First Street. Hanson had never struck me as someone who would fabricate war stories, so I turned around and started doing double-time down the stairs. 'That's it for me. I'll call Lula to come pick me up.'

My progress was halted by a hand grabbing the back of my shirt. 'Guess again,' Ranger said. 'We're in this together.'

'I don't want to get peed on.'

'Just keep your eyes open. If he goes for his dick we'll both jump him.'

'You know I could have lots of good jobs,' I said. 'I don't need to be doing this.'

Ranger had his arm around me, encouraging me to walk up the stairs. 'This isn't just a job. This is a service profession. We uphold the law, babe.'

'Is that why you do this? Because you believe in the law?'

'No. I do this for the money. And because hunting people is what I do best.'

We reached Thompson's door, and Ranger motioned me to one side while he knocked.

'Lousy fuckers,' someone called from inside the room.

Ranger smiled. 'Norvil's home.' He gave another rap. 'Open the door. I need to talk to you.'

'I saw you out on the sidewalk,' Norvil said, the door still closed, 'and I'll open this door when hell freezes over.'

'I'm going to count to three, and then I'm going to break in,' Ranger said. 'One, two . . .' He tried the door-knob, but the door was still locked. 'Three.' No response from inside. 'Damn, stubborn old drunk,' Ranger said. He stepped back and gave the door a solid kick just to the left of the doorknob. There was the sound of splintering wood, and the door crashed open.

'Lousy fuckers,' Norvil yelled.

Ranger cautiously stepped into the doorway, gun in hand. 'It's okay,' he said to me. 'He isn't armed.'

I moved into the room and stood beside Ranger. Norvil was on the far side of the room with his back against the wall. To his right was a chipped Formica table and a single wooden chair. Half the table was taken over with a cardboard box filled with food. Ritz crackers, Count Chocula cereal, a bag of marshmallows, a bottle of ketchup. A dorm-sized refrigerator was on the floor by the table. Norvil was dressed in a faded T-shirt that said 'Get Gas From Bud' and a pair of baggy, soiled khakis. And he was holding a carton of eggs.

'Lousy fuckers,' he said. And before I realized what was happening . . . SPLAT. I got hit in the forehead with an egg. I jumped back, and the ketchup bottle sailed by my ear, smashed on the doorjamb and ketchup splattered everywhere. This was followed by the pickle jar and more eggs. Ranger caught an egg on his arm, and I got one square on my chest. I turned to dodge a jar of mayo and got hit in the back of the head with another egg. Norvil was in a frenzy, throwing whatever he laid hands on . . . crackers, croutons, corn chips, knives and spoons, cereal bowls and dinner plates. A bag of flour exploded in his hands, and flour flew in all directions. 'Rotten pinko, commie bastards,' he shouted, searching through the box for more ammo.

'Now!' Ranger said.

We both lunged for Thompson, going for his arms. Ranger locked a cuff on one wrist. We struggled to secure the other. Norvil took a swing at me, catching me in the shoulder. I lost my footing in the cracker crumbs and flour and went down hard to the floor. I heard the second cuff click closed and looked up at Ranger.

Ranger was smiling. 'You okay?'

'Yeah. I'm just peachy.'

'You have enough food on you to feed a family of four for a week.'

Ranger had none. A small stain on one arm where he'd gotten hit by the egg.

'So why is it you're so clean and I'm such a mess?'

'For one thing, I didn't stand in the middle of the room, making a target of myself. For another thing, I didn't fall on the floor and roll in flour.' He reached a hand out to me and helped me up. 'First rule of combat. If someone throws something at you, step out of the way.'

'Devil whore,' Norvil shouted at me.

'Listen,' I shouted back, 'I was due. And it's none of your business anyway.'

'He calls everyone a devil whore,' Ranger said.

'Oh.'

Norvil planted his feet wide. 'I'm not going anywhere.'

I looked at the stun gun on Ranger's utility belt. 'How about we zap him?'

'You can't zap me,' Norvil said. 'I'm an old man. I got a pacemaker. You screw up my pacemaker and you'll be in big trouble. It could even kill me.'

'Boy,' I said, 'that's tempting.'

Ranger took a roll of duct tape off his gun belt and taped Norvil's legs together at the ankles.

'I'm gonna fall over,' Norvil said. 'I can't stand like this. I got a drinking problem, you know. I fall over sometimes.'

Ranger got Norvil by the armpits and tipped him backward. 'Grab his feet,' he said. 'Let's get him to the car.'

'Help!' Norvil yelled. 'I'm being kidnapped! Call the police. Call the Muslims!'

We got him to the second-floor landing, and he was still yelling and wriggling. I was working hard to hold him. Egg and flour were caked in my hair, I smelled like pickle brine, and I was sweating like a pig. We started down the second flight; I missed a step and slid the rest of the way on my back.

'No problem,' I said, hoisting myself up, wondering how many vertebrae I'd cracked. 'You can't keep Wonder Woman down.'

'Wonder Woman looks a little beat,' Ranger said.

Regina and Deborah were sitting on their stoop when we hauled Norvil out.

'Lord, girl,' Regina said. 'What happened to you? You look like a big corn dog. You've been all breaded up.'

Ranger opened the Range Rover's rear door, and we tossed Norvil inside. I limped around to the passenger side and stared at the pristine leather seat.

'Don't worry about it,' Ranger said. 'You get it dirty I'll just get a new car.'

I was pretty sure he was kidding.

I WAS ON the small front porch, rooting around in my bag, looking for the key to Morelli's house when the door opened.

'I'm not even going to make a guess on this one,' Morelli said.

I pushed past him. 'You know Norvil Thompson?'

'Old guy. Robs stores. Goes nuts when he drinks . . . which is always.'

'Yep. That's Norvil. I helped Ranger bring him in.'

'I take it Norvil wasn't ready to go.'

'Threw everything he had at us.' I looked down at myself. 'I need a shower.'

'Poor baby. I could help.'

'No! Don't come near me!'

'This isn't about the cookie jar, is it?'

I dragged myself up the stairs and into the bathroom. I stripped and stepped under the steaming water. I washed my hair twice and used a cream rinse, but my hair wouldn't come clean. I got out of the shower and took a look at my hair. It was the egg. It had hardened like cement, and little pieces of eggshell were stuck in the cement.

'Why me?' I said.

Morelli was on the other side of the bathroom door. 'Are you all right? Are you talking to yourself?'

I wrenched the door open. 'Look at this!' I said, pointing to my hair.

'Looks like eggshell.'

'It won't come out.'

Morelli leaned closer under the guise of examining my hair, but he was actually looking down my towel. 'Hmm,' he said.

'Listen, Morelli, I need help here.'

'We haven't got much time.'

'Help with my hair!'

'Honey, I don't know how to tell you this, but I think your hair is beyond my help. The best I could do is take your mind off it.'

I searched through the medicine chest and came up with some scissors. 'Cut the egg out.'

'Oh boy.'

Five minutes later Morelli looked up from his job and met my eyes in the mirror. 'That's all of it.'

'How bad is it?'

'You remember when Mary Jo Krazinski had ring-worm?'

My mouth dropped open.

'It's not that bad,' Morelli said. 'Mostly it's just shorter . . . in spots.' His finger traced a line along my bare shoulder. 'We could be a few minutes late.'

'No! I'm not going to be late for your mother. Your mother scares the hell out of me.' His mother scared the hell out of everyone but Joe. Morelli's mother could see around corners. His father had been a drunk and a philan-derer. His mother was beyond reproach. She was a housewife of heroic proportions. She never missed mass. She sold Amway in her spare time. And she didn't take crap from anyone.

Morelli slid his hand under my towel and kissed the back of my neck. 'This'll only take a minute, babe.'

A burning sensation skittered through my stomach

and my toes curled. 'I have to get dressed,' I said. But I was thinking, Ohhhh, this feels good. And I was remembering what he'd done the night before, and *that* had felt even better. His hands found my breasts, and his thumb rubbed across my nipple. He whispered a few things he wanted to do to me, and I felt a little dribble of drool escape from the corner of my mouth.

Half an hour later, I was rushing around my room, searching for clothes to wear. 'I can't believe I let you talk me into that!' I said. 'Look how late we are!'

Morelli was fully clothed and smiling. 'This cohabiting thing isn't so bad,' he said. 'I don't know why I didn't try it out sooner.'

I stepped into my underpants. 'You didn't try it out sooner because you were afraid to make a commitment. And in fact, you still haven't made a commitment.'

'I bought an entire carton of condoms.'

'That's a commitment to sex, not to a relationship.'

'It's a start,' Morelli said.

I glanced over at him. 'Maybe.' I pulled a little cotton sundress out of the closet. It was the color of sun-bleached straw and buttoned in the front like a shirt. I dropped the dress over my head and smoothed over a few wrinkles with my hand.

'Shit,' Morelli said. 'You look great in that dress.'

I checked out his Levi's. He was hard again. 'How did that happen?'

'You want to learn a new game?' Morelli asked. 'It's called Mr. and Mrs. Rover.'

'News flash,' I said. 'I don't iron. I don't eat raw fish. And I don't do dog stuff. You lay a hand on me, and I swear, I'm going for my gun.'

*

MRS. MORELLI OPENED the door to us and smacked Joe on the side of the head. 'Sex fiend. Just like your father, God rest his rotten soul.'

Morelli grinned down at his mother. 'It's a curse.'

'It wasn't my fault,' I said. 'Honestly.'

'Your Grandma Bella and your Aunt Mary Elizabeth are here,' Mrs. Morelli said. 'Watch your language.'

Grandma Bella! My mouth went dry and black dots danced in front of my eyes. Grandma Bella put the curse on Diane Fripp, and Diane had her period nonstop for three months! I rechecked the buttons on the front of my dress and subtly felt to make sure I'd gotten my underwear back on.

Grandma Bella and Aunt Mary Elizabeth were in the living room, sitting side by side on the couch. Grandma Bella is a small white-haired lady dressed in traditional Italian black. She'd come to this country as a young woman, but back then the burg was more Italian than Sicily, so she'd kept her old-country ways. Mary Elizabeth is Bella's younger sister and is a retired nun. They both had highball glasses in their hands and cigarettes hanging out of their mouths.

'So,' Grandma Bella said, 'the bounty hunter.'

I sat on the edge of the seat of a wing-back chair and pressed my knees together. 'Nice to see you, Grandma Bella.'

'I hear you're living with my grandson.'

'I'm . . . renting a room in his house.'

'*Hah!*' she shouted. 'Don't make up fibs to me or I'll put the eye on you.'

I was doomed. I was fucking doomed. Even as I sat there I could feel my period coming on.

CHAPTER TEN

'T HERE'S NO SUCH thing as the eye,' Joe said. 'Don't try to scare Stephanie.'

'You don't believe in anything,' Bella said. 'And I never see you in church.' She shook her finger at him. 'Good thing I pray for you.'

'Dinner's ready,' Mrs. Morelli said. 'Joseph, help your Grandma Bella into the dining room.'

This was the first time I'd been in Mrs. Morelli's house. I'd been in the garage and the backyard. And of course I'd passed by countless times, always speaking in hushed whispers and never dillydallying for fear Mrs. Morelli would come get me by the ear and accuse me of wearing day-old underwear or not brushing my teeth. Her husband was known for not sparing the belt on his sons. Mrs. Morelli needed none of that. Mrs. Morelli could nail you to the wall with a single word. 'Well,' she would say, and the hapless victim would confess to anything. Everyone but Joe. As a kid Joe had run wild and unchecked.

The house was more comfortable than I'd expected. It felt like a family house, used to the noise and confusion of children. First Joe and his siblings, and now there were grandchildren. The furniture was slipcovered and clean. The carpet freshly vacuumed. The tabletops polished.

There was a small wooden toy chest under one of the front windows and a child's rocker beside the chest.

The dining room was more formal. The table was set with a lace cloth. The hutch displayed worn heirloom china. Two bottles of wine sat uncorked and breathing at the head of the table. There were white lace curtains on the windows and a traditional, burgundy Oriental rug under the table.

We all took our seats; and Mary Elizabeth said grace while I eyed the antipasto.

After grace, Grandma Bella raised her wineglass. 'To Stephanie and Joseph. Long life and many bambinos.'

I glanced over at Joe. 'You want to field this one?'

Joe took some ravioli and sprinkled them with grated cheese. 'Only two bambinos. I can't afford a big family on a cop's salary.'

I cleared my throat and glared at Morelli.

'Okay, okay,' Morelli said. 'No bambinos. Stephanie moved in with me because she needs a place to live while her apartment gets repaired. That's all there is to it.'

'What do you think, I'm a fool?' Grandma Bella said. 'I see what goes on. I know what you do.'

Morelli helped himself to chicken. 'Stephanie and I are just good friends.'

I went rigid with my fork halfway to my mouth. He'd used those words to describe his relationship with Terry Gilman. Wonderful. Now what was I supposed to believe? That I was on equal footing with Terry? Well, you pushed him into it, stupid. You forced him to tell Bella this wasn't a serious relationship. Well, yeah, I thought, but he could have made me sound a *little* more important than Terry Gilman!

Bella's head rolled back, and she put her hands palms down on the table. 'Silence!'

Mary Elizabeth made the sign of the cross.

Mrs. Morelli and Joe exchanged long-suffering glances.

'Now what?' I whispered.

'Grandma Bella's having a vision,' Joe said. 'It goes with having the eye.'

Bella's head snapped up, and she pointed two fingers at Joe and me. 'I see your wedding. I see you dancing. And I see after that you will have three sons, and the line will continue.'

I leaned toward Joe. 'Those things you bought . . . they were good quality, right?'

'The best money can buy.'

'I gotta go lay down now,' Bella said. 'I always gotta rest after I have a vision.'

We waited while she left the table and climbed the stairs. The bedroom door clicked closed, and Joe's mother gave an audible sigh of relief.

'Sometimes she gives me the willies,' Mary Elizabeth said.

And then we all dug into the meal, avoiding talk about marriage and babies and crazy old Italian women.

I sipped my coffee and scarfed down a plateful of home-made cookies, keeping one eye on the time. Eddie Kuntz wouldn't show at the bar until nine, but I wanted to be in place earlier than that. My plan was to plant Lula and Sally inside the bar while I did surveillance on the street.

'It was very nice of you to invite me for dinner,' I told Mrs. Morelli. 'Unfortunately, I have to leave early. I have to go to work tonight.'

'Is this bounty hunter work?' Mary Elizabeth wanted to know. 'Are you hunting down a fugitive?'

'Sort of.'

'It sounds exciting.'

'It sounds like a sin against nature,' Grandma Bella said from the hallway, freshly risen from the guest bed. 'No kind of work for someone expecting.'

'Grandma Bella,' I said. 'I'm really not expecting.'

'A lot you know,' she said. 'I've been to the other side. I see these things. I got the eye.'

'OKAY,' I SAID to Morelli when we were half a block from the house, 'just how accurate is this eye thing?'

'I don't know. I never paid much attention to it.' He turned onto Roebling and pulled over to the curb. 'Where are we going?'

'I'm going to the Blue Moon Bar. It's the next point of pickup in Maxine's treasure hunt. Take me back to the house, and I'll get my car.'

Morelli swung out into traffic. 'I'll go with you. Wouldn't want anything to happen to my unborn child.'

'That's not funny!'

'All right. The truth is there's only crap on television tonight, so I might as well come along.'

The Blue Moon Bar was down by the State Complex. There was a public parking lot on the next block, and there was on-street parking in front of the bar. There were small businesses on either side of the bar, but the businesses were closed at this time of the night. The bar had been a disco in the seventies, a sports bar in the eighties, and a year before it had been transformed into a fake micro-brewery. It was basically one large room with a copper vat in the corner, a bar running the entire length of one side and tables in the middle of the room. Besides serving booze, the Blue Moon Bar sold snack food. French fries, onion rings, nachos and fried mozzarella. On Saturday nights it was packed.

It was still early for the bar crowd, and Morelli was able to get a spot on the street, two cars down from the door. 'Now what?' Morelli asked.

'Kuntz's supposed to show up at nine. Then we see what happens.'

'What usually happens?'

'Nothing.'

'Gosh, I can't wait.'

By eight-thirty Lula and Sally were in the building. Kuntz arrived fifteen minutes later. I left Morelli in the truck with a photo of Maxine, and I went in to be with Kuntz.

'You look different,' Kuntz said.

'I had some hair problems.'

'No, that's not it.'

'New dress.'

'No. It's something else. I can't put my finger on it.'

Thank goodness for that.

Lula and Sally came over and stood with us at the bar.

'What's doin'?' Sally said.

'We're wasting more time, that's what's doin',' Kuntz said. 'I hate these dumb treasure hunt things.' His eyes held mine for a moment and then fixed on a point over my shoulder. I turned to see what had caught his attention.

It was Joyce Barnhardt in a very short, very tight black leather skirt and an orange knit tank top.

'Hello, Stephanie,' Joyce said.

'Hello, Joyce.'

She flashed a smile on Kuntz. 'Hello, handsome.'

I turned to Lula, and we made the finger-down-the-throat, tongue-stuck-out gag gesture to each other.

'If I had those breasts I could clean up,' Sally whispered to me. 'I could make enough money in a year to fucking retire. I wouldn't ever have to put on another pair of heels.'

'What are you doing here, Joyce? I thought Vinnie was going to talk to you.'

'It's a free country,' Joyce said. 'I can go where I want. Do what I want. And right now what I want is to get Maxine.'

'Why?'

'Just for the fun of it,' Joyce said.

'Bitch.'

'Slut.'

'Whore.'

'Cunt.'

I kicked Joyce in the shin. I draw the line at *cunt*. And besides, ever since that day I caught her bare-assed on my dining room table with my husband, I've been wanting to kick her.

Joyce responded by grabbing my hair.

'Yow!' I said. 'Let go!'

She wouldn't let go, so I gave her a good pinch in the arm.

'Hold on here,' Lula said. 'I can tell you don't know nothing about fighting. This woman got you by the hair, and all you can do is give her a pinch?'

'Yeah, but it'll leave a bruise,' I said.

Joyce yanked harder at my hair. Then suddenly she gave a squeak, and she was on her back, on the floor.

I glared over at Lula.

'Well, I just wanted to see if the new batteries were working,' Lula said.

'So how much do you think breasts like that would cost?' Sally asked. 'Do you think they'd look good on me?'

'Sally, those are real breasts.'

Sally bent down and took a closer look. 'Damn.'

'Uh oh,' Lula said. 'I don't know how to break this to you, but we're missing someone.'

I looked around. Kuntz was gone. 'Sally, you check the men's room. Lula, you search the room here. I'll see if he's outside.'

'What about Joyce?' Lula said. 'Maybe we should shove her over in the corner where people won't trip on her.'

Joyce's eyes were glazed, and her mouth was open. Her breathing seemed normal enough, considering she'd just taken a few volts.

'Joyce?' I said. 'You okay?'

One of her arms flailed out.

A small crowd had accumulated.

'Dizzy spell,' I told everyone.

'I read in the manual sometimes people wet themselves when they have one of these dizzy spells,' Lula said. 'Wouldn't that be fun?'

Joyce's legs started flopping around, and her eyes came into focus.

Lula hoisted her up and sat her in a chair. 'You should see a doctor about these spells,' Lula said.

Joyce nodded. 'Yeah. Thanks.'

We got Joyce a cold beer and went off to find Kuntz.

I went outside to Morelli. 'You see Eddie Kuntz leave?'

'What's he look like?'

'Five-eleven. Bodybuilder. He was wearing black pleated slacks and a black short-sleeve shirt.'

'Yeah, I saw him. He left about five minutes ago. Drove off in a Chevy Blazer.'

'He alone?'

'Yep.'

'Nobody followed him?'

'Not that I noticed.'

I returned to the bar and stood at the entrance looking for Sally and Lula. The room was crowded, and the noise level had risen considerably. I was jostled forward and then sharply yanked back, face-to-face with an angry woman I didn't recognize.

'I knew it was you!' she said. 'You *bitch*.'

I knocked her hands off me. 'What's your problem?'

'You're my problem. Everything was fine before you came along.'

'What are you talking about?'

'You know what I'm talking about. And if you have any sense in that big bimbo head of yours you'll get out of town. You'll go far away. Because if you don't I'm gonna find you and turn you into a pile of ashes . . . just like your apartment.'

'You set fire to my apartment!'

'Hell no, not me. Do I look crazy enough to do something like that?'

'Yes.'

She laughed very softly, but her eyes were small and hard with emotions that had nothing to do with joy. 'Believe what you want. Just stay away from my boyfriend.' She gave me a rough shove backward and stalked off toward the door, disappearing in the crowd.

I started after her, but the guy next to me moved in. 'So,' he said, 'you want a boyfriend all your own?'

'Jesus,' I said. 'Get a life.'

'Hey,' he said, 'just asking. No reason to get all huffy.'

I shoved my way around him, but the woman was gone. I worked through the room to the door. I looked outside. I went back inside and looked some more. No luck.

I found Sally and Lula at the bar.

'This is impossible,' Lula said. 'There's wall-to-wall people here. You can't hardly even get a drink, much less find someone.'

I told them Morelli saw Kuntz take off in the Blazer, but I didn't tell them about the angry woman. The angry woman was a separate issue. Probably.

'If there's not gonna be any more action here, Sally and me are taking off for this place he knows has good music,' Lula said. 'You want to come with?'

'No thanks, I'm calling it a night.'

Sally and Lula gave each other the elbows.

'SO WHAT HAPPENED?' Morelli asked when I got back to the truck.

'Nothing.'

'Just like always?'

'Yeah, except this was more nothing than usual.' I rummaged through my shoulder bag, found my cell phone and dialed Kuntz. No answer. 'This is too weird. Why would he leave the bar like that?'

'Were you with him the whole time? Maybe someone gave him another clue, and he went off on his own.'

We were still parked at the curb, and I was thinking I

should go back to the bar and ask some questions. 'Wait here,' I told Morelli.

'Again?'

'This will only take a few minutes.'

I went to the bartender who'd been tending bar near us when Joyce went down.

'Do you remember the dark-haired guy I was with?' I asked. 'The one dressed in black.'

'Yeah. Eddie Kuntz.'

'You know him?'

'No. Some woman came in around seven, right after I came on. She gave me a picture of Kuntz and ten dollars to pass him a note.'

'Do you know what the note said?'

'Nope. It was in a sealed envelope. Must have been good, though. He left as soon as he read it.'

Well, duh.

I returned to Morelli, slouched down in the seat and closed my eyes. 'Stick a fork in me, I'm done.'

Morelli turned the key in the ignition. 'You sound bummed.'

'Bummed at myself. I was stupid tonight. I let myself get distracted.' Even more embarrassing, I hadn't immediately thought to question the bartender. And that wasn't all that had me bummed. Morelli had me bummed. He didn't understand about cookie jars. He gave his mother the wrong answer at the table. And I hated to admit it, but that eye thing had me worried. My God, what if Bella was right, and I was pregnant?

I looked over at Morelli. His features were softened by shadow, but even in the dark I could see the paper-thin scar that sliced through his right eyebrow. A few years ago, Morelli had walked into a knife. And he'd probably walk into another. Maybe a bullet. Not a comforting thought. Nor was his love life comforting. In the past, Morelli'd had a short attention span when it came to romance. From time to time, he'd shown flashes of protective tenderness for me, but I wasn't always a priority. I was a friend, like Terry Gilman and the pissed-off woman, whoever the hell she was.

So I was thinking maybe Morelli wasn't prime husband material. Not even counting the fact that he didn't *want* to get married. Okay, now for the big one. Was I in love with Morelli? Hell, yes. I'd been in love with him since I was six years old.

I smacked myself in the forehead with the heel of my hand. 'Unh.'

Morelli gave me a sideways glance.

'Just thinking,' I said.

'Must have been some thought. You almost knocked yourself out.'

The thing is, while I was in love with Morelli for all these years, I'd always known it was best if nothing came of it. Loving Morelli was like loving cheesecake. Hours of misery on the Stairmaster, working off ugly fat, in return for a moment of blissful consumption.

All right, maybe it wasn't as bad as all that. Morelli had matured. How *much* he'd matured I couldn't nail down. Truth is, I didn't know a lot about Morelli. What I knew was that I had a hard time trusting him. Past experience led me to believe blind faith in Morelli might not be a smart thing.

In fact, now that I thought about it, maybe *love* wasn't the right word. Maybe *enamored* was better. I was *definitely* enamored.

We rode in silence for most of the way home. Morelli

had the golden oldies station on, and I was sitting on my hands so I wouldn't rip the knob off the radio.

'You look worried,' Morelli said.

'I was thinking about the note the bartender gave to Eddie Kuntz. He said Kuntz read it and took off.'

'And?'

'The other notes were all in code. Kuntz couldn't figure them out. That's why Sally was brought into it. Sally was always the only one who could read the notes.'

Morelli cruised down his street and parked in front of his house. 'I don't suppose you'd consider turning all this over to the police?'

And cut myself out of a recovery fee and leave the possibility open for Joyce to bring Maxine in? Fat chance. 'Nope. I wouldn't consider it.'

Lights were blinking off in the downstairs windows in Joe's neighborhood. Early to bed, early to rise meant you had a job that allowed you to make the mortgage payment every month. Blocks away cars hummed on Chambers, but there was no traffic on Joe's street.

'I had something else sort of odd happen tonight,' I said. 'I had a run-in with a woman at the bar.'

Morelli unlocked his front door and flipped the light switch. 'And?'

I gave Morelli the details of the conversation. 'So what do you think?' I asked.

'I don't know what to think. Obviously it wasn't Terry.'

'No. It wasn't Terry. There was something familiar about her, though. Like maybe I'd seen her someplace before. You know, like a nameless face in the super- market.'

'You think she firebombed your apartment?'

'I wouldn't write her off the list. You recognize any women going in or out?'

'No. Sorry.'

Our eyes locked, and we both knew the doubt was there.

He tossed his keys on a sideboard, shrugged out of his jacket and tossed it across the lone wooden chair. He moved to the kitchen, where he checked his answering machine, unclipped his gun and his pager and laid them on the counter. 'You need to pass that information about the woman on to the arson squad.'

'Should I call tonight?'

Morelli closed the distance between us and took me in his arms. 'Monday will be soon enough.'

'Hmm,' I said, in a less than encouraging voice.

'What hmm?'

'I'm not sure this is a good idea.'

He kissed me lightly on the mouth. 'This was never a good idea.'

'Exactly. You see, this is exactly what I mean.'

'Oh shit,' Morelli said. 'You're not going to make this all complicated, are you?'

My voice rose an octave. 'Damn right I'm going to make this complicated. What do you think this is here anyway?'

'This is . . . satisfying mutual needs.'

'A good fuck.'

'Well, yeah.'

I shoved him away. 'Don't you ever need more than a good fuck?'

'Not right now! And what about you? You going to tell me you don't need it?'

'I have control over my needs.'

'Yeah, right.'

'I do!'

'That's why your nipples are hard.'

I looked down at my dress. You could see the shape of my nipples behind the cotton fabric. 'They've been like that all day. There's something wrong with them.'

A smile twitched at the corners of Morelli's mouth. 'You want me bad.'

Damn skippy I wanted him. And that made me even more furious. Where were my principles? I wasn't sure I believed his answer about the woman who confronted me at the bar. I sensed a continuing relationship of some sort between him and Terry Gilman. And here I was with hard nipples! Ugh.

'I can do without you just fine,' I said. 'Don't call me. I'll call you.'

'You won't last through the night.'

Egotistical jerk. 'Fifty bucks says I will.'

'You want to bet on this?' He sounded incredulous.

'The first one to crack pays up.'

Morelli's brows lowered and his eyes narrowed. 'Fine. It won't be me, sweetheart.'

'Hah!'

'Hah!'

I whirled around and stomped up the stairs. I brushed my teeth, got into my nightshirt and crawled into bed. I laid there for a half hour in the dark, feeling cranky and lonely, wishing Rex wasn't in the kitchen, wondering what ever possessed me to make that stupid bet. Fear, I thought. That's what possessed me. Fear of being dumped again. Fear of getting screwed over. Fear of defective condoms. Finally I got out of bed and stomped back down the stairs.

Morelli was in the living room, slouched in his favorite chair, watching television. He gave me a long, considering look.

'I came to get Rex,' I said, swishing past him.

Morelli was still watching me when I returned carrying the hamster cage. The look was speculative and quietly unnerving.

'What?' I said.

'Nice nightshirt.'

SUNDAY MORNING I opened my eyes and thought about Maxine Nowicki. I'd been on the case for a week. It felt like three. I dressed in shorts and T-shirt, and without even bothering to comb my hair, carted Rex to the kitchen.

Morelli glanced up from the paper when I padded in. He took in my hair and smiled. 'Trying to help me win the bet?'

I poured out a mug of coffee and looked at the white bakery bag on the table. 'Doughnuts?'

'Yeah. I was going to go to church, but I decided to get doughnuts instead.'

I sat across from him and selected a Boston creme. 'I've been on this Nowicki case for a week, and I don't think I'm making any progress.'

'Imagine how the merry mutilator-murderer feels. He's hacking people up and making no progress.'

'There's that.' I reached behind me for the portable phone and dialed Kuntz. 'No answer.'

Morelli gave a chunk of doughnut to Rex and topped his cup. 'Maybe we should take a ride over there this morning.'

This caught my attention. 'You have one of those cop feelings, don't you?'

'Feels funky.'

I agreed. It felt funky. I ate two doughnuts, read the funnies and went upstairs to take a shower. I left the door unlocked, but Morelli didn't traipse inside. Good, I told myself. This was much better. Yeah, right.

Morelli was waiting for me when I came down the stairs. 'Ready,' I said.

Morelli looked at the big black leather tote bag draped over my shoulder. 'You have a gun in there, don't you?'

'Christ, Morelli, I'm a bounty hunter.'

'You have a permit to carry concealed?'

'You know I don't.'

'Then get rid of the gun.'

'You're wearing a gun!'

'I'm a cop.'

I screwed up my mouth. 'Big deal.'

'Listen,' Morelli said, 'this is just the way it is. I'm a cop, and I can't go out with you when I know you're carrying concealed illegally. Besides, the thought of you with a gun in your hand scares the crap out of me.'

As well it should. 'Fine,' I said, taking the gun out of my bag. 'Just don't come running to me for help.' I looked around. 'So where do I put this?'

Morelli rolled his eyes and put the gun in a drawer in the sideboard. 'You only had one, right?'

'What do I look like, Hopalong Cassidy?'

THE FIRST THING Morelli and I noticed was that Eddie Kuntz's car was nowhere to be seen. The second was that no one was answering the door. Morelli and I looked in the front window. No lights burning. No bodies on the floor. No sign of struggle. No Kuntz.

We were standing there with our noses pressed to the glass when the Lincoln Town Car pulled up.

'What's going on?' Leo wanted to know.

'I'm looking for Eddie,' I said. 'Have you seen him?'

Betty joined us on the porch. 'Is something wrong?'

'They're looking for Eddie,' Leo said. 'When did we see him last? Yesterday?'

'Last night,' Betty said. 'He went out a little after eight. I remember because I was watering my flowers.'

'Was his car here this morning?'

'Now that you mention it, I don't remember seeing it,' Betty said.

'Saturday night,' Leo said. 'You know how it is with a young man.'

Morelli and I looked at each other.

'Could be,' Morelli said.

I gave them my card with my phone and pager numbers. 'Just in case,' I said.

'Sure,' Leo said, 'but don't worry. He's just partying.'

They disappeared into their cool, dark house and the door clicked closed. No cake invitation.

Morelli and I went back to the truck.

'So?' I said.

'It would make sense that the note was personal and not from Maxine. It would explain the fact that it wasn't in code.'

'You really believe that?'

Morelli shrugged. 'It's possible.'

I stared into the Glick front window. 'They're watching us. I can see them standing a few feet back from the window.'

Morelli rolled the engine over. 'You have plans?'

'I thought I might visit Mrs. Nowicki.'

'Isn't that a coincidence? I woke up this morning thinking it would be a good day to go to the shore.'

The temperature was in the eighties. The sky was the color of putty. And the humidity was so high I could feel the air lying on my face. It wasn't a good day to go anywhere . . . unless it was out of Jersey.

'You aren't going to play Buddy Holly all the way to Point Pleasant, are you?'

'What's wrong with Buddy Holly?'

I grimaced. He probably liked the Three Stooges, too.

IT STARTED RAINING when we hit Point Pleasant. A nice steady soaker that chased everyone off the beach. It was the sort of rain farmers liked. Except there weren't any farmers in Point Pleasant—only bummed-out vacationers.

I directed Morelli to the Nowicki house, and we sat outside for a while, watching. There were no cars in the driveway. No lights on inside. No sign of activity.

'Looks a lot like Eddie Kuntz's house,' I said.

'Yeah,' Morelli said. 'Let's go take a look.'

We ran for the shelter of the porch and rang the bell. Neither of us expecting an answer. When we didn't get one, we snooped in the windows.

'We missed the party,' Morelli said.

The front room was a mess. Lamps knocked over, tables on end, chair cushions askew. Not from Joyce, either. This was a different mess.

I tried the door, but it was locked. We ran around back and crowded onto the small stoop. No luck with that door, either.

'Damn,' I said. 'I bet there are clues inside. Maybe even bodies.'

'One way to find out.' Morelli smashed the door window with his gun butt.

I jumped back. 'Shit! I don't believe you did that. Didn't you watch the O.J. trial? Cops can't just bust into places.'

Morelli had his arm through the hole in the glass. 'It was an accident. And I'm not a cop today. It's my day off.'

'You should team up with Lula. You'd make a great pair.'

CHAPTER ELEVEN

M ORELLI OPENED THE door, and we carefully picked our way around the broken glass. He looked under the sink, found a pair of rubber gloves, put them on and wiped his prints off the doorknobs. 'You don't need to worry about prints,' he said. 'You were here legitimately two days ago.'

We did a fast walk-through just to make sure there were no bodies, dead or alive. Then we methodically worked our way through the rooms. Closets, drawers, hidden places, garbage bags.

All of their clothes were gone, and as far as I could tell, so were the prizes they'd won. They'd been in a hurry. Beds were unmade. Food had been left in the fridge. There'd been a struggle in the living room, and no one had bothered to make repairs. We didn't find anything that might hint at a new address. No sign of drugs. No bullets embedded in woodwork. No bloodstains.

My only conclusion was that they weren't great housekeepers and were probably going to end up with diverticulitis. They ate a lot of bologna and white bread, smoked a lot of cigarettes, drank a lot of beer and didn't recycle.

'Gone,' Morelli said, snapping the gloves off, returning them to the sink.

'Any ideas?'

'Yeah. Let's get out of here.'

We ran to the truck, and Morelli drove to the board-walk. 'There's a pay phone at the top of the ramp,' he said. 'Call the police and tell them you're a neighbor, and you noticed a back window was broken in the house next door. I don't want to leave that house open for vandalism or robbery.'

I took stock of myself and decided I couldn't get much wetter, so I sloshed through the rain to the phone, made the call and sloshed back.

'Everything go okay?' he asked.

'They didn't like that I wouldn't tell them my name.'

'You're supposed to make something up. Cops expect it.'

'Cops are weird,' I said to Morelli.

'Yeah,' he said, 'cops scare the hell out of me.'

I took my shoes off and buckled myself in. 'You want to hazard a guess on what happened in the living room back there?'

'Someone came after Maxine, chased her around the living room and got hit from behind by a blunt instrument. When he woke up the three women were gone.'

'Maybe that someone was Eddie Kuntz.'

'Maybe. But that doesn't explain why he's still missing.'

THE RAIN STOPPED halfway home, and Trenton showed no sign of relief from the heat. The hydrocarbon level was high enough to etch glass, and the highways hummed with road rage. Air conditioners were failing, dogs had diarrhea, laundry mildewed in hampers, and sinus cavities felt filled with cement. If the barometric pressure dropped any lower everyone's guts would be sucked through the soles of their feet into the bowels of the earth.

Morelli and I barely noticed any of this, of course, because we were born and raised in Jersey. Life is about survival of the fittest, and Jersey is producing the master race.

We stood dripping in Morelli's foyer, and I couldn't decide what I wanted to do first. I was starving, I was soaked, and I wanted to call and see if Eddie Kuntz had turned up. Morelli prioritized my actions by stripping in the hall.

'What are you doing?' I asked.

He'd removed his shoes and socks and shirt and had his thumbs stuck in his shorts. 'I don't want to track water all through the house.' A smile tugged at his mouth. 'You have a problem with this?'

'No problem at all,' I said. 'I'm taking a shower. Does that give you any problems?'

'Only if you use all the hot water.'

He was on the phone when I came downstairs. I was clean, but I couldn't get dry. Morelli didn't have air, and at this time of the day it was possible to work up a sweat doing nothing. I prowled through the refrigerator and decided on a ham-and-cheese sandwich. I slapped it together and ate standing at the counter. Morelli was writing on a pad. He looked up at me, and I decided this was cop business.

When he got off the phone he picked at the deli ham I'd left out. 'That case I was working on has just been reopened. Something new turned up. I'm going to take a fast shower, and then I'm going to have to go out. I'm not sure when I'll be back.'

'Today? Tomorrow?'

'Today. I just don't know when.'

I finished my sandwich and straightened the kitchen. Rex had crawled out of his soup can and was looking neglected, so I gave him a small chunk of cheese and a crust of bread. 'We're not doing too good here,' I told him. 'I keep losing people. Now I can't find the guy I'm working for.'

I tried calling Eddie Kuntz. No answer. I looked up Glick in the phone book and called Betty.

'Have you seen Eddie yet?' I asked.

'No.'

I hung up and did some pacing. Someone knocked on the front door.

It was a little Italian lady.

'I'm Joe's godmother, Tina Ragusto,' she said. 'You must be Stephanie. How are you, dear? I just heard. I think it's wonderful.'

I didn't know what she was talking about, and I suspected it was better that way. I made a vague gesture toward the stairs. 'Joe's in the shower.'

'I can't stay. I'm on my way to a jewelry party.' She handed me a white shirt box. 'I just wanted to drop this off.' She lifted the lid and spread the tissue paper, so I could see what lay beneath. Her round face smoothed with her smile. 'You see?' she said. 'Joseph's christening outfit.'

Ulk.

She gave me a pat on the cheek. 'You're a good Italian girl.'

'Half Italian.'

'And a good Catholic.'

'Umm . . .'

I watched her walk to her car and drive away. She

thought I was pregnant. She thought I was marrying Joe Morelli, the man voted 'least trustworthy male to date my daughter' by mothers statewide. And she thought I was a good Catholic. How had this happened?

I was standing in the foyer, holding the box, when Joe came down. 'Was someone here?'

'Your godmother. She brought me your christening outfit.'

Morelli picked it out of the box and looked at it. 'Good grief, it's a dress.'

'What do you want me to do with it?'

'Put it in a closet somewhere, and I'd appreciate it if you kept the dress part quiet.'

I waited until Morelli was out of sight, and then I looked down at my stomach, 'No way,' I said. I looked at the christening dress. It was kind of pretty. Old-fashioned. Very Italian. Damn, I was getting all choked up over Morelli's dress. I ran upstairs with the dress, put it on Morelli's bed, ran out of the room and slammed the door closed.

I went to the kitchen and called my best friend, Mary Lou, who had two kids and knew about pregnancy.

'Where are you?' Mary Lou wanted to know.

'I'm at Morelli's.'

'Ommigod! It's true! You're living with Morelli! And you didn't tell me! I'm your best friend. How could you do this to me?'

'I've only been here for three days. And it's no big deal. My apartment burned up, and Morelli had an extra room.'

'You did it with him! I can hear it in your voice! How was it? I want details!'

'I need a favor.'

'Anything!'

'I need one of those pregnancy test things.'

'Ommigod! You're pregnant! Ommigod. Ommigod!'

'Calm down. I'm not pregnant. I just want to make sure. You know, peace of mind. And I don't want to buy one myself, because if anybody sees me it'll be all over.'

'I'll be right there. Don't move.'

Mary Lou lived about a half mile away. Her husband, Lennie, was okay but he had to be careful not to drag his knuckles when he walked. Mary Lou never cared much about intelligence in a man. Mary Lou was more into packaging and stamina.

Mary Lou and I have been friends since the day we were born. I was always the flake, and Mary Lou was always the underachiever. Maybe *underachiever* isn't the right word. It was more that Mary Lou had simple goals. She wanted to get married and have a family. If she could marry the captain of the football team, even better. And that's exactly what she did. She married Lennie Stankovic, who was captain of the football team, graduated high school and went to work for his father. Stankovic and Sons Plumbing and Heating.

I wanted to marry Aladdin so I'd get to fly on his magic carpet. So you can see that we were coming from different places.

Ten minutes later Mary Lou was at the front door. Mary Lou is four inches shorter than me and five pounds heavier. None of her weight is fat. Mary Lou's solid. Mary Lou's built like a brick shithouse. If I ever do tag team wrestling, Mary Lou's going to be my partner.

'I've got it!' she said, barreling into the foyer, brandishing the test kit. She stopped short and looked around. 'So this is Morelli's house!'

This was said in hushed tones of awe usually reserved for Catholic miracles like weeping statues of the Virgin.

'Oh man,' she said. 'I always wanted to see the inside of Morelli's house. He isn't home, right?' She took off up the stairs. 'I want to see his bedroom!'

'It's the one to the left.'

'This is it!' she shrieked, opening the door. 'Ommigod! Did you do it on this bed?'

'Yeah.' And on my bed. And on the couch, the hall floor, the kitchen table, in the shower . . .

'Holy shit,' Mary Lou said, 'he's got a carton of condoms. What is he . . . a fucking rabbit?'

I took the little brown bag from her hand and peeked inside. 'So this is it?'

'It's simple. All you have to do is pee on the plastic strip and wait for it to change color. Good thing it's summer and you're wearing a T-shirt, because the hard part is not getting your sleeve wet.'

'Darn,' I said. 'I don't have to go right now.'

'You need beer,' Mary Lou said. 'Beer always works.'

We went to the kitchen, and we each had two beers.

'You know what's missing in this kitchen?' Mary Lou said. 'A cookie jar.'

'Yeah, well, you know how it is with men.'

'They don't know anything,' Mary Lou said.

I opened the box and removed the foil packet. 'I can't get this open. I'm too nervous.'

Mary Lou took it from me. Mary Lou had nails like razor wire. 'We gotta time this. And don't tip the plastic strip. You have to collect the pee in that little indentation.'

'Ick.'

We went upstairs, and Mary Lou waited outside the

door while I did the test. Friendship among women does not include viewing each other's urine.

'What's happening?' Mary Lou yelled through the door. 'Do you see a plus sign or a negative sign?'

My hand was shaking so badly I was lucky I didn't drop the whole thing in the toilet. 'I don't see anything yet.'

'I'm timing,' Mary Lou said. 'It takes three minutes max.'

'Three minutes,' Mary Lou yelled again, and she opened the door. 'Well?'

Little black dots were dancing in front of my eyes and my lips felt numb. 'I'm going to faint.' I sat down hard on the floor and put my head between my knees.

Mary Lou took the test strip. 'Negative. Yes!'

'God, that was close. I was really worried. We used condoms every single time, but Bella said—'

'Joe's Grandma Bella?' Mary Lou gasped. 'Oh shit! Bella didn't give you the eye, did she? Remember when she put it on Raymond Cone and all his hair fell out?'

'Worse than that, she told me I was pregnant.'

'Then that's it,' Mary Lou said. 'The test is wrong.'

'What do you mean the test is wrong? The test isn't wrong. Johnson and Johnson doesn't make mistakes.'

'Bella knows these things.'

I got up off the floor and splashed water on my face. 'Bella's a crackpot.' Even as I said it I was mentally doing the sign of the cross.

'How far overdue are you?'

'I'm not actually overdue yet.'

'Wait a minute. You can't take this test if you aren't overdue. I thought you knew that.'

'What?'

'It takes time to develop the hormone. When's your period?'

'I don't know. In about a week, I guess. Are you telling me this test isn't valid?'

'That's what I'm telling you.'

'Fuck!'

'I gotta go,' Mary Lou said. 'I told Lennie I'd bring pizza home for supper. You want to eat with us?'

'No. Thanks anyway.'

After Mary Lou left I slouched in the chair in the living room and stared at the blank television screen. Taking the pregnancy test had exhausted me.

I heard a car pull up and footsteps on the pavement outside the house. It was another little Italian lady.

'I'm Joseph's Aunt Loretta,' she said, handing me a foil-topped casserole. 'I just heard. And don't worry, dear, these things happen. We don't talk about it, but Joseph's mother had sort of a hurry-up wedding, too, if you know what I mean.'

'It's not what it seems.'

'The important thing is that you eat good food. You aren't throwing up, are you?'

'Not yet.'

'Don't worry about getting the dish back to me. You can give it to me at the shower.'

My voice rose an octave. 'The shower?'

'I gotta go,' she said. 'I gotta visit my neighbor in the hospital.' She leaned forward and lowered her voice. 'Cancer,' she whispered. 'Terrible. Terrible. She's rotting away. Her insides are rotted, and now she's got sores all over her body. I had a cousin once who rotted like that. She turned black and just before she died her fingers fell off.'

'Eee*euw*.'

'Well,' she said, 'you enjoy the casserole.'

I waved good-bye and carted the warm casserole off to the kitchen. I set it on the counter and banged my head against the cabinet door a couple of times. 'Argh.'

I lifted a corner of the foil and peeked inside. Lasagna. Smelled good. I cut a square for myself and scooped it onto a plate. I was thinking about seconds when Morelli came home.

He looked at the lasagna and sighed. 'Aunt Loretta.'

'Yep.'

'This is out of control,' he said. 'This has to stop.'

'I think they're planning a shower.'

'Shit.'

I got up and rinsed my plate, so I wouldn't be tempted to cut another wedge of lasagna. 'How'd things go today?'

'Not that good.'

'Want to talk about it?'

'Can't. I'm working with the Feds. It's not supposed to go public.'

'You don't trust me.'

He cut a slab of lasagna and joined me at the table. 'Of course I trust you. It's Mary Lou I don't trust.'

'I don't tell Mary Lou everything!'

'Look, it's not your fault. You're a woman, so you blab.'

'That's disgusting! That's so sexist!'

He took a bite of lasagna. 'I have sisters. I know women.'

'You don't know *all* women.'

Morelli considered me. 'I know you.'

I could feel my face get warm. 'Yeah, well, we should talk about that.'

He pushed back in his chair. 'It's your nickel.'

'I don't think I'm cut out for irresponsible sex.'

He thought about that for a beat and gave an almost imperceptible nod. 'We have a problem then, because I don't think I'm cut out for marriage. At least not now.'

Wow. Big surprise. 'I wasn't proposing marriage.'

'What were you proposing?'

'I wasn't proposing anything. I guess I was just setting boundaries.'

'You know, you're one of those women who drive men nuts. Men drive off bridges and drink too much because of women like you. And it was your fault in the bakery, too.'

I narrowed my eyes. 'You want to explain that to me?'

Morelli smiled. 'You smelled like a jelly doughnut.'

'You jerk! That's what you wrote on the bathroom wall in Mario's Sub Shop. You said I was warm and sweet and good to eat. And then you went on to describe how you did it! It got back to my parents, and I was grounded for three months. You have no scruples!'

His eyes darkened. 'Don't confuse me with that eighteen-year-old kid.'

We glared at each other for a couple of beats, and the silence was shattered by the sound of something smashing through Morelli's living room window.

Morelli bolted from his chair and ran for the front room. I was close behind, almost slamming into him when he stopped short.

A bottle lay in the middle of his living room floor, and there was a fire-blackened rag stuck into the mouth of the bottle. A Molotov cocktail that had burned itself out because the bottle hadn't broken on impact.

Morelli skirted the bottle, rushed into the hall and out the door.

I got to the door in time to see Morelli aim and fire at a retreating car. Only the gun didn't fire. It went *click, click, click*. Morelli looked at the gun in disbelief.

'What's wrong?' I asked.

'This is your gun. I got it out of the sideboard when I ran through the hall. It hasn't got any bullets in it!'

'Bullets are creepy.'

Morelli looked dazed. 'What good is a gun without bullets?'

'It's good for scaring people. Or you can hit people with it. Or you can use it to break windows . . . or crack walnuts.'

'You recognize that car?'

'No. You get a look at the driver?'

Morelli shook his head. 'No.' He stalked through the house, took his gun and pager off the kitchen counter and clipped them to his belt. He called the dispatcher and gave him the car description. Then he called someone else with the plate number. He took an extra clip out of a kitchen drawer and put it in his pocket while he waited on the plate.

I was standing behind him, and I was trying hard to stay calm, but I was shaking inside, and I was having flashbacks of my ruined apartment. If I'd been home, in bed, when the bottle had exploded, I'd have been killed, charred beyond recognition. As it was I'd lost just about everything I owned. Not that it was much . . . but it was all I had. And now it had almost happened again.

'That was for me,' I said, relieved that my voice didn't tremble and give me away.

'Probably,' Morelli said. He murmured something into the phone and hung up. 'The car was reported stolen a couple hours ago.'

He gingerly picked up the bottle with a kitchen towel and put it in a paper bag. Then he set the bag on the kitchen counter. 'Fortunately, this guy didn't choose his bottle wisely, and when he threw it, it landed on carpet.'

The phone rang, and Morelli snatched at it.

'It's for you,' he said. 'It's Sally.'

'I need help,' Sally said. 'I have a gig tonight, and I can't figure out this makeup shit.'

'Where's Sugar?'

'We had another fight, and he took off.'

'Okay,' I said, reacting more than thinking, still feeling numbed by the second attempt to end my life. 'I'll be right over.'

'Now what?' Morelli asked.

'I need to help Sally with his makeup.'

'I'll go with you.'

'Not necessary.'

'I think it is.'

'I don't need a bodyguard.' What I really meant was *I don't want to get you killed, too.*

'Then consider this to be a date.'

WE KNOCKED TWICE, and Sally just about ripped the door off its hinges when he yanked it open. 'Shit,' he said, 'it's you.'

'Who'd you think it would be?'

'I guess I was hoping it was Sugar. Look at me. I'm a wreck. I don't know how to do any of this shit. Sugar always gets me dressed. Christ, I haven't got the right hormones for this fucking shit, you know what I mean?'

'Where'd Sugar go?'

'I don't know. We had another fight. I don't even know

how it started. Something about me not appreciating his coffee cake.'

I looked around. The house was beyond immaculate. Not a speck of dust anywhere. Nothing out of place. Through the kitchen door I could see the kitchen counters neatly lined with cakes, pies, loaves of bread, glass jars filled with cookies and homemade fudge.

'I didn't even realize he was all that upset,' Sally said. 'He got dressed and left when I was in my bubble bath.'

Morelli arched an eyebrow. 'Bubble bath?'

'Hey, give me a break here. RuPaul says you're supposed to take a goddamn bubble bath, so that's what I do. Gets you in touch with your fuckin' female side.'

Morelli grinned.

Sally was wearing black bikini Calvins and panty hose, and he was holding a contraption that looked like a corset with breasts. 'You gotta help me,' he said. 'I can't get into this by myself.'

Morelli held up a hand. 'You're on your own.'

Sally looked over at him. 'What, are you homophobic?'

'Nope,' Morelli said. 'I'm Italian. There's a difference.'

'Okay,' I said. 'What do I have to do?'

Sally wiggled into the corset and got it in place. 'Tighten this fucker up,' he said. 'I need to get a waist.'

I pulled at the strings, but I couldn't get them to go together. 'I can't do this. I haven't got enough hand strength.'

We both looked at Morelli.

Morelli gave a disgusted sigh. 'Shit,' he said, heaving himself off the couch. He took hold of the strings, put his foot to Sally's butt and yanked.

'Oof,' Sally said. He looked over his shoulder at Morelli. 'You've done this before.'

'Dolan used to wear one of these when he went undercover.'

'I don't suppose you did Dolan's makeup?'

'Sorry,' Morelli said, 'makeup's way out of my league.'

Sally looked to me.

'No sweat,' I said. 'I'm from the burg. I was putting makeup on Barbie before I could walk.'

Half an hour later I had him appropriately slutted up. We tugged on his wig and did some last-minute combing. Sally zipped himself into a short black leather skirt and a black leather top that looked like Madonna meets the Hell's Angels. He slipped his size-fourteen feet into a pair of platform heels, and he was ready to go.

'How are you doing on time?' I asked.

He grabbed his guitar case. 'I'm cool. So how do I look? Am I pretty?'

'Well, uh . . . yeah.' If you like almost-seven-feet-tall, slightly bow-legged, hook-nosed guys with hairy chests and arms dressed up like the bride of the Valkyries.

'You should come with me,' Sally said. 'I'll introduce you to the rest of the band, and you could stay and watch the show.'

'Do I know how to take a girl on a date, or what?' Morelli said.

We took the elevator with Sally and followed him out of the lot. He looped around down by the river and got on Route 1 north.

'That was nice of you to help him with his corset,' I said.

'Yeah,' Morelli said. 'I'm Mr. Sensitivity.'

Sally went about fifteen miles and put his blinker on, so we'd know he was turning. The club was on the right side of the highway, all lit up in red and pink neon lights.

Already there were a lot of cars in the lot. The sign on the rooftop advertised an all-girl review. I guessed that was Sally.

Sally crawled out of the Porsche and straightened his skirt. 'We've played here for four weeks now,' he said. 'We're like fucking regulars.'

Regular what I didn't know.

Morelli looked around the lot. 'Where's Sugar's car?'

'The black Mercedes.'

'Sugar does okay.'

Sally grinned. 'You ever see him in drag?'

We both shook our heads no.

'When you see him you'll understand.'

We followed Sally in through the kitchen entrance.

'If I go through the front I'll get fucking mobbed,' he said. 'These people are animals.'

We went down a dreary narrow hall to a back room. The room was filled with smoke and noise and the Lovelies. All five of them. All dressed in various forms of leather . . . with the exception of Sugar. Sugar was wearing a blood-red satin dress that fit him like his own skin. It was short and tight and so smooth in front I thought he must have been surgically altered. His makeup was flawless. His lips were full and pouty, painted in high gloss to match the dress. He wore the Marilyn wig, and on my best day I never looked that good. I slid a sideways glance at Morelli, and he obviously was caught in the same dumbstruck fascination that I was experiencing. I shifted my attention back to Sugar and realization suddenly hit me.

'The woman in the bar was Sugar,' I whispered to Morelli. 'It was a different blond wig, but I'm sure it was Sugar.'

'Are you kidding me? He was right in front of you, and you didn't recognize him?'

'It happened so fast, and the room was dark and crowded. And besides, look at him! He's beautiful!'

Sugar saw the three of us come into the room, and he was on his feet, calling Sally an ungrateful slut.

'Christ,' Sally said, 'what's he talking about? Don't you have to be a chick to be a slut?'

'You *are* a chick, you dumb shit,' one of the other drag queens said.

Sally grabbed his package and gave it a hike up.

'I'd like to talk to you in private,' Morelli said to Sugar.

'You don't belong here, and I'm not talking to you,' Sugar said. 'This is the band's dressing room. Now get the hell out.'

Morelli crossed the room in three strides, backing Sugar into a corner. They stood talking like that for a few minutes, and then Morelli eased off. 'Nice meeting you,' he said to the other band members, who were shuffling foot to foot in awkward silence. 'Talk to you later,' he said to Sally.

When we left Sugar was still in the corner, his eyes small and glittery, not a part of his baby doll face.

'Jeez,' I said. 'What did you say to him?'

'I asked him if he was involved in the firebombings.'

'And what did he tell you?'

'Not much.'

'He sure makes a beautiful woman.'

Morelli gave his head a small shake of amazement. 'Christ, for a minute there I didn't know whether I wanted to punch him in the face or ask him for a date.'

'We going to stay to watch the band?'

'No,' Morelli said. 'We're going out to the lot to check out the Mercedes, and then we're going to run a check on Sugar.'

THE MERCEDES WAS clean, and so was Sugar. No priors for Gregory Stern. When we got back to Morelli's house there were two cop cars parked in front and several people milling around on the sidewalk. Morelli parked the truck and got out and walked over to the nearest uniform, who happened to be Carl Costanza.

'Been waiting for you,' Carl said. 'Didn't know if you wanted us to board your window.'

'No. It'll be okay for tonight, and tomorrow I'll get a glass guy over here.'

'You coming in, or you gonna do the report in the morning?' Carl asked.

'I'll do it in the morning.'

'Congratulations,' Costanza said to me. 'I hear you're preggers.'

'I'm *not* preggers!'

Costanza draped an arm around me and leaned close. 'Would you like to be?'

I rolled my eyes.

'Okay, but remember me in case you change your mind,' Carl said.

An old man in a bathrobe came up to Morelli and gave him the elbow. 'Just like old times, huh? I can remember when Ziggy Kozak's house got machine-gunned into Swiss cheese. Boy, I tell you, those were the days.'

Morelli went into the house, got the firebomb and gave it to Carl. 'Have this checked for prints and put it in the lockup. Anybody canvass the neighborhood for a witness?'

'No witnesses. We did every house.'

'How about the car?'

'Hasn't turned up yet.'

The cops got into their cars and drove off. The people dispersed. I followed Morelli into the living room, where we both stood looking at the glass shards scattered over the floor.

'I'm really sorry,' I said. 'This is my fault. I shouldn't have come here.'

'Don't worry about it,' Morelli said. 'Life was getting dull.'

'I could move out.'

Morelli grabbed me by the front of my shirt and pulled me to him. 'You're just afraid you're going to cave and have to pay me fifty dollars.'

I felt a smile come on. 'Thanks.'

Morelli leaned in and kissed me. He had his knee between my legs and his tongue in my mouth, and I got a hot rush that dropped my stomach about six inches.

He backed off and grinned at me. 'Good night.'

I blinked. 'G'nite.'

The grin widened. 'Gotcha.'

I narrowed my eyes. 'I'm going to bed.'

'I'll be down here if you get lonely. I'm going to sleep on the couch tonight just to make sure no one crawls through my window and walks off with my television.'

CHAPTER TWELVE

I WAS UP early, but Joe was up earlier. He'd cleaned the glass away and was eating lasagna for breakfast when I trooped into the kitchen.

I poured coffee and gave the lasagna a wistful glance.

'Go for it,' Morelli said.

If I ate the lasagna I'd have to do something physical, like jog a couple of miles. Not my favorite activity. I preferred to get my exercise by walking through a shopping mall. Okay, what the hell, I should probably go out for a run anyway. Keep in shape, and all that crap.

I sat across from him and dug in. 'You back on the mystery case today?'

'Surveillance.'

I hated surveillance. Surveillance meant you sat in a car all by yourself until your ass fell asleep. And if you left to go to the bathroom all hell broke loose and you missed it.

Morelli pushed his empty plate away. 'What are your plans?'

'Find Maxine.'

'And?'

'And that's it. I have no ideas. I'm out of leads. Everyone's disappeared. Eddie Kuntz's probably dead. For all I know Mrs. Nowicki, Margie and Maxine are dead. Dead and buried.'

'Boy, it's nice to see you so positive this morning.'

'I like to start out right.'

Morelli got up and rinsed his plate. 'I have to go to work. If you were an ordinary person I'd tell you to be careful. Since you are who you are, I'll just wish you good luck. Oh, yeah, and someone's supposed to show up at nine to fix the window. Can you hang around until he's done?'

'No problem.'

He kissed me on the top of the head and left.

I looked at Rex. 'This feels a little strange,' I said. 'I'm not used to being a housewife.'

Rex sat on his haunches and stared at me. At first glance you might think he was contemplating what I'd just said. More likely he wanted a grape.

For lack of something better to do I called Eddie Kuntz. No answer. 'Dead,' I said to Rex. I wanted to drive over and have another chat with Betty, but I had to wait for the glass to get fixed. I had a second cup of coffee. And then I had a second piece of lasagna. At nine o'clock the glazier arrived, and he was followed by yet another Italian lady bearing food. A chocolate cake this time. I ate half while I waited for the windows.

I DIDN'T HAVE to knock on the door to know Eddie Kuntz wasn't home. No car out front. No lights any-where. Windows and doors closed up tight. The only thing missing was black crepe.

I knocked on Betty's door instead.

'What can I tell you?' Betty said. 'He's not home. Like I told you before, last I saw him was Saturday.'

She didn't look worried or confused. What she looked was pissed. Like I was bothering her.

'Does he do this a lot? Do you think we should notify the police?'

'He's on a bender,' Leo said from his chair in front of the TV. 'He picked up one of his trashy girlfriends, and they're shacked up somewhere. That's the end of it. He'll be home when he's home.'

'You're probably right,' I said. 'Still, it might not hurt to do a little investigating. Maybe it would be a good idea if we checked out his apartment. You have a key?'

Leo was more adamant this time. 'He's on a bender, I'm telling you. And you don't go snooping around in a man's home just because he goes on a bender. Anyway, why are you so interested in finding Eddie? I thought you were looking for Maxine Nowicki.'

'Eddie's disappearance might be related.'

'For the last time, I'm telling you it's not a disappearance.'

Sounded like denial to me, but what do I know? I went back to the Buick and drove to Mrs. Nowicki's house. It looked even worse than it had the first time I saw it. No one was cutting the grass, and a dog had done number two right in the middle of the sidewalk. Just for the hell of it I walked around the house and looked in the windows. No sign of life.

I got back in the car and headed for Margie's house. I took New York to Olden, turned onto Olden and spotted the beat-up Fairlane Morelli uses for surveillance. He was parked across the street from the 7-Eleven where Helen Badijian had worked before her death. Morelli was working with the Feds, so I assumed it was drugs, but really it could be anything from running guns to black-market babies. Or maybe he'd stopped there to have lunch and take a nap.

Margie's house looked better kept than Nowicki's, but empty all the same. I looked in the windows, and I wondered what Margie had done with her cat.

The next-door neighbor stuck her head out her front door and caught me peeking in Margie's window.

'I'm looking for Margie,' I said. 'I work with her at the diner, and I haven't seen her for a couple days, so I got worried. She doesn't seem to be home.'

'She went on vacation. She said it was too hard to work with her finger cut like that, so she took some time off. I think she went to the shore. I'm surprised you didn't know.'

'I knew she wasn't working. I didn't know she went to the shore.' I looked around. 'Where's her cat? She take it with her?'

'No. They don't allow cats in the house she rented. I'm feeding the cat. It's no bother.'

I was half a block away when it hit me. The finger! She'd have to have it looked at. She'd have to get her stitches removed. And Maxine's mother probably needed medical attention, too. She'd still had her head all wrapped up when I saw her in Point Pleasant.

I hustled to the office so I could use the by-street directory. Connie was doing her nails, and Lula had her ears plugged into a Walkman. Lula's back was to me, and her beads were clicking around her head, and her ass was going side to side in some jive step. She caught me in her peripheral vision and turned the Walkman down.

'Uh oh,' she said. 'You're not getting any.'

'How do you know that?' I yelled. I threw my hands into the air. 'I don't believe this!'

Vinnie poked his head around the corner. 'What's all the racket about?'

'Stephanie's here,' Connie said.

Vinnie had a cigar in his mouth that I'm willing to bet was twice the size of his dick. 'Where's Maxine? I forfeit my money in five days, for crissake. I should never have taken Barnhardt off.'

'I'm closing in.'

'Right,' Vinnie said. 'Closing in on my liver.' He ducked into his office and slammed the door.

I traced Margie's address in the directory and came up with her last name. There are three hospitals in the Trenton area. Helen Fuld is a short distance from Nowicki's neighborhood. Margie's address is equal distance between Helen Fuld and St. Francis.

I went home to Joe's house, helped myself to another wedge of chocolate cake and called my cousin Evelyn, who works at Helen Fuld. I gave her the two names and asked her to nose around. Neither Margie nor Mama Nowicki was wanted by the police, so (assuming they were alive) they had no reason not to return to their doctors. Their only concern was keeping me from following them back to Maxine.

IT WAS THREE o'clock, and I was sort of hoping another Italian lady would stop around with something new for dinner. I kept looking out the window, but I didn't see any big black cars bearing food. This posed a problem because the idea of being in Morelli's kitchen, making him dinner, felt like a Doris Day movie.

Evelyn called and told me it was my lucky day. Both women had been treated at Fuld. Both women would go to their own doctors for follow-up. She gave me the names of the attending physicians and also the names listed for primary care through their medical plans. I told her I owed her. She said a detailed description of Morelli in bed would do the trick.

I called the doctors and lied my ass off to their receptionists, telling them I'd forgotten my appointment time. Both women had Wednesday appointments. Shit, I was good.

Morelli dragged in with a sweat stain the length of his gray T-shirt. He went to the refrigerator and stuck his head in the freezer. 'I've gotta get air in this house.'

I thought the weather was pretty good compared to yesterday. Today you could sort of see a yellow glow where the sun was behind the layer of funk air.

He pulled his head out of the freezer, tossed his gun on the counter and got a beer.

'Bad day?'

'Average.'

'I saw you in north Trenton.'

'You made me?'

'I recognized the car. I figured you were watching the 7-Eleven.'

'And watching, and watching, and watching.'

'Drugs?'

'Funny money.'

'I thought you weren't supposed to tell me.'

'Fuck it. Treasury has this case so screwed up it doesn't matter. There've been bogus twenties coming out of Trenton for five years that we know of . . . probably more. Treasury has everything in place. They go in to get the guy. No plates where the plates are supposed to be. No paper. No nothing. Including no funny money traffic. We can't even make an arrest. We look like a bunch of fucking amateurs. Then all of a sudden, yesterday, a couple of the twenties get passed at the convenience store on Olden. So we start all over, looking to see who goes in that store.'

'The clerk didn't know who passed them?'

'They were discovered at the bank when the teller was counting them out for deposit.'

'What do you think?'

'I think we had the right guy the first time. Some fluky thing happened and the stuff wasn't there.'

'I just had a weird thought. We attributed Helen Badijian's death to her connection with Maxine. Maybe it didn't have anything to do with Maxine. Maybe it had to do with the funny money.'

'I thought of that, too, but the MO ties it to Maxine. Cause of death to Badijian was a blow to the head, but she also had one of her fingers chopped off.'

I had an even weirder thought, but I didn't want to say it out loud and sound like a dunce.

The phone rang, and Morelli answered. 'Yes, Mrs. Plum,' he said.

I jumped out of my chair and started to run for the front door. I was halfway through the dining room when Morelli snagged me by the back of my shirt and stopped my progress with a sharp yank that had me pressed against his chest.

'Your mother,' he said, handing me the phone.

'Stephanie,' my mother said. 'What is this I hear about your being pregnant?'

'I'm not pregnant. This is a living arrangement, not a marriage.'

'Everybody's talking. Everybody thinks you're pregnant. What should I tell Mrs. Crandle?'

'Tell her I'm not pregnant.'

'Your father wants to talk to you.'

I could hear the phone being transferred and then some breathing.

'Dad?'

'Yeah,' he said. 'How's the Buick running? You gotta give it high test, you know.'

'Don't worry. I always give it high test.' I *never* gave it high test. It didn't deserve high test. It was ugly.

He gave the phone back to my mother, and I could hear my mother rolling her eyes at him.

'I have a nice pot roast on the stove,' she said. 'With peas and mashed potatoes.'

'Okay,' I said. 'I'll come for dinner.'

'And Joseph.'

'No. He can't make it.'

'Yes, I can,' Joe said.

I gave a big sigh. 'He'll come, too.'

I disconnected and gave him the phone. 'You'll be sorry.'

'NOTHING LIKE BEING pregnant to give a woman a glow,' Grandma said.

'I may be glowing, but I'm not pregnant.'

Grandma looked down at my stomach. 'You look pregnant.'

It was all that damn Italian food. 'It's cake,' I said.

'You might want to get rid of that cake before the wedding,' Grandma said. 'Or you're going to have to buy one of them empire gowns that don't have a waist.'

'I'm not getting married,' I said. 'There's no wedding.'

Grandma sat up straighter. 'What about the hall?'

'What hall?'

'We figured you'd hold your reception at the Polish National Hall. It's the best place for it, and Edna Majewski said they had a cancellation, but you'd have to act fast.'

'You didn't hire a hall!'

'Well, we didn't put down no deposit,' Grandma said. 'We weren't sure of the date.'

I looked to Joe. 'You explain it.'

'Stephanie's apartment got damaged in the fire, and she's renting a room from me until her apartment's repaired.'

'How about sex?' Grandma asked. 'Are you having sex?'

'No.'

Not since Saturday.

'If it was me, I'd have sex,' Grandma said.

'Christ,' my father said, at the head of the table.

My mother passed me the potatoes. 'I have forms for you to fill out for the insurance. Ed was over at your apartment and said there was nothing left of it. He said the only thing that was left was the cookie jar. He said the cookie jar was fine.'

I silently dared Morelli to say something about the cookie jar, but Morelli was busy cutting his meat. The phone rang and Grandma went to the kitchen to answer it.

'It's for you, Stephanie,' Grandma yelled.

'I been calling all over, trying to track you down,' Lula said. 'I got some news. Joyce Barnhardt called Vinnie just before we were getting ready to leave, and Connie listened in. Joyce told Vinnie she'd make him bark like a dog if he put her back on the case and guess what?'

'I can guess.'

'Yeah, so then she goes on to tell Vinnie how she's getting her leads on Maxine. And now we know the name of the little jack-off that's helping Joyce.'

'*Yes!*'

'So I figure maybe you and me should pay him a visit.'

'Now?'

'You got something better to do?'

'No. Now will be fine.'

'I'll pick you up then on account of I'm not riding in that Buick.'

Everyone stopped eating when I returned to the table.

'Well?' Grandma said.

'It was Lula. I'm going to have to eat and run. We have a lead on a case.'

'I could go, too,' Grandma said. 'Like last time.'

'Thanks, but I'd rather you stayed home and entertained Joe.'

Grandma winked at Morelli, and Morelli looked like a snake that just swallowed a cow and got it stuck in his throat.

Ten minutes later, I heard a car pull to the curb outside. Rap music thumped through the house, the music cut off and in moments Lula was at the door.

'We got a lot of pot roast,' Grandma said to Lula. 'You want some?'

My mother was on her feet, setting an extra plate.

'Pot roast,' Lula said. 'Boy, I like pot roast.' She pulled a chair up and shook out her napkin.

'I always wanted to eat with a Negro,' Grandma said.

'Yeah, well, I always wanted to eat with a boney-assed

old white woman,' Lula said. 'So I guess this works out good.'

Grandma and Lula did some complicated handshake thing.

'Bitchin',' Grandma said.

IT WAS THE first time I'd ridden in the new Firebird, and I was feeling envious.

'How can you afford a car like this working as a file clerk? And how come your insurance came through, and I'm still waiting?'

'First off, I got low overhead where I'm living. And second, I just keep leasing these suckers. You barbecue a car and they give you a new one. No sweat.'

'Maybe I should look into that.'

'Just don't tell them about how your cars keep getting blown up. They might think you're a risk, you know what I'm saying?' Lula had taken High to Hamilton. 'This guy, Bernie, works at the supermarket on Route Thirty-three. When he's not stacking oranges he's selling wacky tobaccy, which is the common link between Barnhardt and Mama Nowicki. Nowicki talks to Bernie, then Bernie talks to Barnhardt.'

'Joyce said it was a retail connection.'

'Ain't that the truth.'

'From what Connie got on the phone it seems he's also visually challenged.'

'Blind?'

'Ugly.'

She turned into the supermarket lot and rolled to a stop in a front slot. Not many people were shopping at this time of the night.

'Joyce said he was a horny little troll, so if you don't want to buy dope maybe you can promise him favors.'

'As in sexual favors?'

'You don't have to deliver,' Lula said. 'All you gotta do is promise. I'd do it, but I think he's more your type.'

'What type is that?'

'White.'

'How do I find him?'

'Name's Bernie. Works in Produce. Looks like a horny little troll.'

I pulled the visor mirror down, fluffed my hair and applied fresh lip gloss. 'Do I look okay?'

'From what I hear, this guy won't care if you bark and chase cars.'

I didn't have trouble finding him. He was stickering grapefruits with his back to me. He had a lot of curly black hair on the back and sides of his head and none on the top. The top of his head looked like a big pink egg. He was just under five feet, and built like a fireplug.

I put a sack of potatoes in my cart, and I cruised over to him. 'Excuse me,' I said.

He turned, tilted his head back and looked at me. His fat fish lips parted slightly, but no words came out.

'Nice apples,' I said.

He made a gurgling sound, and his eyes slid down to my chest.

'So,' I said, 'you have any dope?'

'What are you kidding me? What do I look like?'

'A friend of mine said I could get some dope from you.'

'Oh yeah? Who's your friend?'

'Joyce Barnhardt.'

This got his eyes to light up in a way that told me Joyce probably hadn't paid cold cash for her marijuana.

'I know Joyce,' he said. 'But I'm not saying I sold her any dope.'

'We have another mutual friend.'

'Who's that?'

'Her name's Nowicki.'

'I don't know anybody named Nowicki.'

I gave him a description.

'That must be Francine,' he said. 'She's a pip. I just never knew her last name.'

'Good customer?'

'Yeah. She buys lots of fruit.'

'See her lately?'

His voice got crafty. 'What's it worth to you?'

I didn't like the sound of this. 'What do you want?'

Bernie made a smoochy sound.

'Gross!'

'It's because I'm short, isn't it?'

'No. Of course not. I like short men. They, um, try harder.'

'Then it's the hair, right? You want a guy with hair.'

'Hair doesn't matter. I couldn't care less about hair. And besides, you have plenty of hair. It's just not on the top of your head.'

'Then what?'

'You don't just go around making smoochy sounds at women! It's . . . cheap.'

'I thought you said you were friends with Joyce.'

'Oh yeah. I see your point.'

'So how about it?'

'The truth is, I'm not actually attracted to you.'

'I knew it. I could tell all along. It's my height.'

Jeez, the poor schnook really had a thing about his height. I mean, it wasn't as if he could help being born short or having a head like a bowling ball. I didn't want to compound his problem, but I didn't know what to say. And then I thought of Sally! 'It's not your height,' I said. 'It's me. I'm a lesbian.'

'You're shitting me!'

'No. Really.'

He looked me up and down. 'Are you sure? Christ, what a waste! You don't look like a lesbian.'

I guess he thought lesbians had a big *L* burned into their foreheads, or something. Although, since I don't know any lesbians I'm not exactly an authority.

'You have a girlfriend?' he asked.

'Yeah, sure. She's . . . waiting in the car.'

'I want to see her.'

'Why?'

'Because I don't believe you, I think you're just trying to be nice to me.'

'Look, Bernie, I want some information on Nowicki.'

'Not until I see your girlfriend.'

This was ridiculous. 'She's shy.'

'Okay, I'll go out there.'

'No! I'll go get her.' Jesus!

I jogged out to the parking lot and leaned in the window at Lula. 'I'm in kind of a bind here. I need you to help me out. I need a lesbian girlfriend.'

'You want me to find you one? Or you want me to be one?'

I explained the situation to her, and we hoofed it back to Bernie, who was rearranging his grapefruits.

'Hey, little dude,' Lula said. 'What's the word?'

Bernie looked up from the grapefruits and almost jumped out of his shoes. 'Whoa!'

Guess Bernie hadn't expected my girlfriend to be a two-hundred-pound black woman wearing pink spandex.

'Jeez!' Bernie said. 'Jeez!'

'So Stephanie tells me you know old lady Nowicki.'

Bernie vigorously nodded his head. 'Yeah.'

'You see her lately?'

Bernie just stared at Lula.

'Earth to Bernie,' Lula said.

'Unh?'

'You see old lady Nowicki lately?'

'Yesterday. She came in to get some, you know, fruit.'

'How often does she like to buy fruit?'

Bernie chewed on his lower lip. 'Hard to say. She's not regular.'

Lula draped an arm around Bernie and almost smothered him in her right breast. 'See, the thing is, Bern, we'd like to talk to Nowicki, but we're having a hard time finding her on account of she's not staying in her house. Now if you could help us out here, we'd be grateful. *Real* grateful.'

A bead of sweat rolled down the side of Bernie's face, from his bald dome to in front of his ear. 'Oh crap,' he said. And I could tell from the way he said it that he wanted to help us out.

Lula gave him another squeeze. 'Well?'

'I dunno. I dunno. She never says much.'

'She always come in alone?'

'Yeah.'

I gave him my card. 'If you remember something, or if you see Nowicki, you give me a call right away.'

'Sure. Don't worry.'

We got to the car, and I had another one of those weird thoughts. 'Wait here,' I said to Lula. 'I'll be right back.'

Bernie had been standing in the front of the store, watching us through the glass. 'Now what?' he said. 'You forget something?'

'When Nowicki bought her fruit from you, did she pay you with a twenty?'

He sounded surprised at the question. 'Yeah.'

'You still have it?'

He stared at me blank-faced for a minute. 'I guess . . .' He took his wallet from his back pocket and looked inside. 'Here it is. It's the only twenty I got. It must be it.'

I rooted around in my shoulder bag and found some money. I counted out two tens. 'I'll trade you.'

'Is that it?' he asked.

I gave him a sly smile. 'For now.'

'You know, I wouldn't mind just watching.'

I patted him on the top of his head. 'Hold that thought.'

'We didn't find out much,' Lula said when I got into the car.

'We know she was in Trenton yesterday.'

'Not many places three women can stay in Trenton,' Lula said. 'Not like down the shore where there's lots of motels and lots of houses to rent. Hell, the only hotels we got charge by the hour.'

That was true. It was the state capital, and it didn't actually have a hotel. This might leave people to think no one wanted to stay in Trenton, but I was sure this was a wrong assumption. Trenton is cool. Trenton has everything . . . except a hotel.

Of course, just because Nowicki was doing business with Bernie didn't mean she had to be in Trenton proper.

We took one last spin past Eddie Kuntz's house, the Nowicki house and Margie's house. All were dark and deserted.

Lula dropped me off in front of Morelli's house and shook her head. 'That Morelli got one fine ass, but I don't know if I'd want to live with a cop.'

My sentiments exactly.

The windows were open to bring air into the house, and Morelli's television carried out to the street. He was watching a ball game. I felt the truck hood. Warm. He'd just gotten home. His front door was open like the windows, but the screen door was locked.

'Hey!' I yelled. 'Anybody home?'

Morelli padded out barefoot. 'That was fast.'

'Didn't seem all that fast to me.'

He relocked the screen and went back to the television.

I don't mind going out to the ballpark. You could sit in the sun and drink beer and eat hot dogs, and the whole thing was an event. Baseball on television put me into a coma. I dug into my pocket, found the twenty and passed it over to Morelli. 'I stopped for a soda in north Trenton and got this in change. I thought it'd be fun to check its authenticity.'

Morelli looked up from the game. 'Let me get this straight. You bought a soda, and you got a twenty in change. What'd you give her, a fifty?'

'Okay, so I don't want to tell you where I got it right now.'

Morelli examined the bill. 'Goddamn,' he said. He turned it over and held it to the light. Then he patted the couch cushion next to him. 'We need to talk.'

I sat down with reservation. 'It's phony, isn't it?'

'Yep.'

'I had a hunch. Is it easy to tell?'

'Only if you know what to look for. There's a small line in the upper right corner where the plate is scratched. They tell me the paper isn't exactly right, either, but I can't see it. I only know by the scratch mark.'

'Was the guy you tried to bust from north Trenton?'

'No. And I was pretty sure he was working alone. Counterfeiting like this is usually a mom-and-pop deal. Very small.' He draped his arm over the back of the couch and stroked the nape of my neck with a single finger. 'Now, about the twenty . . .'

CHAPTER THIRTEEN

I T WAS HOPELESS. Morelli was going to worm this out of me.

'The twenty came from Francine Nowicki, Maxine's mother,' I said. 'She passed it to a dope dealer yesterday.'

I told him the rest of the story, and when I was done he had a strange expression on his face.

'How do you walk into these things? It's . . . spooky.'

'Maybe I have the eye.'

As soon as I said it I regretted it. The eye was like the monster under the bed. Not something to tempt out of hiding.

'I really thought it was a one-man operation,' Morelli said. 'The guy we were watching fit the profile. We watched him for five months. And we never pegged anyone as being an accomplice.'

'It would explain a lot about Maxine.'

'Yeah, but I still don't get it. During that five-month period this guy never made physical contact with Kuntz or Maxine.'

'Did you actually see him passing the money?'

'No. That was part of the problem. Everything we had on him was circumstantial and coincidence.'

'Then why did you move?'

'It was the Feds' call. There were events that led us to believe he was printing.'

'But he wasn't.'

'No. Not money, anyway.' Morelli looked at the twenty again. 'It's very possible there are just a bunch of these twenties floating around, and Nowicki's mother inadvertently passed one on.'

There was a knock on the door, and Morelli went to get it.

It was Sally. 'He's bananas!' Sally said. 'He tried to kill me! The poor dumb sonnovabitch tried to fucking kill me.'

Sally looked like an overgrown, demented, testosterone-gone-berserk schoolgirl. Plaid pleated skirt, crisp white blouse, grungy sweat socks and beat-up Reeboks. No makeup, no wig, two day beard, hairy chest peeking out the top of the blouse.

'Who's trying to kill you?' I asked. I assumed it was his roomie, but with the way Sally was dressed it could be most anyone.

'Sugar. He's freaked out. Stormed out of the club after the gig on Sunday night and didn't come home until about an hour ago. Walked in the door with a gallon of gasoline and a Bic lighter and said he was going to torch the place, claiming he was in love with me. Can you believe it?'

'Go figure.'

'He was ranting on about how everything was fine until you showed up, and then I stopped paying attention to him.'

'Doesn't he know you're not gay?'

'He said if you hadn't interfered I would have developed an attraction for him.' Sally ran his hand through his Wild Man of Borneo hair. 'My luck, someone goes fucking gonzo over me, and it's a guy.'

'Could have something to do with the way you dress.'

Sally looked down at his skirt. 'I was trying this on when he barged in. I'm thinking of changing my image to wholesome.'

Morelli and I both bit into our lower lips.

'So what happened?' Morelli asked. 'Did he set fire to the apartment?'

'No. I wrestled the gas can out of his hands and threw it out the window. He tried to set fire to the rug with his Bic, but the rug wouldn't burn. All he did was make big black melt spots and stink the place up. Synthetic fibers, you know. Finally he gave up and ran away to get more gas. I decided I wasn't going to wait around to get turned into a briquette, so I stuffed a bunch of clothes into a couple of garbage bags and took off.'

Morelli had a grim expression on his face. 'And you came here.'

'Yeah. I thought with the way you handled him in the club, and with you being a cop and all, this was a safe place to stay.' He held up his hands. 'Just for a couple days! I don't want to impose.'

'Shit,' Morelli said. 'What does this look like, a halfway house for potential victims of homicidal maniacs?'

'It might not be such a bad idea,' I said. 'If Sally let it be known he was living here, we might draw Sugar in.'

Truth is, I was enormously relieved to know the identity of the firebomber. And I was sort of relieved to find it was Sugar. Better than the mob. And better than the guy who cuts off fingers.

'Two things wrong with that,' Morelli said. 'Number one, I can't get excited about my house being turned into an inferno. Number two, grabbing Sugar won't do much good if we can't convict him of a crime.'

'No problem there,' Sally said. 'He told me about how he firebombed Stephanie's apartment and how he tried to burn down this house, too.'

'You willing to testify to that?'

'I can do better than testify. I've got his diary out in the car. It's filled with juicy details.'

Morelli leaned against the counter, arms crossed over his chest. 'The only way I'll agree to this is if neither of you actually stays here. You put the word out that you're living with me, and twice a day you go in and out the front door, so it looks real. Then I put you in a safe house for the night.'

'Put Sally in a safe house,' I said. 'I'll help with surveillance.'

'No way,' Sally said. 'I'm not being left out on all the fun.'

'Neither of you does surveillance,' Morelli said. 'And it's not open to debate. It's my way or it's no way.'

'What safe house did you have in mind?'

Morelli thought about it a minute. 'I could probably put you with one of my relatives.'

'Oh no! Your grandmother would find me and give me the eye.'

'What's the eye?' Sally wanted to know.

'It's a curse,' I said. 'It's one of those Italian things.'

Sally shivered. 'I don't like that curse stuff. One time I was down in the islands, and I accidentally ran over this voodoo person's chicken, and the voodoo person said she was gonna make my dick fall off.'

'Well?' Morelli asked. 'Did it fall off?'

'Not yet, but I think it might be getting smaller.'

Morelli grimaced. 'I don't want to hear this.'

'I'll go home to my parents,' I said. 'And Sally can come with me.'

We both looked at Sally in the skirt.

'You have any jeans in the car?' I asked.

'I don't know what I have. I was in a real rush. I didn't want to be there when Sugar got back with more gasoline.'

Morelli put in a call to have Sugar picked up, and then we dragged Sally's clothes in from his car. We left the Porsche parked at the curb, behind the Buick, and we pulled the shades on the front downstairs windows. Then Morelli called his cousin, Mooch, to come get Sally and me at nine in the alley behind his house.

Thirty minutes later Morelli got a call from Dispatch. Two uniforms had gone over to check on Sally's apartment and had found it on fire. The building had been evacuated without injury. And Dispatch said the fire was under control.

'He must have come back right away,' Sally said. 'I didn't think he'd set fire to everything if I was gone. It must have just about killed him to torch all of those cakes and pies.'

'I'm really sorry,' I said. 'Do you want me to go over there with you? Do you want to see it?'

'I'm not going anywhere near that place until Sugar's strapped to a bed in the loony bin. Besides, it wasn't even my place. I was renting from Sugar. All the furniture was his.'

'You see, this is much better,' my mother said, opening the door for me. 'I have your bedroom all ready. As soon as you called we put on new sheets.'

'That's nice,' I said. 'If it's okay with you, I'll let Sally sleep in my room, and I'll bunk with Grandma Mazur. It'll only be for a day or two.'

'Sally?'

'He's just behind me. He had to get his bags out of the car.'

My mother looked over my shoulder and froze as Sally ambled into the foyer.

'Yo, dudes,' Sally said.

'What's happening?' Grandma chimed back.

'Jesus H. Christ,' my father said, from his chair in the living room.

I carted Rex off to the kitchen and set his cage on the counter. 'No one's supposed to know Sally and I are living here.'

My mother looked pale. 'I won't tell a soul. And I'll kill anyone who does.'

My father was on his feet. 'What kind of getup is that?' he asked, pointing at Sally. 'Is that a kilt? Are you a Scot?'

'Heck no,' Grandma said. 'He's no Scot. He's a transvestite . . . only he doesn't strap down his dingdong on account of it gives him a rash.'

My father looked at Sally. 'You mean you're one of them Tinkerbell boys?'

Sally stood up a little taller. 'You got a problem with that?'

'What kind of car you drive?'

'Porsche.'

My father threw his hands in the air. 'You see? A Porsche. Not even an American car. That's what's wrong with you weirdos. You don't want to do nothing like you're supposed to. There wasn't anything wrong with this country when everybody was buying American cars. Now everywhere you look it's some Japanese piece of caca and look at the trouble we're in.'

'Porsche is German.'

My father rolled his eyes. 'German! Now there's a country. They can't even win a war. You think they're gonna help me get what I got coming to me from Social Security?'

I grabbed one of the garbage bags. 'Let me help you get this upstairs.'

Sally followed after me. 'You sure this is okay?'

I had the bag halfway to the second floor. 'Yeah. My father likes you. I could tell.'

'No, I don't,' my father said. 'I think he's a fruit-cake. And any man who looks that bad in a skirt has a patriotic duty to stay in the closet where no one can see him.'

I pushed the bedroom door open, set the bag inside, and gave Sally fresh towels.

Sally was standing in front of the mirror I had on the back of my door.

'You think I look bad in this skirt?' Sally asked.

I studied the skirt. I didn't want to hurt his feelings, but he looked like a mutant from Planet of the Apes. He was probably the hairiest transvestite ever to wear a garter belt. 'It's not terrible, but I think you're more of a straight skirt kind of guy. And leather is good on you.'

'Dolores Dominatrix.'

More like Wanda the Werewolf. 'You could go with the wholesome look,' I said, 'but it would require a lot of shaving.'

'Fuck that,' Sally said. 'I hate shaving.'

'You could try a body waxing.'

'Man, I did that once. Shit, it hurt like hell.'

Good thing he didn't have ovaries.

'Now what?' Sally said. 'I can't go to bed this early. I'm a night person.'

'We don't have a car so we're sort of limited, but Morelli's only about a half mile from here. We could walk over and see if anything's happening. Look through your stuff and see if you have something dark.'

Five minutes later Sally came downstairs in black jeans and a faded black T-shirt.

'We're going for a walk,' I said. 'Don't feel like you have to wait up. I have a key.'

Grandma sidled up to me. 'Do you want the "big boy"?' she whispered.

'No, but thanks for offering.'

SALLY AND I strained our eyes and ears all the way to Morelli's neighborhood. Unlike Lula, who never admitted to being scared, Sally and I were perfectly comfortable with the knowledge that Sugar had us ready to jump out of our skin.

We stopped at the corner of Morelli's block and looked things over. There were cars on either side of the street. No vans. Morelli's truck was parked, so I guessed Morelli was home. Shades were still drawn, and the lights were on. I assumed there was someone watching the outside of the house, but I couldn't pick him out.

This was a nice neighborhood. Similar to my parents'. Not as prosperous. Houses were mostly occupied by seniors who'd lived there all their adult lives or by young couples just starting out. The seniors were on fixed incomes, clipping coupons, buying tennis shoes on sale at

K-mart, doing only the most essential house maintenance, thankful their mortgages were paid and they could stay in their homes for taxes. The young couples painted and papered and filled their houses with furniture from Sears. And they marked time while they built equity and hoped their properties would appreciate, so they could buy bigger tract houses in Hamilton Township.

I turned to Sally. 'Do you think Sugar will come here looking for you?'

'If he doesn't come for me, he'll come for you. He was fucking flipped out.'

We walked to the middle of the block and stared across the street at Morelli's house. A shoe scuffed on the stoop behind us, and a figure slid from deep shadow. Morelli.

'Out for a stroll?' he asked.

I looked beyond him at the bike parked on the small yard. 'Is that a Ducati?'

'Yeah. I don't get to ride it much.'

I moved closer. It was the 916 Superbike. Red. The motorcycle to die for. Smart choice for tailing someone who'd just firebombed your house. Faster and better maneuverability than a car. I found myself liking Morelli more now that I knew he owned a Duc.

'You out here alone?' I asked.

'For now. Roice is coming on at two.'

'I guess they weren't able to pick Sugar up.'

'We're looking for the car, but so far it's a big zero.'

Headlights appeared at the end of the street, and we all shrank back against the house. The car rolled past us and turned two blocks down. We eased forward, out of hiding.

'Sugar have friends outside of the band?' Morelli asked Sally.

'Lots of casual friends. Not many close ones. When I first joined the band, Sugar had a lover.'

'Would Sugar go to him for help?'

'Not likely. It wasn't a happy parting.'

'How about the band? You have anything scheduled?'

'Rehearsal on Friday. Club date on Saturday.'

That seemed like a millennium away. And Sugar would have to be a fool to show up. It had been stupid of him to attack Morelli. Cops get touchy when someone drops a firebomb in a fellow officer's house.

'Get in touch with the other band members,' Morelli said to Sally. 'Let them know you're staying with Stephanie and me. Ask if they've seen Sugar.'

I looked over at Morelli. 'You'll call me if anything happens?'

'Sure.'

'You have my pager number?'

'Committed to memory.'

I'd done this drill before. He wouldn't call me. Not until it was all over.

Sally and I crossed the street, entered Morelli's house, walked the length of it and exited the back door. I stood for a moment in the yard and thought about Morelli, lost in shadow again, his street appearing deserted. It gave me a creepy feeling. If Morelli could disappear, so could Sugar.

ONCE A WEEK Grandma Mazur went to the beauty parlor and had her hair shampooed and set. Sometimes Dolly would use a rinse and Grandma would have hair the color of an anemic apricot, but mostly Grandma lived with her natural color of steel gray. Grandma kept her hair short and permed with orderly rows of curls marching across her shiny pink scalp. The curls stayed miraculously tidy until the end of the week, when they'd begin to flatten and blend together.

I'd always wondered how Grandma had managed this feat. And now I knew. Grandma rolled her pillow under her neck so barely any skull touched the bed. And Grandma slept like the dead. Arms crossed over her chest, body straight as a board, mouth open. Grandma never moved a muscle, and she snored like a drunken lumberjack.

I crawled out of bed at six A.M. bleary-eyed and rattled from my night's experience. I'd had maybe thirty minutes of sleep, and that had been accumulated time. I grabbed some clothes and dressed in the bathroom. Then I crept downstairs and made coffee.

An hour later I heard movement overhead and recognized my mother's footsteps on the stairs.

'You look terrible,' she said. 'You feel okay?'

'You ever try to sleep with Grandma?'

'She sleeps like the dead.'

'You got it.'

Doors opened and slammed shut upstairs, and my grandmother yelled for my father to get out of the bathroom.

'I'm an old lady,' she yelled. 'I can't wait all day. What are you doing in there anyway?'

More doors slamming, and my father clomped into the kitchen and took his place at the breakfast table. 'I gotta go out with the cab this morning,' he said. 'Jones is in Atlantic City, and I said I'd cover his shift.'

My parents owned their house free and clear, and my father got a decent pension from the post office. He didn't need the money from hacking. What he needed was to get out of the house, away from my mother and my grandmother.

The stairs creaked, and an instant later Sally's frame filled the doorway. His hair stood out from his head in snarls, his eyes were half closed and he stood stoop shouldered and barefoot, hairy arms dangling from my too-small, fuzzy pink robe.

'Man,' he said, 'this house is frantic. I mean, like, what time is it, dude?'

'Oh jeez,' my father said, grim-faced, 'he's wearing ladies' clothes again.'

'It was in the closet,' Sally said. 'Guess the clothes fairy left it for me.'

My father opened his mouth to say something, my mother gave him a sharp look, and my father snapped his mouth shut.

'What's that you're eating?' Sally asked.

'Cereal.'

'Far out.'

'Would you like some?'

He shuffled to the coffeemaker. 'Just coffee.'

Grandma Mazur hustled in. 'What's going on? I didn't miss anything, did I?'

I was sitting at the table, and I could feel her breath on the back of my head. 'Something wrong?'

'Just looking at this new-style hairdo you got. Never seen anything like it, what with these big chunks cut outta the back.'

I closed my eyes. The egg. 'How bad is it?' I asked my mother.

'If you have some free time you might want to go to the beauty parlor.'

'I thought it was some punk thing,' Sally said. 'It'd be rad if it was purple. Maybe spiked out.'

AFTER BREAKFAST, SALLY and I took another walk over to Morelli's house. We stood in the alley behind the house, and I dialed Morelli on my cell phone.

'I'm in your yard,' I told him. 'I didn't want to walk through your back door and get blown away.'

'No problem.'

Morelli was at the sink, rinsing out his coffee mug. 'I was just getting ready to take off,' he said. 'They found Kuntz's car parked in the farmers' market lot by the tracks.'

'And?'

'That's it.'

'Blood? Bullet holes?'

'Nope,' Morelli said. 'A-one condition. At first glance doesn't look like anything was stolen. No vandalism. No sign of struggle.'

'Was it locked?'

'Yep. My guess is it was left there sometime early this morning. Any sooner than that and it would have been stripped clean.'

'Anything happen here last night?'

'Nothing. Very quiet. What are you up to today?'

I picked at my hair. 'Beauty parlor.'

A grin tugged at the corners of Morelli's mouth. 'Going to ruin my handiwork?'

'You didn't take any more hair off than you absolutely had to, right?'

'Right,' Morelli said, the grin still in place.

Usually, I got my hair done by Mr. Alexander at the mall. Unfortunately, Mr. Alexander couldn't work me into his busy schedule today, so I opted for Grandma's salon, the Clip and Curl on Hamilton. I had a nine-thirty appointment. Not that it mattered. My gossip rating was so high I could walk into Clip and Curl any time of the day or night, no waiting necessary.

We left through the front door, and I noticed the van parked across the street.

'Grossman,' Morelli said.

'He have a Duc in that van?'

'No. He's got a two-way radio, a crossword puzzle book, and a jelly jar.'

I had my eye on the Porsche and the butter-soft leather seats. And I knew I'd look very cool in the Porsche.

'Forget it,' Morelli said. 'Take the Buick. If you get into trouble the Buick is built like a tank.'

'I'm going to the beauty parlor,' I said. 'I'm not going to get into trouble.'

'Cupcake, your middle name is trouble.'

Sally was standing between the Porsche and the Buick. 'So, like, what's it gonna be?' he asked.

'The Porsche,' I said. 'Definitely the Porsche.'

Sally buckled himself in. 'This car does zero to a hundred in a fucking second.' He cranked the engine over and catapulted us off the curb.

'Yow!' I said. 'This is a family neighborhood. Slow down!'

Sally looked at me from behind reflector shades. 'I like speed, man. Speed is good.'

I had my hands braced on the dashboard. 'Stop street! *Stop street!*'

'Stops on a dime,' Sally said, stomping on the brake.

I jerked against the shoulder harness. 'Ulk.'

Sally laid an affectionate hand on the steering wheel. 'This car is like a total engineering experience.'

'Are you on drugs?'

'No way. Not this early in the day,' Sally said. 'What do I look like, a bum?'

He turned onto Hamilton and lead-footed it to Clip and Curl. He parked and looked at the shop over the tops of his glasses. 'Retro.'

Dolly had converted the downstairs part of her two-story house into a beauty parlor. I'd come here as a little girl to get my bangs cut, and nothing had changed since then. If it was midday or Saturday, the place would be packed. Since it was early morning only two women were under dryers. Myrna Olsen and Doris Zayle.

'Ommigod,' Myrna said, shouting over the noise of the dryer. 'I just heard the news about you marrying Joseph Morelli. Congratulations.'

'I always knew you two would get married,' Doris said, pushing the dryer off her head. 'You were made for each other.'

'Hey, I didn't know you dudes were married,' Sally said. 'Way to go.'

Everyone gaped at Sally. Men didn't come into the Clip and Curl. And Sally pretty much looked like a man today . . . with the possible exceptions of his lip gloss and two-inch dangly rhinestone earrings.

'This is Sally,' I told them.

'Chill,' Sally said, giving them a rapper fist kind of greeting. 'Thought maybe I'd get a manicure. My nails are like trashed.'

They looked confused.

'Sally's a drag queen,' I said.

'Isn't that something,' Myrna said. 'Imagine.'

Doris leaned forward. 'Do you wear dresses?'

'Mostly skirts,' Sally said. 'I'm too long-waisted for dresses. I don't think they're flattering. Of course, I have a couple gowns. Gowns are different. *Everyone* looks good in a gown.'

'Being a drag queen must be so glamorous,' Myrna said.

'Yeah, well, it's okay until they start to throw beer bottles at you,' Sally said. 'Getting hit with beer bottles is a fucking bummer.'

Dolly examined my hair. 'What on earth happened to you? It looks like someone cut big chunks out of your hair.'

'I got egg stuck in it, and it got hard, and it had to get cut out.'

Myrna and Doris rolled their eyes at each other and went back under the dryers.

An hour later Sally and I slid back into the Porsche. Sally had cherry-red nails, and I looked like Grandma Mazur. I looked at myself in the visor mirror and felt tears pooling behind my eyes. My naturally curly hair was cut short, and perfect Tootsie Roll curls covered my head.

'Massive,' Sally said. 'They look like fucking dog turds.'

'You should have told me she was doing this!'

'I couldn't see. I was drying my nails. Excellent manicure.'

'Take me to Joe's house. I'm going to get my gun and kill myself.'

'It just needs to be a little mussed,' Sally said. He reached over. 'Let me fix it up for you. I'm good at this.'

I looked in the mirror when he was done. '*Eeeeek!*' I looked like Sally.

'See,' he said. 'I know just how to do it. I have naturally curly hair, too.'

I took another look. I guessed it was better than the dog turds.

'Maybe we should cruise over to north Trenton,' I said. 'Check out Eddie Kuntz. Make sure he isn't sitting in his kitchen having lunch.'

Sally stepped on the gas, and my head snapped back.

'Jackrabbit start,' he said.

'How long have you had this car?'

'Three weeks.'

My radar was tingling. 'You have a license?'

'Used to.'

Oh boy.

THE LINCOLN TOWN Car was in front of the Glick half of the house. Of course, Kuntz's half was without car.

'This doesn't feel good,' I said to Sally.

'Like maybe ol' Eddie Kuntz is fish food.'

I imagined, now that Eddie's car had been found abandoned, his aunt and uncle would be wringing their hands. Maybe they'd be distraught enough to let me into Eddie's apartment to snoop around.

Leo Glick opened his front door before I had a chance to knock.

'Saw you drive up,' he said. 'What kind of cockamammy car is that anyway? Looks like a big silver egg.'

'It's a Porsche,' Sally said.

Leo squinted at him. 'What's with the earrings?'

'I felt like being pretty today, man,' Sally said, shaking

his head to give Leo the full effect. 'See how they sparkle in the sun? Fucking awesome, huh?'

Leo backed up a step, as if Sally might be dangerous. 'What do you want?' he asked me.

'I don't suppose you've heard from Eddie?'

'Don't suppose I have. And I gotta tell you I'm getting sick of people asking about him. First the cops come this morning to tell us about his car. Big deal. He left his car somewhere. Then some bimbo comes around asking about him. And now here you are on my doorstep with Miss America.'

'What kind of bimbo? Do you remember her name?'

'Joyce.'

Great. Just what I need. More Joyce.

'Who is it?' Betty called from inside the house. She looked around Leo's shoulder. 'Oh, it's you. Why do you keep bothering us? Why don't you just mind your own business?'

'I'm surprised you aren't more worried about your nephew. What about his parents? Aren't his parents worried?'

'His parents are in Michigan. Visiting. We got relatives there,' Leo said. 'And we aren't worried, because Eddie's a bum. He does this all the time. The only reason we put up with him is because he's blood. We give him cheap rent, but that don't mean we have to baby-sit him.'

'You mind if I look around?'

'Damn right I mind,' Leo said. 'I don't want no one creeping around my house.'

'As it is, I've had the phone ringing ever since the police were here. Everyone wanting to know what's going on,' Betty said.

'Next thing you know there'll be TV trucks pulling

up, and I'll be on the evening news because *her* nephew's a bum.'

'He's your nephew, too,' Betty said.

'Only by marriage, and that don't hardly count.'

'He's not so bad,' Betty said.

'He's a bum. *A bum!*'

CHAPTER FOURTEEN

Sally AND I stood at the curb by the Porsche and watched the Glicks making shooing motions at us.

'They're like . . . lame people,' Sally said.

'When I first met them I had the feeling they liked Kuntz. At least Betty. In the beginning she was inviting me in for pound cake. And she was warm. Sort of motherly.'

'Maybe they're the ones who offed ol' Eddie. Maybe he didn't pay his rent. Maybe he insulted Betty's pound cake.'

I didn't think they offed Eddie Kuntz, but I did think they were acting odd. If I had to pin down emotions I'd say they were scared and angry. They definitely didn't want me sticking my nose into their business. Which meant either they had something to hide or else they didn't like me. Since I couldn't imagine anyone not liking me, I was going to assume they had something to hide. And the most obvious thing they would have to hide would be knowledge of Eddie Kuntz. Like maybe whoever snatched him had gotten in touch with Uncle Leo and Aunt Betty and had scared the beejeebers out of them.

Or here's another thought. Maybe Kuntz's mixed up with the counterfeit stuff and has gone underground. Maybe the note passed through the bartender was to warn him. And maybe Kuntz told Uncle Leo that he's okay and that Leo should keep his mouth shut and not let anybody come snooping . . . or else. Jesus, maybe his closets are filled with stacks of twenties!

Betty was still making the shooing sounds, but now she was mouthing the word *go*.

'How about I drive,' I said to Sally. 'I've always wanted to drive a Porsche.' Also, I've always wanted to live.

My pager went off, and I looked at the number. It wasn't familiar. I hauled my cell phone out of my shoulder bag and dialed.

The voice at the other end was excited. 'Jeez, that was fast!'

I squinted at the phone. Like squinting would help me to think better. 'Who is this?'

'Bernie! You know, the vegetable guy. And I got news for you. Francine Nowicki just came in. She wanted some special produce, if you get my drift.'

Yes! 'Is she there now?'

'Yeah. I was real smart. I told her I couldn't get anything for her until I went on my break, and then I called you right away. I figured your friend said she'd be grateful and all.'

'I'm on my way. Make sure Mrs. Nowicki stays there until I arrive.'

'Your friend's with you, right?'

I disconnected and jumped into the car. 'We just got a break!' I said, buckling myself in, plugging the key into the ignition. 'Mama Nowicki's shopping for fruit.'

'Far out,' Sally said. 'Fruit is cosmic.'

I didn't want to tell him what sort of fruit Bernie was selling. I was afraid he'd clean Bernie out and there wouldn't be any left for Maxine's mother.

I took off from the curb with my foot to the floor.

'*Wow!* Warp speed Mr. Sulu,' Sally said. 'Excellent.'

Ten minutes later, give or take a few seconds, I cruised into the supermarket lot and parked. I wrote a note to Bernie telling him to give Francine Nowicki enough 'produce' for only one day, and instructed him to tell her she'd have to come back tomorrow for the rest. Just in case I lost her today. I signed it 'Love and kisses, your new friend, Stephanie.' And then I added that Lula sent her love, too.

'There's a little guy in the produce department who looks like R2D2,' I told Sally. 'Give him this note and take off. If you see Maxine's mother, don't go near her. Just give Bernie the note and come back here, so we can follow her when she leaves.'

Sally loped across the lot on his long legs, earring glittering in the sunlight, rat's nest hair bobbing as he walked. He swung through the big glass doors and turned toward Produce. I lost sight of him for a moment and then he was back in my line of vision.

'She was there,' he said, folding himself into the little car. 'I saw her standing by the apples. You can't miss her with that big bandage on her head. She's got it covered with a scarf, but you can still see it's a bandage underneath.'

I'd chosen a spot off to the side, next to a van so we'd be less visible. We fell into silence, watching the door.

'There!' Sally yelped. 'She's coming out!'

We scrunched down in our seats, but it wasn't necessary. Mrs. Nowicki was parked in the front on the other side of the lot. And she wasn't being careful. Just another day in the life of a housewife. Out to do the marketing, scoring some dope from Businessman Bernie.

She was driving an old, beat-up Escort. If she was flush with funny money, she sure wasn't spending it on transportation. I let her get some space on me, and then I crept out of the lot after her. After a half mile I had a depressing feeling about her destination. After another half mile I was sure. She was going home. Maxine wasn't Albert Einstein, but I also didn't think she was dumb enough to hide out at her mother's house.

Mrs. Nowicki parked in front of her house and shuffled inside. If I thought Maxine was on the premises I had the right as a bounty hunter to break down the door and go in guns drawn. I wasn't going to do this because, first off, I didn't have a gun with me. And secondly, I'd feel like an idiot.

'Guess it wouldn't hurt to talk to her,' I said.

Sally and I knocked on the door and Mrs. Nowicki swayed into view. 'Look what the cat drug in,' she said.

'How's your head?' This was my friendly approach, designed to throw drunken, pothead Mrs. Nowicki off guard.

She drew on her cigarette. 'My head's peachy. How's your car?'

So much for friendly. 'The insurance company felt sorry for me, so they gave me this Porsche.'

'Yeah, up your ass,' she said. 'The Porsche belongs to the freak.'

'Seen Maxine lately?'

'Not since she took off at the beach.'

'You left the house early.'

'Got tired of sand,' Mrs. Nowicki said. 'What's it to you?'

I moved past her, into her living room. 'You don't mind if I look around?'

'You got a search warrant?'

'Don't need one.'

Her eyes followed me as I moved through the house. 'This is harassment.'

It was a small bungalow. All on one floor. Easy to see Maxine wasn't there. 'Looks like you're packing.'

'Yeah, I'm cleaning out my Dior stuff. I decided I was only wearing Versace from now on.'

'If you see Maxine . . .'

'Right. I'm gonna call you.'

There was an end table and chair by the door. A .38 had been placed on the end table.

'You think you need that?' I asked.

Mrs. Nowicki stubbed her cigarette out in the ashtray by the gun. 'Doesn't hurt to be careful.'

We got back in the car and my pager beeped, displaying my mother's number.

Grandma answered my callback. 'We just wanted to know if you'll be home for dinner,' Grandma said.

'Probably.'

'And what about Sally?'

'Sally, too.'

'I saw he was wearing rhinestones when he went out today. You think I should get dressed up for supper?'

'Not necessary.'

I took off and drove back to the supermarket. I had one last detail to check out with Bernie.

Sally and I staggered through the heat into the air-conditioned store. Bernie was ripping leaves off heads of lettuce when he saw us. His eyes got round, and by the time we got up to him, he was jiggling around, unable to stand still.

'Oh man,' Bernie said, 'you're back! Holy cow!' He

was beaming at Sally, and he was wringing his hands. 'I thought I recognized you, but I wasn't sure. And then when I saw you just now I knew! You're Sally Sweet! Jeez, I'm a big fan. A *big* fan! I go to the club all the time. I love that all-girl review. Boy, you guys are great. And that Sugar. She's the best. I could really go for her. She's the most beautiful woman I've ever seen.'

'Sugar's a guy,' I said.

'Get out!'

'Hey,' I said. 'I know about these things.'

'Oh yeah. I forgot. You look so normal.'

'Did Francine Nowicki pay you with another twenty?'

'Yep. I got it right here.' He took it out of his shirt pocket. 'And I did what you said. I only gave her a couple pieces of fruit. Too bad, too, because I could have made a real killing. She had a lot of money on her. She took out a roll of twenties big enough to choke a horse.'

I took the twenty from him and looked at it. It had the scratch mark in the corner.

Bernie was on tiptoe, trying to see the bill. 'What's with the interest in the twenty. It marked or something?'

'No. Just checking to see if it's real.'

'Well? Is it?'

'Yep.' Real counterfeit.

'We need to go now,' I said. 'Thanks for calling me.'

'My pleasure.' He was gaping at Sally again. 'It's been a real treat to meet you,' he said. 'I don't suppose I could have your autograph.'

Sally took the black marking pen out of Bernie's shirt pocket and wrote 'Best wishes from Sally Sweet' on Bernie's bald dome.

'There you go, dude,' Sally said.

'Oh man,' Bernie said, looking like he'd burst with happiness. 'Oh man! This is so great.'

'You do that a lot?' I asked Sally.

'Yeah, but usually when I do head writing I have to write a lot smaller.'

'Hmm.'

I wandered over to the cookie aisle to pick out some lunch, and I wondered if Morelli was still watching the 7-Eleven. I could save him a lot of trouble. I was pretty sure Maxine's mother had been the one to pass the phony twenties. It was her neighborhood store. And she didn't seem shy about floating the bad bills. The upside to telling Morelli about Francine Nowicki passing another bogus twenty dollars was that he'd probably abandon the store and watch Francine for me. The flip side was that if anything went down I couldn't trust him to include me. And if he brought Maxine in, and I wasn't along for the ride, neither Vinnie nor I would get our money.

Sally and I settled on a box of Fig Newtons and a couple of sodas. We went through checkout and ate in the car.

'So, lay this marriage gig on me,' Sally said. 'I always thought Morelli was just nailing you.'

'We're not married. And he's not *nailing* me.'

'Yeah, right.'

'Okay, so he used to be nailing me. Well, actually, he only nailed me for a very short time. And it wasn't nailing. Nailing sounds like body piercing. What we had was . . . uh, consensual sex.'

'Consensual sex is excellent.'

I nodded agreement and popped another Fig Newton into my mouth.

'I guess you got a thing going for Morelli though, huh?'

'I don't know. There's something there. I just can't figure out what it is.'

We chewed Fig Newtons and thought about that for a while.

'You know what I don't get?' Sally said. 'I don't understand why everyone was working so hard to throw us off the trail five days ago, and now old lady Nowicki is back in her house. We walked right up to her, and she didn't care.'

He was right. Obviously something had changed. And my fear was that Maxine was good-bye. If Maxine was safely on her way to a new life, Mrs. Nowicki could afford to take more chances. And so could Margie. I hadn't stopped at Margie's house, but I was sure she was there, packing her valuables, explaining to her cat why Mommy was going to be gone for a long, long time. Probably paying the cat-sitting neighbor off in bad twenties.

But of course she wasn't ready to leave yet. She had a doctor's appointment. And so did Francine. Good thing for me, because I'd be hard-pressed to do surveillance. I wasn't exactly the FBI. I didn't have any of their cool surveillance equipment. For that matter, I didn't even have a car. A silver Porsche, a '53 Buick, and a red Firebird weren't gonna cut it as primo stealth vehicles. I was going to have to find a car that would go unnoticed, so I could sit in front of the Nowicki house tomorrow.

'No!' Morelli said. 'You can't borrow my pickup. You're death on cars.'

'I am *not* death on cars!'

'Last time you used my car it got blown up! Remember that?'

'Well, if you're going to hold that against me . . .'

'And what about your pickup? And your CRX? Blown up!'

'Technically, the CRX caught fire.'

Morelli scrunched his eyes closed and smacked the heel of his hand against his forehead. 'Unh!'

It was a little after four. Sally was watching television in the living room, and Morelli and I were in the kitchen. Morelli'd just gotten in, and he looked like he'd had another one of those days. Probably I should have waited for a better time to ask him about the truck, but I had to be at my mother's in an hour for dinner. Maybe I should try a different approach. I ran my fingertip across his sweat-soaked T-shirt and leaned *very* close. 'You look . . . hot.'

'Honey, I'm about as hot as a man can get.'

'I might be able to do something about that.'

His eyes narrowed. 'Let me get this straight. Are you offering sex for the use of my truck?'

'Well, no, not exactly.'

'Then what *are* you offering?'

I didn't know what I was offering. I'd intended this to be sort of playful, but Morelli wasn't playing.

'I need a beer,' Morelli said. 'I've had a really long day, and it's going to be even longer. I have to relieve Grossman in an hour.'

'Anything new turn up on Kuntz's car?'

'Nothing.'

'Anything happen at the 7-Eleven?'

'Nothing.' He pulled on his beer. 'How was your day?'

'Slow. Not a lot going on.'

'Who you want to watch?'

'Mrs. Nowicki. She moved back into her house. I went in to talk to her, and she was packing.'

'Doesn't mean she's going to take you to Maxine,' Morelli said.

I shrugged. 'It's all I've got.'

'No, it's not,' Morelli said. 'You're sitting on something.'

I raised an eyebrow. It said, Oh yeah?

Morelli chucked the empty beer bottle into the recycling bin. 'This better not have to do with the counterfeiting case I'm on. I'd hate to think you were withholding evidence.'

'Who me?'

He took a step closer and pinned me to the counter. 'So, how bad do you want my truck?'

'Pretty bad.'

His gaze dropped to my mouth. '*How* bad?'

'Not that bad.'

Morelli gave a disgusted sigh and backed off. 'Women.'

Sally was watching MTV, singing along with the groups, doing his head-banger thing.

'Jesus,' Morelli said, looking into the living room, 'it's a wonder he doesn't shake something loose.'

'I CAN'T LOAN you my car,' my father said. 'It's gotta go in to get serviced tomorrow. I got an appointment. What's wrong with the Buick you're driving?'

'The Buick is no good for surveillance,' I said. 'People stare at it.'

We were at the table, and my mother was serving out

stuffed cabbage. *Plop*, onto my plate, four cabbage rolls. I opened the button on my shorts and reached for my fork.

'I need a new car,' I said. 'Where's my insurance money?'

'You need a steady job,' my mother said. 'Something that pays benefits. You're not getting any younger, you know. How long can you go chasing hoodlums all over Trenton? If you had a steady job you could finance a car.'

'Most of the time my job is steady. I just got stuck with a lemon of a case here.'

'You live from hand to mouth.'

What could I say; she was right.

'I could get you a job driving a school bus,' my father said, digging into his dinner. 'I know the guy does the hiring. You make good money driving a school bus.'

'One of them daytime shows did a thing on school bus drivers,' Grandma said. 'And two of the drivers got bleeding hemorrhoids on account of the seats weren't any good.'

My eye had started to twitch again. I put my finger to it to make it stop.

'What's wrong with your eye?' my mother asked. 'Do you have that twitch back?'

'Oh, I almost forgot,' Grandma said. 'One of your friends came looking for you today. I said you were out working, and she gave me a note for you.'

'Mary Lou?'

'No, not Mary Lou. Someone I didn't know. Real pretty. Must have been one of those makeup ladies at the mall, because she was wearing a ton of makeup.'

'Not Joyce!'

'No. I'm telling you it was someone I didn't know. The note's in the kitchen. I left it on the counter by the phone.'

I pushed away from the table and went to get the note. It was in a small, sealed envelope. 'STEPHANIE' had been printed in neat block letters on the face of the envelope. It looked like an invitation to a shower or a birthday party. I opened the envelope and put a hand to the counter to steady myself. The message was simple. 'DIE BITCH.' And in smaller script it said when I least suspected it he'd make his move. It was written on a recipe card.

What was even more disturbing than the message in the note was the fact that Sugar had waltzed right into my parents' house and handed the envelope to Grandma.

I returned to the table and wolfed down three cabbage rolls. I didn't know how to handle this. I needed to warn my family, but I didn't want to scare them half to death.

'Well?' Grandma said. 'What's in the note? Looked like an invitation.'

'That was someone I know from work,' I said. 'Actually, she's not a nice person, so if you ever see her again, don't let her in the house. In fact, don't even open the door to her.'

'Ommigod,' my mother said. 'Another lunatic. Tell me she doesn't want to shoot you.'

'Actually . . .'

My mother made the sign of the cross. 'Holy Mary, mother of God.'

'Don't get going with the Holy Mary stuff,' I said to my mother. 'It's not that bad.'

'So what should I do if I see her again?' Grandma asked. 'You want me to put a hole in her?'

'No! I just don't want you to invite her in for tea!'

My father helped himself to more cabbage rolls. 'Next time put in less rice,' he said.

'Frank,' my mother said, 'are you listening to this?'

My father picked up his head. 'What?'

My mother smacked herself on the forehead.

Sally had been bent over his plate, shoveling in cabbage rolls like there was no tomorrow. He paused and looked at me, and I could hear the gears grinding in his brain. Pretty girl. Lots of makeup. Note. Bad person. 'Uh oh,' Sally said.

'I'm going to have to eat and run,' I said to my mother. 'I have to work tonight.'

'There's chocolate chip cookies for desert.'

I laid my napkin on the table. 'I'll put them in a bag.'

My mother jumped to her feet. 'I'll do it.'

We had labor laws in the burg. Mothers do brown bags. That's it. No exceptions. All over the country people were looking for ways to get out of work. In the burg, housewives militantly guarded their responsibilities. Even working mothers refused to relinquish the assembling of lunch or leftovers. And while other family members might from time to time be recruited to mop the kitchen floor, do the laundry, polish the furniture, no one performed the task to housewife standards.

I took the cookie bag and ushered Sally out of the house. It was early, and we really didn't need to leave, but I didn't think I'd hold up to the grilling. There was no good way to tell my mother I was being stalked by a homicidal drag queen.

My mother and grandmother were at the door, watching us get in the car. They stood backs straight, hands clasped. Lips pressed tight together. Good Hungarian women. My mother wondering where she went wrong, wondering why I was riding around with a man wearing rhinestone earrings. My grandmother wishing she was with us.

'I have a key,' I called to them. 'So, it probably would be a good idea to lock up.'

'Yeah,' Sally added, 'and don't stand in front of any open windows.'

My mother did another sign of the cross.

I started the car. 'We need to end this,' I told Sally. 'I'm fed up with being scared, worrying that Sugar's going to jump out at me and set my hair on fire.'

'I talked to all the guys in the band, and no one's heard from him.'

I drove toward Chambers. Truth is, I'd abdicated dealing with Sugar. 'Tell me about Sugar,' I said. 'Tell me the stuff you told the police.'

'We were roommates for about six months, but I don't know a whole lot about him. His family's in Ohio. They couldn't deal with the gay thing, so Sugar split. I've been with the band for about a year, but in the beginning I mostly hung with the guys from Howling Dogs.

'About six months ago Sugar had this knock-down, drag-out fight with his boyfriend, John. John moved out, and I moved in. Only I wasn't like John, you know. I was like just a roommate.'

'Sugar didn't think so.'

'Guess not. Man, this is a real piece of shit, on account of we were like the perfect roommates. Sugar's a neat freak. Always cleaning, cleaning, cleaning. And I'm like, not into that, so it was cool. I mean, man, we didn't fight over who got to do the fucking vacuuming. And he's real good with the girl shit. He knows all about foundation and blush and the best hair spray. You should have seen me before I moved in with him. I was like a fucking barbarian. I mean, I've like lived with a couple chicks, but

I never paid any attention to how they got the fucking eyeliner on. This girl shit is complicated.

'Sugar knew all about it. He even helped me pick out clothes. That was the one thing we did together. Shop. He was a fucking shopping fool. Sometimes he'd bring clothes home for me. Like I wouldn't even have to go with him.'

So now I understood the shorts with the ass hanging out.

'He was in drag when he gave the note to Grandma,' I said. 'It takes special equipment to look like a woman, and it's unlikely Sugar had time to take anything out of the apartment. So either he has a second apartment or else he bought new.'

'Probably bought new,' Sally said. 'Sugar makes lots of money. Five times what I'm making. Some of the things you need to get in New York, but that's not a real problem.'

'Too bad he torched the apartment. We might have been able to find something there.'

'And the police have the diary.'

Common sense told me to give this over to Joe, but when I ran through the benefits they didn't add up. The department was already motivated to find Sugar. They were probably already putting out the maximum effort. What we needed here was talent from a different direction. What we needed was Ranger.

I called his private number, his pager, and finally connected on his car phone.

'Help,' I said.

'No kidding.'

I filled him in on recent harrowing events.

'Bummer,' Ranger said.

'Yeah, so what do you think I should do?'

'Increase his discomfort. Invade his space and do whatever makes him crazy.'

'In other words, set myself up as a target.'

'Unless you know where he lives. Then we go there and take him down. But I figure you don't know where he lives.'

I looked in my rearview mirror and saw Ranger's black BMW slide to the curb behind me about half a block away.

'How did you find me?' I asked.

'I was in the neighborhood. Saw you turn onto Chambers. Is that guy wearing rhinestones?'

'Yep.'

'Nice touch.'

'Okay, we'll go to Sugar's favorite hangouts. See what we can stir up.'

'I'm in the wind, babe.'

Whatever the hell that meant.

'I HAVE IT all mapped out,' Sally said, pulling into a small parking lot next to a downtown restaurant. 'This is the first stop.'

I looked at the sign on the side of the building. DANTE'S INFERNO. Like, oh boy.

'Don't worry about the name,' Sally said. 'It's just a restaurant. Serves spicy food. Sugar likes spicy food.'

The restaurant was basically one large room. Walls were decorated with faux frescoes depicting various scenes where satyrs and minotaurs frolicked in hell and other hot places. No Sugar.

Two men waved to Sally, and Sally waved back.

'Hey, dudes,' Sally said, moving through the room to their table. 'I'm looking for Sugar. Don't suppose you've seen him tonight?'

'Sorry,' they said. 'Haven't seen Sugar all week.'

After Dante's we did a full circuit of bars and restaurants with no luck.

'I know we're out here doing this looking for Sugar thing,' Sally finally said, 'but the truth is I'd crap in my pants if he all of a sudden popped up. I mean, he's crazy. He could, like, fucking Bic me.'

I was trying not to think about it. I was telling myself Ranger was out there . . . somewhere. And I was trying to be careful, staying alert and on guard, always looking, ready to react. I thought if Sugar wanted to get in my face and slash me to ribbons, I'd stand a chance. If he just wanted to get rid of me, he could probably do it. Hard to avoid a bullet from a man who thinks he has nothing left to lose.

The sun had set and dusk had settled around us, not doing much for my nervous stomach. Too many shadows now. Sally had known someone in almost every place we'd visited. No one had admitted to having seen Sugar, but that didn't mean it was true. The gay community was protective of its own, and Sugar was well liked. My hope was that someone had been lying and a phone call had been made that would send Sugar out prowling.

'We have many places left to try?' I asked Sally.

'A couple clubs. We'll save the Ballroom for last.'

'Would Sugar go out in drag?'

'Hard to say. Depends on his mood. He'd probably feel safer in drag. I know I always do. You put that makeup on, and it's *watch out world*!'

I could relate to that. My makeup always increases

with my insecurity. In fact, at that very moment I had an overwhelming desire to crayon my lids with bright blue eye shadow.

We stopped in at the Strip, Mama Gouches, and Curly's. Only one place left. The Liberty Ballroom. Appropriately named. If you didn't have balls, you didn't want to go there. I figured I had balls when I needed them, so there was no problem.

I drove past the State Complex, which always felt weirdly deserted at night. Acres of unoccupied parking spaces, eerily lit by halogen light. Empty buildings with black glass windows, looking like the death star.

The Ballroom was on the next block, next to the high-rise seniors' housing known to one and all as the Warehouse.

All night long Sally had been telling people we'd end up at the Ballroom. And now that we were here my skin was crawling and all my little hairs were standing on end. It was fear and dread premonition, plain and simple. I knew Sugar was in there. I knew he was waiting for us. I parked and looked around for Ranger. No Ranger in sight. That's because he's in the wind, I told myself. You can't see the wind. Or maybe the wind went home to watch Tuesday night fights.

Sally was cracking his knuckles next to me. He felt it, too. We looked at each other and grimaced.

'Let's do it,' I said.

CHAPTER FIFTEEN

SALLY AND I stood inside the door and looked around. Bar and cocktail tables in the front. Small dance floor to the rear. Very dark. Very crowded. Very noisy. My understanding was that the Ballroom was a gay place, but clearly not everyone here was gay.

'What are all these ungay people doing here?' I asked Sally.

'Tourists. The guy who owns this place was going bust. It was a gay bar, but there weren't enough gay men in Trenton to make a go of it. So Wally got this great idea . . . he hired some guys to come in and dance and get all smoochy with each other, so the place would look *really* gay. Word got out, and the place started filling up. Like you could come here to see homos and be fucking politically correct.' Sally smiled. 'Now it's trendy.'

'Like you.'

'Yeah. I'm fucking trendy.'

Sally waved to someone. 'See that guy in the red shirt? That's Wally, the owner. He's a genius. The other thing he does is give the first drink free to day-trippers.'

'Day-trippers?'

'Yuppies who want to be gay-for-a-day. Like suppose you're a guy, and you think it'd be a kick to get dressed up in your wife's clothes and go out to a bar. This is the place!

You get a free drink. And on top of that, you're trendy, so it's all okay. You can even bring your wife, and she can try out being dyke-for-a-day.'

The woman standing next to me was dressed in a black leather vest and black leather hot pants. She had an expensive perm that gave her perfect red curls all over her head, and she was wearing brown lipstick.

'Hi!' she said to me, all cheery and chirpy. 'Want to dance?'

'No thanks,' I said. 'I'm just a tourist.'

'Me too!' she squealed. 'Isn't this place too much? I'm here with my husband, Gene. He wants to see me slow dance with a woman!'

Gene looked very preppy in Dockers and a plaid sport shirt with a little horse stitched onto the pocket. He was swilling a drink. 'Rum Coke,' he said to me, leaning across his wife. 'Want one?'

I shook my head no. 'I have a gun in my shoulder bag,' I said. 'A big one.'

Gene and his wife moved away and disappeared in the crowd.

Sally had an advantage at 6'4". He was swiveling his head, looking the crowd over.

'See him?' I asked.

'No.'

I didn't like being stuck in the Liberty Ballroom. It was too crowded, too dark. People were jostling me. It would be easy for Sugar to come up on me here . . . like Jack Ruby shooting Lee Harvey Oswald. That could be me. One shot to the gut and I'd be history.

Sally put his hand to my back to steer me forward, and I jumped and shrieked. 'Yikes!'

'What? *What?*' Sally yelled, looking around panic-stricken.

I had my hand to my heart. 'I might be a tad nervous.'

'My stomach's a mess,' Sally said. 'I need a drink.'

Sounded like a good idea to me, so I trailed behind him to the bar. Every time he'd push through people they'd turn and look and go, 'Hey, it's Sally Sweet! I'm a real fan.' And Sally would go, 'Shit, man, that's cool.'

'What do you want?' Sally asked.

'Beer in a bottle.' I figured if Sugar attacked me, I could brain him with my beer bottle. 'I didn't realize you were so famous,' I said to Sally. 'All these people know you.'

'Yeah,' Sally said, 'probably half the people in this room have slipped a five under my garter belt. I'm like regional.'

'Sugar's here somewhere,' the bartender said, passing drinks to Sally. 'He wanted me to give you this note.'

The note was in the same tidy little invitation-sized envelope Sugar had given Grandma. Sally opened the envelope and read the note card.

' "Traitor." '

'That's it?' I asked.

'That's all it says. "Traitor." ' He shook his head. 'He's wigged, man. Beyond Looney Tunes. Looney Tunes is funny. This isn't funny.'

I belted back some beer and told myself to stay calm. Okay, so Sugar was a little over the edge. It could be worse. Suppose the guy who was going around chopping off fingers was after me? That would be worrisome. *He'd* already killed someone. We didn't know for sure if Sugar was a killer. Arson didn't necessarily mean he was a killer type. I mean, arson was remote, right? So no point to getting all freaked out ahead of time.

Ranger moved next to me. 'Yo,' Ranger said.

'Yo yourself.'

'Is the man here?'

'Apparently. We haven't spotted him yet.'

'You armed?'

'Beer bottle.'

He gave me a wide smile. 'Good to know you're on top of things.'

'No grass growing here,' I said.

I introduced Ranger and Sally to each other.

'Shit,' Sally said, gaping at Ranger. 'Jesus shit.'

'Tell me what I'm looking for,' Ranger said.

We didn't exactly know.

'Blond Marilyn wig, red dress with short skirt,' the bartender said.

Same outfit he had been wearing onstage at the club.

'Okay,' Ranger said. 'We're going to walk through the room and look for this guy. Pretend I'm not here.'

'You going to be the wind again?' I asked.

Ranger grinned. 'Wiseass.'

Women spilled drinks and walked into walls at the sight of Ranger grinning. Good thing he didn't want to be the wind. The wind would have had a hard time with this group.

We cautiously elbowed our way to the back, where people were dancing. Women were dancing with women. Men were dancing with men. And a man and a woman in their seventies, who must have been from a different planet and had accidentally landed on Earth, were dancing together.

Two men stopped Sally to tell him Sugar was looking for him.

'Thanks,' Sally said, ashen faced.

Ten minutes later, we'd circled the room and had come up empty.

'I need another drink,' Sally said. 'I need drugs.'

The mention of drugs made me think of Mrs. Nowicki. No one was watching her. I just hoped to God she was hanging around for her doctor's appointment. Priorities, I told myself. The apprehension money wouldn't do me much good if I was dead.

Sally went off to the bar, and I went off to the ladies' room. I pushed through the door labeled Rest Rooms and walked the length of a short hall. Men's room on one side. Ladies' room on the other. Another door at the end of the hall. The door closed behind me, locking out the noise.

The ladies' room was cool and even more quiet. I had a moment of apprehension when I saw it was empty. I looked under the three stall doors. No size-ten red shoes. That was stupid, I thought. Sugar wouldn't go to the ladies' room. He was a man, after all. I went into a stall and locked the door. I was sitting there enjoying the solitude when the outer door opened and another woman came into the room.

After a moment I realized I wasn't hearing any of the usual sounds. The footsteps had stopped in the middle of the room. No purse being opened. No running water. No opening and closing of another stall door. Someone was silently standing in the middle of the small room. Great. Caught on the toilet with my pants down. A woman's worst nightmare.

Probably my overactive imagination. I took a deep breath and tried to steady my heartbeat, but my heartbeat wouldn't steady, and my chest felt like it was on fire. I did a mental inventory of my shoulder bag and realized the only genuine weapon was a small canister of pepper spray.

There was the scrape of high heels on the tile floor, and a pair of shoes moved into view. Red.

Shit! I clapped a hand over my mouth to keep from whimpering. I was on my feet now. And I was dressed. And I felt sick to my stomach.

'Time to come out,' Sugar said.

I reached for my bag, hanging on the hook on the back of the door, but before I could grab it the bolt popped off and the door was wrenched open, taking my bag with it.

'I did everything for him,' Sugar said, tears streaming down his cheeks. 'I kept the apartment clean, and I made all his favorite food. And it was working—until you showed up. He liked me. I know he did. You ruined everything. Now all he thinks about is this bounty hunter business. I can't sleep at night. I worry all the time that he's going to get hurt or killed. He has no business being a bounty hunter.'

He held a gun in one hand, and he swiped at his tears with the other. Both hands were shaking, and he was scaring the hell out of me. I had my doubts that he was a killer, but an accidental gunshot wound is just as deadly as an intentional one.

'You've got this all wrong,' I said. 'Sally just decodes messages for me. He doesn't do anything dangerous. And besides, he really does like you. He thinks you're terrific. He's outside. He's been looking for you all night.'

'I've made up my mind,' Sugar said. 'This is the way it's going to be. I'm going to get rid of you. It's the only way I can protect Sally. It's the only way I can get him back.' He motioned to the door with the gun. 'We need to go outside now.'

This was good, I thought. Going outside was a break. When we walked through the Ballroom, Ranger would kill him. I carefully inched my way to the door and stepped out into the hall, moving slowly, not wanting to spook Sugar.

'No, no,' Sugar said. 'You're going the wrong way.' He pointed to the door at the other end of the hall. '*That* way.'

Damn.

'Don't think about trying something dumb. I'll shoot you dead,' he said. 'I could do it, too. I could do anything for Sally.'

'You're in enough trouble. You don't want to add murder to the list.'

'Ah, but I do,' he said. 'I've gone too far. Every cop in Trenton is looking for me. And do you know what will happen to me when I'm locked up? No one will be gentle. I'm better off on death row. You get your own room on death row. I hear they let you have a television.'

'Yes, but eventually they *kill* you!'

More tears streaked down his cheek, but his eyeliner didn't smudge. The man knew makeup.

'No more talking,' he said, pulling the hammer back on the revolver. 'Outside. Now. Or I'll shoot you here. I swear I will.'

I opened the door and looked out. There was a small employee parking lot to the right and two Dumpsters to the left. A single overhead bulb lit the area. Beyond the Dumpsters was a blacktopped driveway. Then a grassy lawn and the seniors' building. It was a really good place for him to shoot me. It was private and sound wouldn't carry. And he had several exits. He could even choose to go back into the building.

My heart was going ka-*thunk*, ka-*thunk*, and my head felt spongy. 'Wait a minute,' I said. 'I need to go back inside. I forgot my shoulder bag.'

He closed the door behind him. 'You don't need your shoulder bag where you're going.'

'Where's that?'

'Well, I don't know exactly. Wherever you go when you're dead. Climb into the Dumpster so I can shoot you.'

'What are you nuts? I'm not climbing into the Dumpster. That thing is disgusting.'

'Okay, fine, then I'll just shoot you here.' He pulled the trigger and *click*.

No bullet in the chamber. Standard safety procedure.

'Darn,' he said. 'I can't do anything right.'

'You ever shoot a gun before?'

'No. But it didn't seem like it'd be all that complicated.' He looked at the gun. 'Ah, I see the problem. The guy I borrowed the gun from left one of the bullets out.'

He sighted the gun at me, and before he had time to pull the trigger, I jumped behind one of the Dumpsters. *Bang, zing.* A bullet hit the Dumpster. *Bang, zing* again. We were both so panicked we were acting unreasonably. I was running between Dumpsters like a tin duck in a shooting gallery, and Sugar was firing at shadows.

He got off five rounds, and then there was the telltale *click* again. He was out of bullets. I peeked out from my hiding place.

'Shit,' he said. 'I'm such a loser I can't even shoot somebody. Damn.' He plunged his hand into his red purse and came out with a knife.

He was between me and the back door. My only real

option was to run like hell around the building or across the grass to the seniors' building. He looked more athletic than me, but he was in heels and a skirt, and I was wearing shorts and sneakers.

'I'm not giving up,' he said. 'I'll do it with my bare hands if I have to. I'll rip your heart out!'

I didn't like the sound of that, so I took off across the grass for all I was worth, running full out for the seniors' building. I'd been in the building before. There was always a guard at the door at this time of the night. The front of the building was well lit. There were two double glass doors, and then the guard. Beyond the guard was a lobby where the old folks sat.

I could hear Sugar laboring behind me, breathing heavily and shrieking for me to stop so he could kill me.

I barreled through the doors and hollered for the guard, but no guard came running. I looked over my shoulder and saw the knife arc down at me. I spun to the side, and the knife blade sliced through the sleeve of my Rangers jersey.

The lobby couches were filled with seniors.

'Help!' I yelled. 'Call the police! Get the guard!'

'No guard,' one woman explained. 'Budget cuts.'

Sugar lunged again.

I jumped away, grabbed a cane from an old geezer and started slashing at Sugar.

I'm one of those people who imagine themselves acting heroically at disasters. Saving children from school buses dangling precipitously from bridges. Performing first aid at car wrecks. Rescuing people from burning buildings. The truth is, I totally lose my cool in an emergency, and if things turn out okay, it's through no effort of mine.

I was blindly slashing at Sugar. My nose was running and I was making animal sounds, and by sheer accident I connected with the knife and sent it sailing through the air.

'You bitch!' Sugar shrieked. 'I hate you! I hate you!' He hurled himself at me, and we went down to the ground.

'In my day, you'd never see two women fighting like that,' one of the seniors said. 'It's all of that violence on television. That's what does it.'

I was rolling around with Sugar, and I was shouting 'Call the police, call the police.' Sugar grabbed me by my hair and yanked, and when I jerked back I caught him with my knee and pushed his gonads a good six inches into his body. He rolled off me into a fetal position and threw up.

I flopped over onto my back and looked up at Ranger.

Ranger was grinning again. 'Need any help?'

'Did I wet my pants?'

'No sign of it.'

'Thank God.'

RANGER, SALLY AND I stood on the sidewalk in front of the seniors' building and watched the police drive off with Sugar. I'd pretty much stopped shaking, and my skinned knees had stopped bleeding.

'Now what am I going to do?' Sally said. 'I'm never going to be able to get into that corset all by myself. And what about makeup?'

'It's not easy being a drag queen,' I said to Ranger.

'Fuckin' A,' Ranger said.

We walked back to the club parking lot and found

our cars. The night was humid and starless. The air-conditioning system droned from the club roof, and canned music and muffled conversation spilled out the open front door into the lot.

Sally was unconsciously bobbing his head in time to the music. I loaded him into the Porsche and thanked Ranger.

'Always enjoy seeing you in action,' Ranger said.

I drove out of the lot and headed for Hamilton. I noticed my knuckles were white on the wheel and made another effort to relax.

'Man, I'm really stoked,' Sally said. 'I think we should do more clubs. I know this great place in Princeton.'

I'd just almost been shot, slashed, and choked to death. I wasn't feeling all that stoked. I wanted to sit someplace quiet and non-threatening and eat my mother's cookies.

'I need to talk to Morelli,' I said. 'I'm going to pass on the clubs, but you can go on your own. You don't have to worry about Sugar now.'

'Poor little guy,' Sally said. 'He isn't really a bad person.'

I supposed that was true, but I was having a hard time finding a lot of sympathy for him. He'd destroyed my car and my apartment and had tried to kill me. And if that wasn't enough, he'd ruined my Gretzky Rangers jersey. Maybe I'd feel more generous tomorrow, when I'd regained my good humor. Right now, I was tending toward grouchy.

I turned at Chambers and wound my way to Morelli's. The van was no longer on his street, and I didn't see the Duc. Lights were on in the downstairs part of Morelli's house. I assumed he'd been told about Sugar and had ended the stake-out. I took my cookies and angled out of the Porsche.

Sally slid over to the driver's seat. 'Later, dude,' he said, taking off with his foot to the floor.

'Later,' I said, but the street was already empty.

I knocked on the screen door. 'Yo!' I hollered above the TV.

Morelli padded out and opened the door for me. 'Were you really rolling around on the floor at the senior citizens' home?'

'You heard.'

'My mother called. She said Thelma Klapp phoned her and told her you just beat the crap out of some pretty blond woman. Thelma said that since you were pregnant and all she thought you shouldn't be rolling around like that.'

'The pretty blond woman wasn't a woman.'

'What's in the bag?' Morelli wanted to know.

Morelli could sniff out a cookie a mile away. I took one and handed the bag over to him. 'I have to talk to you.'

Morelli flopped onto the couch. 'I'm listening.'

'About Francine Nowicki, Maxine's mother . . .'

Morelli went still. 'Now I'm *really* listening. What about Francine Nowicki?'

'She passed another phony twenty. And my informant tells me Francine had a roll of them.'

'That's why you were so hot to put her under surveillance. You think she's mixed up in this counterfeiting thing and she's going to take off . . . along with Maxine.'

'I think Maxine might already be gone.'

'Why are you still interested if you think Maxine's gone?'

I took another cookie. 'I don't know for sure that she's gone. And maybe she's not so gone that I can't find her.'

'Especially if her mother or her friend rats on her.'

I nodded. 'There's always that possibility. So what do you say, can I use your truck?'

'If she's still there in the morning I'll put a van in place.'

'Her doctor appointment's at three.'

'Why did you decide to tell me?'

I slouched lower on the couch. 'I need help. I don't have the right equipment to do any kind of decent surveillance. And I'm tired. I hardly slept last night, and I've had a nightmare day. This guy emptied a revolver at me tonight, and then he chased me with a knife in his hand. I hate it when people do that!' I was trying to eat a cookie, but my hand was shaking so bad I could hardly get it to my mouth. 'Look at me. I'm a wreck!'

'Adrenaline surplus,' Morelli said. 'As soon as it wears off you'll sleep like the dead.'

'Don't say that!'

'You'll feel better in the morning.'

'Maybe. Right now I'm happy for whatever assistance you can give me.'

Morelli got up and shook out cookie crumbs. 'I'm going to get a glass of milk. Want one?'

'Sure.'

I stretched out the length of the couch. He was right about the adrenaline. I'd stopped shaking and now I was exhausted.

I HAD A moment of disorientation when I opened my eyes. And then I realized I'd fallen asleep on Morelli's couch. And now it was morning. Sunlight was streaming through the front windows, and I could smell coffee brewing in the kitchen. Morelli had removed my shoes and covered me with a summer quilt. I did a quick check to make sure the rest of my clothes were intact before feeling too grateful.

I shuffled into the kitchen and poured out some coffee.

Morelli was buckling his gun onto his belt. 'I've gotta run,' he said. 'I called your mother last night and told her you were here. I figured she'd worry.'

'Thanks. That was nice of you.'

'Help yourself to whatever. If anything comes up today, you can get me on my pager.'

'Are you watching Nowicki?'

Morelli paused. 'She's gone. I had someone check last night. The house is empty.'

'Damn!'

'We might still get her. There's an alert out for her. The Treasury has resources.'

'The doctor—'

'Nowicki canceled her appointment yesterday.'

He gulped the rest of his coffee, put the mug in the sink and took off. He got to the middle of the dining room, stopped and stared down at his shoe for a minute. Thinking. I saw him give his head a single shake. He turned, strode back into the kitchen, pulled me to him and kissed me. Lots of tongue. Hungry hands.

'Jesus,' he said, backing off. 'I'm in really bad shape.'

And he was gone.

MY MOTHER LOOKED up expectantly when I came into the kitchen. Well? the look said. Did you sleep with him?

My grandmother was at the table with a cup of tea. My father was nowhere to be seen. And Sally was at the head of the table, eating chocolate chip cookies, once again wearing my bathrobe.

'Hey, dude,' Sally said to me.

'Sally was telling us all about last night,' Grandma said. 'Boy, I sure wish I'd been there. Sally said you were the bomb.'

'Of all places,' my mother said, 'the senior citizens' home. What were you thinking? You know how they talk!'

'We've had three phone calls so far this morning,' Grandma said. 'This is the first chance I've had to sit down with my tea. It's just like we're movie stars!'

'So what's new?' I asked Sally. 'You have plans for the day?'

'I'm moving. Got a new place to live. Ran into some friends last night who were looking to replace a roommate. They've got a house in Yardley.'

'Dang,' Grandma said. 'I'm going to miss seeing you sitting there in that pink bathrobe.'

I puttered around until Sally was out of the house. Then I took a shower and straightened my room. I didn't like that I'd lost Mrs. Nowicki. All because I hadn't told Morelli the whole story soon enough. *'Damn!'* I yelled out. Now all I needed was for Joyce Barnhardt to haul Maxine in. *'Shit!'*

My mother knocked on my bedroom door. 'Are you all right in there?'

I opened the door. 'No, I'm not all right. I'm bummed! I've screwed this case up, and now I have to worry about Joyce Barnhardt making my apprehension.'

My mother gave a sharp inhale. 'Joyce Barnhardt!

Joyce Barnhardt couldn't carry your water pail! You're better than Joyce Barnhardt!'

'You think so?'

'Just go fix whatever it is you botched. I'm sure it isn't that bad. This woman you're after has to be out there somewhere. People don't just disappear.'

'It isn't that easy. I've lost all my leads.' With the exception of Bernie the horny drug dealer, who I wasn't crazy about seeing again.

'Do you know that for sure?'

Actually, no.

'You're right,' I said. 'It wouldn't hurt to check a few things out.' I grabbed my shoulder bag and headed for the stairs.

'Will you be home for supper?' my mother asked. 'We're having fried chicken and biscuits and strawberry shortcake.'

'I'll be home.'

My enthusiasm did another dip when I saw the Buick waiting for me. It was hard to be Wonder Woman in the Buick. It would be much easier to be Wonder Woman on a Duc, for instance.

I crawled onto the big bench seat and peered over the steering wheel at the powder-blue hood stretching endlessly in front of me. I turned the key and accelerated. *Bzzzzzzzup*, the car sucked gas and rolled up the street.

Morelli had covered Mrs. Nowicki's house, but he hadn't gone to see Margie. There was a slim chance that Mrs. Nowicki might be with Margie.

I didn't feel encouraged when I pulled up at Margie's house. Her car wasn't there, and neither was Mrs. Nowicki's. I went to the door and found it locked. No one answered my knock. I tiptoed around and looked in windows and saw no sign of life. No breakfast dishes left on the kitchen counter. No socks left lying on the floor. No cat curled in an armchair. The neighbor didn't pop out. Maybe she was used to me snooping.

I crossed the lawn and rapped on the neighbor's door.

She looked puzzled at first, then she placed me. 'You're Margie's friend!' she said.

'Yes, and I'm still looking for Margie.'

'You just missed her. She was home for a day, and now she's gone again.'

'Do you know where she went?'

'I didn't ask. I just assumed it was back to the shore.'

'Well, thanks,' I said. 'I'll catch up with her one of these times.'

I went back to the car and sat there berating myself for a few minutes. 'Stupid, stupid, *stupid*!' I said.

I was on the road, so I thought, What the hell, I'll make a last-ditch effort and double-check on Maxine's mother. No stone unturned.

I didn't see a car in front of her house, either, but I parked and went to her door. I knocked, and the door swung open. 'Hello?' I called. No answer. I went room to room and was relieved not to find anyone dead, or scalped, or hacked into little pieces.

Maxine's mother hadn't lived well. The double bed mattress sagged miserably in the middle. The sheets were threadbare. A faded chenille spread served as blanket and bedspread. Both were littered with burns from cigarettes. The furniture was old and scarred, beyond polish. Rugs were soiled. Sinks were stained and chipped. The kitchen wastebasket was filled with booze bottles. And the house reeked from stale smoke and mildew.

There were no scribbled notes indicating travel plans.

No magazine pages dog-eared to cruise advertisements. No fake twenties carelessly discarded. Mrs. Nowicki was gone and didn't expect to be back. I thought the open door was a blatant message. Let the wipe-ass scavengers pick this shit over, the door said. I'm movin' on.

I went back to the Buick and tried to piece things together, but I didn't have nearly enough information. What I knew was that Margie, Maxine's mother and Maxine were sticking together. I knew that Francine Nowicki had a bunch of bad twenties. I suspected that Eddie Kuntz wanted Maxine for more than love letters. And I knew someone wanted information on Maxine bad enough to kill for it.

I thought the most confusing element in all of this was the disappearance of Eddie Kuntz. He'd been missing for four days. I thought he'd have floated in on the tide by now.

I've checked on Margie and Maxine, I thought. I should check on Eddie Kuntz, too. Trouble was, I hated to tangle with Betty and Leo again. It was getting unpleasant. Of course, I could just ride by. Stopping could be optional.

I put the Buick in gear and cruised over to Muffet Street, pausing in front of the Glicks' house. Didn't look like anybody was home in either side. No Lincoln Town Car parked at the curb. I could feel my fingers getting twitchy, wanting to see if Eddie's front door would swing open like Francine's. Maybe since no one was around I could even *help* it swing open.

My heart did a little tap dance. Stephanie, Stephanie, Stephanie, don't even think what you're thinking! What if you get caught inside! Okay, I have to admit, getting caught inside would be a downer. I needed a lookout. I needed Lula. The office was about ten minutes away.

I hauled out my cell phone and dialed the office.

'Yeah, sure,' Lula said. 'I'm good at lookout shit. I'll be right there.'

'I'm going to try to get inside,' I told her. 'I'll take my cell phone with me. You sit across the street and be cool and call me if Betty or Leo comes home. Then I'll go out the back door.'

'You can count on me,' Lula said.

I drove to the end of the block, turned the corner and parked. Then I walked back to the Glicks' house and marched up the stairs to the porch. Just to be sure I knocked on the Glicks' door. No answer. I looked in the window. No one walking around. I did the same on the Kuntz side. I tried the door. Locked. I ran around to the back. No luck there, either. I should have called Ranger instead of Lula. Ranger had a way with locks. I used to carry a set of lock picks, but I could never get them to work, so I threw them away.

I glanced over at Eddie's back window, next to the door. It was cracked open! No air-conditioning in the Kuntz side. You could probably bake bread on the kitchen floor. I slunk off the porch and gave the window a nudge. Stuck. I looked around. There was no activity in the neighborhood. No dogs barking. No neighbors watering grass. No kids playing. Too hot. Everyone was inside, running their air conditioners, watching television. Good for me.

I discreetly dragged a garbage can over to the window and climbed on. I balanced on my knees, gave the window a good hard shot and *ZZZING!* The window sailed open. I didn't hear anybody yelling 'Hey, you!

What are you doing?' so I figured everything was cool. I mean, it wasn't like I was breaking and entering, because I hadn't actually broken anything.

I slid the window back down and ran to the front of the house to make sure the Glicks hadn't come home. When I didn't see the Lincoln I felt a little more comfortable, so that my heart slowed down to almost normal. I did the upstairs first, methodically going room by room. When I got to the downstairs I looked out the window and saw the red Firebird parked two houses down. I searched the kitchen last. Milk in the refrigerator. And upstairs in his bedroom there'd been dirty clothes on the floor. Things that would lead me to believe he hadn't intended to go on a trip.

I found two key rings in the junk drawer by the sink. One key ring held several keys. Car key, house key, a locker key. The other key ring only held one key. My mother lived in a duplex like this, and her junk drawer held two key rings, too. One was an extra set of keys. The other was the key to next door.

CHAPTER SIXTEEN

I LOOKED AT my watch. I'd been in the house for a half hour. Probably I shouldn't push my luck, but I really wanted to take a quick tour of the Glick half. It'd be helpful to find a ransom note left lying on the Glicks' kitchen counter. The key was in the drawer calling to me. *Use me. Use me.* Okay, what was the worst that could happen? The Glicks would catch me, and I'd be embarrassed. But that wouldn't happen because Lula was watching.

I pocketed the key, closed the window to within an inch of the sill, slipped out the door and stuck the key in the Glicks' lock. Bingo. The door clicked open.

The first thing I noticed was the wash of cool air. It had to be forty degrees in Betty Glick's kitchen. It was like walking into a refrigerator. The no-wax linoleum floor was spotless. The appliances were new. The countertops were Formica butcher block. The theme was country kitchen. Wooden hearts painted barn red and Newport blue, inscribed with homey messages, were hung on the walls. A small pine turned-leg table had been positioned under the back window. The toaster snuggled under a crafts fair toaster cover. Pot holders and dish towels sported rooster designs, and in a colorful, hand-painted bowl was the essential orange-scented potpourri.

Only problem was that the potpourri did nothing to disguise the fact that Betty Glick's kitchen smelled bad. Betty needed some baking soda down her sink drain. Or maybe Betty needed to empty the garbage. I did a quick look through the cupboards and drawers. Nothing unusual there. Also no dead rats or rotting chicken carcasses. The waste container was scrubbed clean and lined with a plastic bag. So *what* was that smell? There was a kitchen telephone, but no answering machine to snoop on. The sticky pad beside the telephone was blank, waiting for an important message. I looked in the refrigerator and the broom closet, which had been converted into a small pantry.

The smell was stronger on the broom closet side of the room, and suddenly I knew what I was smelling. Uh oh, I thought, take me out of here, feet! But my feet weren't listening. My feet were creeping closer to the source of the smell. My feet were heading for the cellar door next to the broom closet.

My cell phone was in my shoulder bag, and my shoulder bag was hung on my shoulder. I looked inside the bag to make sure the LED was lit. Yep. The phone was working.

I opened the cellar door and flipped the light switch. 'Hel-*lo*-o,' I called. If I'd have gotten an answer, I'd have fainted.

I crept halfway down the stairs and saw the body. I'd expected it would be Eddie or maybe Maxine. This body was neither. It was a man in a suit. Late fifties, early sixties, maybe. Very dead. He'd been placed on a tarp. No blood anywhere. I wasn't a forensics expert, but from the way this guy's eyes were bulging and his tongue was sticking out I'd say he hadn't died of natural causes.

So what the hell did this mean? Why would Betty have a corpse in her basement? I know it sounds crazy, but it struck me as especially odd since Betty was such a tidy housekeeper. The basement had been finished off with tile flooring and an acoustical ceiling. Laundry area to one side. Storage to the other, including some large equipment under another tarp. An average basement . . . except for the dead guy.

I stumbled back up the stairs and popped into the kitchen just as Betty and Leo came through the front door.

'What the hell?' Leo said. 'What the hell is this?'

I didn't know what was going on, but it didn't feel healthy to hang around in Betty's kitchen. So I bolted for the back door.

BANG! A bullet sailed past my ear and embedded itself in the doorjamb.

'Stop!' Leo shouted. 'Stop right where you are.'

He'd dropped the box he'd been carrying, and he was aiming a semiautomatic at me. And he was looking much more professional with a gun in his hand than Sugar had looked.

'You touch that back door, and I'll shoot you,' Leo said. 'And before you die I'll chop your fingers off.'

I stared at him bug-eyed and open-mouthed.

Betty rolled her eyes. 'You and those fingers,' she said to Leo.

'Hey, it's my trademark, okay?'

'I think it's silly. And besides, they did it in that movie about that short person. Everyone will think you're a copycat.'

'Well, they're wrong. I did it first. I was clipping fingers years ago in Detroit.'

Betty retrieved the box Leo had dropped, carted it into

the kitchen and set it on the counter. I read the printing on the side. It was a new chainsaw. Black and Decker, 120 horsepower, portable.

Eek.

'You're not going to believe this,' I said, 'but there's a dead guy in your cellar. Probably you should call the police.'

'You know when things start to go wrong, it all turns to crapola,' Leo said. 'You ever notice that?'

'Who is he?' I asked. 'The man down there.'

'Nathan Russo. Not that it matters to you. He was my partner, and he got nervous. I had to settle his nerves.'

My phone rang inside my shoulder bag.

'Christ,' Leo said, 'what is that? One of those cellular phones?'

'Yeah. I should probably answer it. It might be my mother.'

'Put your bag on the counter.'

I put it on the counter. Leo rummaged through it with his free hand, found the phone and shut it off.

'This is a real pain in the ass now,' Leo said. 'Bad enough I have to get rid of *one* body. Now I have to get rid of *two*.'

'I told you not to do it in the cellar,' Betty said. 'I *told* you.'

'I was busy,' Leo said. 'I didn't have a lot of time. I didn't notice you helping any to get the money together. You think it's easy to get all that money?'

'I know this is a sort of dumb question,' I said. 'But what happened to Eddie?'

'Eddie!' Leo threw his hands in the air. 'None of this would have happened if it wasn't for that bum!'

'He's just young,' Betty said. 'He's not a bad person.'

'Young? He ruined me! My life's work . . . pooof! If he was here I'd kill him, too.'

'I don't want to hear that kind of talk,' Betty said. 'He's blood.'

'*Hah*. Wait until you're out on the street because your no-good nephew blew our pension plan. Wait until you need to get into a nursing home. You think they're gonna let you into assisted living on your good looks? No sirree.'

Betty put her grocery bag on the small kitchen table and started to unpack. Orange juice, bread, bran flakes, a box of three-ply jumbo-sized trash bags. 'We should have gotten two boxes of these trash bags,' she said.

This made me swallow hard. I had a pretty good idea what they were going to do with the trash bags and chain saw.

'So go back to the store,' Leo said. 'I'll start downstairs, and you can go get more bags. We forgot to get steak sauce anyway. I was gonna grill steaks tonight.'

'My God,' I said. 'How can you think of grilling steaks when you've got a dead man in your basement?'

'You gotta eat,' Leo said.

Betty and Leo were standing with their backs to the side window. I looked over Leo's shoulder and saw Lula bob up and look in the window at us, her hair beads flopping around.

'Do you hear funny clicking sounds?' Leo asked Betty.

'No.'

They both stood listening.

Lula bobbed up a second time.

'There it is again!'

Leo turned, but Lula was gone from the window.

'You're hearing things,' Betty said. 'It's all this stress.'

We should take a vacation. We should go to someplace fun like Disney World.'

'I know what I heard,' Leo said. 'And I heard something.'

'Well, I wish you'd hurry up and kill her,' Betty said. 'I don't like standing here like this. What if one of the neighbors comes over? How will it look?'

'Downstairs,' Leo said to me.

'And don't make a mess,' Betty said. 'I just cleaned down there. Choke her like you did Nathan. That worked out good.'

It was the second time in twenty-four hours someone had pointed a gun at me, and I was beyond scared. I was vacillating between cold, stark terror and being truly pissed. My stomach was hollow from fear, and the rest of my body was spastic with the need to grab Leo by his shirtfront and rap his head against the wall until his fillings fell out of his teeth.

I imagined Lula was scrambling to help, calling the police. And I knew what I needed was to stall for time, but it was hard to think coherently. I was sweating in Betty's forty-degree kitchen. It was the cold sweat of someone facing death badly. Not ready to go.

'I don't g-g-get it,' I said to Leo. 'Why are you doing all this killing?'

'I only kill when I have to,' Leo said. 'It's not like it's indiscriminate. I wouldn't have killed that salesclerk, but she pulled Betty's ski mask off.'

'She seemed like such a nice girl, too,' Betty said. 'But what could we do?'

'I'm a n-n-nice girl,' I said.

'We didn't even get any information from her,' Leo said. 'I cut off her finger to show I was serious, and she still wouldn't talk. What kind of a person is that? All she said was that Maxine was in Point Pleasant. Big deal. Point Pleasant. Maxine and twenty thousand other people.'

'Maybe that was all she knew.'

Leo shrugged.

I did a panicked search for another question. 'You know what else I don't get? I don't get why you scalped Mrs. Nowicki. Everybody else had their finger cut off.'

'I forgot my clippers,' Leo said. 'And all she had in the house was this dinky paring knife. You can't do real good work with a paring knife. Not unless it's supersharp.'

'I keep telling you, you should take ginko,' Betty said. 'You don't remember anything anymore.'

'I'm not taking any damn ginko. I don't even know what ginko is.'

'It's an herb,' Betty said. 'Everybody takes it.'

Leo rolled his eyes. 'Everybody. Unh.'

Lula bobbed up at the window again. And this time she had a gun in her hand. She squinted and sighted and bam! The window shattered, and a rooster pot holder hanging from a hook on the opposite wall jumped in place.

'Jesus H. Christ,' Leo said, dodging aside, whirling around to face the window.

'Drop your gun, you punk-ass old coot,' Lula yelled. 'You don't drop your gun, I'm gonna bust a cap up your ass!'

Leo shot at the window. Lula returned fire, taking out the microwave. And Betty and I dove under the table.

Sirens whooped in the distance.

Leo ran for the front door, where there was more gunfire and a lot of cussing from both Leo and Lula. Police strobes flashed through the front windows, and there was more shouting.

'I hate this part,' Betty said.

'You've done this before?'

'Well, not exactly like this. It was much more orderly last time.'

Betty and I were still under the table when Morelli came in.

'Excuse me,' Morelli said to Betty. 'I'd like to speak to Ms. Plum in private.'

Betty crawled out and stood and looked like she didn't know where to go.

I crawled out, too. 'You might want to detain her,' I said to Morelli.

Morelli passed her off to a uniform and glared at me. 'What the hell's going on here? I answer my pager and it's Lula screaming how someone's shooting you.'

'Well, he didn't actually get around to shooting me.'

Morelli sniffed. 'What's that smell?'

'Dead guy in the basement. Leo's partner.'

Morelli wheeled around and went downstairs. A minute later he came up smiling. 'That's Nathan Russo.'

'And?'

'He's our friendly neighborhood funny money distributor. He's the guy we've been watching.'

'Small world.'

'There's a press down there, too. Under a tarp.'

I felt my face crumple and my eyes fill with tears. 'He wanted to kill me.'

'I know the feeling,' Morelli said. He put an arm around me and kissed the top of my head.

'I hate to cry,' I said. 'I get all blotchy, and it makes my nose run.'

'Well, you're not blotchy right now,' Morelli said. 'Right now you're white. The guy downstairs has more color than you.' He guided me through the house to the porch, where Lula was pacing, looking like she'd break out in hives any minute. Morelli sat me down on the step and told me to put my head between my legs.

After a minute the clanging stopped in my head, and I didn't feel like throwing up anymore. 'I'm okay,' I said. 'I feel better.'

Lula sat next to me. 'First time I ever saw a white person who really was white.'

'Don't go anywhere,' Morelli said. 'I need to talk to both of you.'

'Yessir, boss,' Lula said.

Morelli squatted next to me and lowered his voice. 'You weren't in this house illegally, were you?'

'No.' I shook my head for emphasis. 'The door was open. I was invited in. The wind blew the door . . .'

Morelli narrowed his eyes. 'You want to pick one?'

'Which one do you like?'

'Christ,' Morelli said.

He went back into the house, which was now filled with cops. An EMS truck had arrived. No need for that. No one had been hurt, and the body in the basement would go home with the coroner in his body snatcher truck. Neighbors had collected on the sidewalk by the EMS truck. Others stood on porches across the street. Betty and Leo were sitting in two separate blue-and-whites. They'd be kept apart from now on and questioned independently.

'Thanks for coming to my rescue,' I said to Lula. 'Boy, you really nailed that pot holder.'

'Yeah, only I was aiming for Leo. Sorry I didn't call you

in time. I kept getting interference. Lucky I got through to Morelli right away.'

At the end of the block a black Jeep screeched to a halt and a naked man jumped out.

'Goddamn!' Lula said. 'I know that naked mother-fucker.'

I was on my feet and running. The naked mother-fucker was Eddie Kuntz! Eddie saw the crowd in front of his house and immediately scurried behind some shrubbery. I skidded to a stop directly in front of the shrub and stared. Kuntz was tattooed head to toe with colorful messages like 'pencil dick,' and 'woman beater,' and 'I like to be butt-fucked.'

'Ommigod,' I said, trying hard not to be obvious about comparing messages with equipment displayed.

Kuntz was rabid. 'They've been holding me hostage. They tattooed my entire body!'

Lula was next to me. 'Think they been generous with the pencil dick,' she said. 'Think you're more a stubby eraser.'

'I'm going to kill her,' Kuntz said. 'I'm going to find her and kill her.'

'Maxine?'

'And don't think you're getting your thousand dollars, either.'

'About the car you just got out of . . .'

'It was that other bounty hunter. The one with the knockers. Said she'd picked up a police call on her scanner and was heading over here. She picked me up on Olden. That's where Maxine dumped me off. Olden! In front of the 7-Eleven!'

'Do you know where Maxine was going?'

'The airport. All three of them. They're in a blue

Honda Civic. And I take that back about the thousand. You bring that cunt to me, and I'll make you goddamn rich.'

I whirled around and ran for the Firebird.

Lula was pounding pavement behind me. 'I'm on it,' she was saying. 'I'm on it!'

We both jumped in the car, and Lula rocketed away before I even had my door closed.

'They'll take Route One,' she said. 'That's why they dropped him off on Olden. They were heading for One.' She cornered Olden with two wheels touching pavement, took the turnoff and hit Route 1 north.

I'd been so excited I'd forgotten to ask which airport. Like Lula, I'd just assumed it was Newark. I looked over at the speedometer and saw it hovering at ninety. Lula put her foot to the floor, and I braced myself and turned my face away.

'They got that little prick good,' Lula said. 'I almost hate to pick Maxine up. You gotta admire her style.'

'Creative,' I said.

'Damn skippy.'

Actually, I thought the tattooing might be a little excessive.

I didn't like Eddie Kuntz but I had to wince at the thought of Maxine needling him head to foot.

I was looking for the blue Honda, and I was also looking for Joyce. Wouldn't you know, Joyce would happen on Eddie Kuntz. If there was a naked man anywhere near Joyce, she'd find him.

'There they are!' I yelled. 'On the side of the road.'

'I see 'em,' Lula said. 'Looks like Maxine got stopped by the cops.'

Not the cops. They got stopped by Joyce Barnhardt,

who'd stuck a portable red flasher on the roof of her Jeep. We pulled in behind Joyce and ran to see what was happening.

Joyce was standing on the shoulder of the road, holding a gun on Maxine, Mrs. Nowicki and Margie. The three women were spread-eagled on the ground by Joyce with their hands cuffed behind their backs.

Joyce smiled when she saw me. 'You're a little late, sweetie-pie. I've already made the apprehension. Too bad you're such a loser.'

'Hunh,' Lula said, slitty eyed.

'You've got three people cuffed, Joyce, and only one of them is a felon. You have no right to manhandle the other two women.'

'I can manhandle whoever I want,' Joyce said. 'You're just pissy because I got your collar.'

'I'm pissy because you're being an unprofessional jerk.'

'Careful what you say to me,' Joyce said. 'You get me annoyed and you and lard butt might find yourselves on the ground with these three. I've got a couple more cuffs left.'

'Excuse me,' Lula said. 'Lard butt?'

Joyce trained her gun on Lula and me. 'You've got thirty seconds to get your fat asses out of here. And you should both look for new jobs, because it's clear I'm the primo bounty hunter now.'

'Yeah,' Lula said. 'We don't deserve to have a cool job like bounty hunter. I've been thinking maybe I'd get a job at that new place just opened, Lickin' Chicken. They tell me you work there you get to eat whatever you want. You even get them biscuits when they're fresh out of the oven. Here, let me help you get these women into your car.'

Lula hoisted Maxine to her feet, and when she handed her over to Joyce, Joyce made a sound like 'Ulk' and crumpled to the ground.

'Oops,' Lula said. 'Another one of them dizzy spells.'

Helped along by a few volts from Lula's stun gun.

There was a medium-sized duffel bag on the back seat in Joyce's car. I searched through the bag and found the keys to the cuffs. I unlocked Mrs. Nowicki's cuffs and then Margie's cuffs. I stepped away. 'You're on your own,' I told them. 'I'm not authorized to arrest you, but Treasury is looking for you, and you'd be smart to turn yourselves in.'

'Yeah, sure,' Mrs. Nowicki said. 'I'm gonna do that.'

Lula got Maxine to her feet and dusted her off, while Mrs. Nowicki and Margie shuffled uncomfortably on the side of the road.

'What about Maxie?' Margie asked. 'Can't you let Maxie go, too?'

'Sorry. Maxine has to report back to the court.'

'Don't worry about it,' Maxine said to her mother and Margie. 'It'll work out okay.'

'Don't feel right to leave you like this,' Mrs. Nowicki said.

'It's no big deal,' Maxine said. 'I'll meet up with you after I get this straightened out.'

Mrs. Nowicki and Margie got into the blue Honda and drove away.

Joyce was still lying on the ground, but she'd started to twitch a little, and one of her eyes was open. I didn't want Joyce to get accosted while she was coming around, so Lula and I picked Joyce up and stuffed her into the Jeep. Then we took the Jeep keys and locked Joyce in, nice and snug and safe. The little red light was still flashing on the roof of her car, so chances were good that a cop would stop to investigate. Since the little red light was illegal, it was possible that Joyce might get arrested. But then, maybe not. Joyce was good at talking cops out of tickets.

MAXINE WASN'T FEELING talkative on the way to the station, and I suspected she was composing her story. She looked younger than she had in her photo. Less trampy. Maybe that's what happens when you tattoo out anger. Like breathing life back into a drown victim. In goes the good air, out comes the bad air. Or maybe it was the hundred-dollar haircut and color, and the seventy-five-dollar DKNY T-shirt. Maxine didn't look like she was hurting for money.

The Trenton Police Station is on North Clinton. The building is red brick and utilitarian. The parking lot is Brooklyn south . . . about an acre of second-rate blacktop surrounded by ten-foot-high chain-link fencing. The hope is that the fencing will prevent the theft of police cars, but there's no guarantee.

We pulled into the police lot and saw there were two cruisers backed up to the drop-off behind the building. Leo Glick was helped from one of the cars. He looked our way. His gaze was piercing and angry.

'No sense making a big scene,' I said to Lula. 'We'll take Maxine in through the front so she doesn't have to deal with Leo.'

Sometimes, if court was in session, I could take my apprehension directly to the judge, but court was adjourned for the day, so I walked Maxine back to the docket lieutenant. I gave him my paperwork and handed Maxine over.

'I have a message for you,' he said. 'Morelli called in

about five minutes ago and left this number. Wants you to call him back. You can use the phone in the squad room.'

I made the call and waited for Morelli to come on the line.

'Since you're at the station I assume you brought Maxine in,' Morelli said.

'I always get my man.'

'That's a scary thought.'

'I was speaking professionally.'

'I need a rundown on what happened at the house here.'

I skipped over the part about using Kuntz's key to get into the house and told him the rest.

'How did you get to me so fast today?' I asked.

'I was back on surveillance at the 7-Eleven.' There was a moment of silence between us when I could hear people talking in the background. 'Kuntz is being cooperative,' Morelli said. 'He's so pissed off he's willing to tell us anything we want to know. He said Maxine was on her way to the airport.'

'Yeah. I got her on Route One.'

'She alone?'

'Nope.'

'I'm waiting,' Morelli said.

'Margie and Mrs. Nowicki were with her.'

'And?'

'And I let them go. I wasn't authorized to arrest them.' And I didn't especially want to see them caught. I had a hard time believing they were involved in the counterfeiting. For that matter, I hadn't especially wanted to bring Maxine in, either. What I suspected was that they'd extorted money from Leo and were on their way to the good life. This was really terrible, but something inside me wanted them to succeed.

'You should have told me right away. You knew I wanted to talk to Maxine's mother.'

Morelli was mad. He was using his cop voice.

'Anything else?' I asked.

'That's it for now.'

I stuck out my tongue at the phone and hung up. I was feeling very mature.

MY FATHER WAS slouched in his chair, watching baseball on television. My grandmother was asleep sitting up, head back on the couch, and my mother was next to her, crocheting. This was a nightly pattern, and there was comfort in the ritual. Even the house itself seemed to fall into a satisfied stupor when the dishes were done and the only sound was the drone of the ball game.

I was outside, on my parents' steps, doing nothing. I could have been doing something deep, like thinking about my life, or Mother Teresa's life, or life in general, but I couldn't get turned on by that. What turned me on right now was the luxury of doing nothing.

After I'd handed Maxine over, I'd gone to see my apartment and had been surprised to find repairs were already under way. I'd visited with Mrs. Karwatt and Mrs. Delgado, and then I'd gone back to Morelli's house and packed up my few possessions. The threat of danger was gone, and staying with Morelli now would have smacked of relationship. What was wrong was that there was no relationship. There was great sex and some genuine affection, but the future was too far in the future to feel comfortable. And on top of that, Morelli made me nuts.

Morelli pushed all my buttons without even trying. Not to mention Grandma Bella. Not to mention all those Morelli sperms swimming upstream, trying to bash their way through the end of the condom. My eye started to twitch, and I put my finger to it. You see? That's what Morelli does to me . . . gives me an eye twitch.

Better to live with my parents than Morelli. If I could just make it through a few weeks with my parents, I could move back into my own apartment, and then my life will get back to normal. And then my eye will stop twitching.

It was almost ten, and there was no activity on the street. The air was still and dense. The temperature had dropped. There were a few stars overhead, struggling to shine through Trenton's light pollution, not having much luck with it.

Someone was bouncing a basketball blocks away. Air conditioners hummed, and a lone cricket chirped in the side yard.

I heard the whine of a motorcycle, and I thought there was a slim chance I knew the biker. The sound was mesmerizing. Not the thunder of a hog. This was the sound of a crotch rocket. The bike drew closer, and finally I saw the outline under the streetlight at the end of the block. It was a Ducati. All speed and agility and Italian sexiness. The perfect bike for Morelli.

He eased the Duc to the curb and removed his helmet. He was wearing jeans and boots and a black T-shirt, and he looked like the sort of man a woman had to worry about. He kicked the stand out and strolled over to me.

'Nice night to be sitting out,' he said.

I was reminded of the time I went to Girl Scout camp and sat too close to the fire and my boots started smoking.

'Thought you'd want to know how the interrogation went.'

I leaned forward, greedy with curiosity. Of course I wanted to know!

'It was a total bitchfest,' Morelli said. 'I've never seen so many people so eager to incriminate themselves. It turns out that Leo Glick has a record a mile long. He grew up in Detroit, working for the Angio family. Was an enforcer. Twenty years ago he decided he was getting too old to do muscle work, so he apprenticed himself to a printer he met in prison. The printer, Joe Costa, had a set of really good plates. Leo spent three years with Costa, learning the business, and then one day Costa got dead. Leo doesn't know how this happened.'

I rolled my eyes.

'Yeah,' Morelli said. 'That's what I think, too. Anyway, Leo and Betty left Detroit and moved to Trenton, and after a couple years they set up shop.

'Leo knew Nathan Russo from Detroit. Nathan was a bag man for the Angios. Leo got Nathan to relocate and launder for him. It was all pretty clever. Nathan runs a dry-cleaning business. Betty was the go-between, and she made all the exchanges in bundles of laundry. Very sanitary.'

'That's terrible.'

Morelli grinned.

'What about Maxine?' I asked.

'Maxine was in love with Kuntz, but Kuntz is a real asshole. Slaps women around. Maxine isn't the first. Abuses them in other ways, too. Kept telling Maxine she was stupid.

'So one day they have a real bad fight and Maxine takes off with Kuntz's car. Kuntz figures he'll show her, so he presses charges and has her arrested. Maxine gets out on bail and is berserk. She goes back to Kuntz and pretends to be lovey, but what she really wants is to get even. Kuntz has been bragging about what a big gangster he is and how he has this counterfeit operation going. Maxine goads him into showing her the plates, and Eddie, with his very small brain, goes next door when Leo and Betty are at the supermarket and gets the plates and the account book and a duffel bag of twenties. Then Maxine screws his brains out, sends him into the shower to get ready for round two, and takes off with everything.'

'Maxine is the shit.'

'Yes,' Morelli said. 'Maxine is definitely the shit. In the beginning it was just supposed to be a revenge game. You know, make Kuntz sweat. Send him on a treasure hunt from hell. But Leo finds out about it and sets off to find Maxine, Detroit style. He interrogates Marge and Maxine's mother, and they don't know anything about anything.'

'Even after he encourages them to talk by slicing off a body part.'

'Yeah. Leo's not too good at character analyses. He doesn't know he can't get blood from a stone. Anyway, when Maxine finds out about the finger and the scalping, she's outraged, and she decides to cut her mother and Marge in and go for the gold.

'She's gone through the account books by now, so she knows she's dealing with Leo. She calls him up and gives him the terms. A million in real money for the plates and the account book.'

'Did Leo have that kind of money?'

'Apparently. Of course, Maxine's denying the extortion part of the story.'

'Where's the million?'

Morelli looked like he really liked this part. 'Nobody knows. I think it's out of the country. It's possible the only charges that'll stick against anyone is the original auto theft and the failure to appear against Maxine. There isn't actually any proof of extortion.'

'What about kidnapping Eddie Kuntz?'

'No charges pressed. If you had "pencil dick" tattooed all over your ass would you want to go public? Besides, most of those tattoos weren't permanent. The first night Eddie was kidnapped Maxine locked him in a room with a bottle of gin. He got stinking drunk and passed out and when he woke up he was Mr. Tattoo.'

I was looking at the Duc, and I was thinking that it was very cool and that if I had a Duc I'd *really* be the shit.

Morelli nudged my knee with his. 'Want to go for a ride?'

Of course I wanted to go for a ride. I was dying to get my legs around those 109 horses and feel them wind out.

'Do I get to drive?' I asked.

'No.'

'Why not?'

'It's *my* bike.'

'If I had a Ducati, I'd let *you* drive.'

'If you had a Ducati you probably wouldn't talk to a lowlife like me.'

'Remember when I was six and you were eight, and you conned me into playing choo-choo in your father's garage?'

Morelli's eyes narrowed. 'We aren't going to go through this again, are we?'

'I never got to be the train. *You* were always the train. *I* always had to be the tunnel.'

'I had better train equipment.'

'You owe me.'

'I was eight years old!'

'What about when I was sixteen, and you seduced me behind the eclair case at the bakery?'

'What about it?'

'I never got the top. I was only the bottom.'

'This is entirely different.'

'This is no different! This is the same thing!'

'Jesus,' Morelli said. 'Just get on the damn bike.'

'You're going to let me drive, right?'

'Yeah, you're going to drive.'

I ran my hand over the bike. It was sleek and smooth and red.

Morelli had a second helmet strapped to the back seat. He unhooked the cord and gave me the helmet. 'Seems a shame to cover up all those pretty curls.'

I buckled on the helmet. 'Too late for flattery.'

It had been a while since I'd driven a bike. I settled myself onto the Duc and looked things over.

Morelli took the seat behind me. 'You know how to drive this, right?'

I revved the engine. 'Right.'

'And you have a license?'

'Got a bike license when I was married to Dickie. I've kept it current.'

He held me at the waist. 'This is going to even the score.'

'Not nearly.'

'Entirely,' he said. 'In fact, this ride's going to be so good you're going to owe *me* when it's done.'

Oh boy.

extracts reading groups
competitions books new
discounts extracts
competitions
books new
events books
extracts new reading groups
interviews
events extracts
discounts
new books events
events new
discounts extracts discounts
www.panmacmillan.com
extracts events reading groups
competitions books extracts new